THE ZOMBIE COMBAT MANUAL

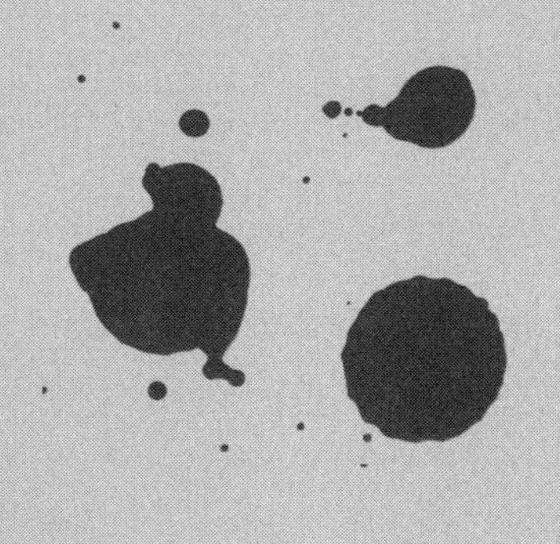

THE ZOMBIE COMBAT MANUAL

A GUIDE TO FIGHTING THE LIVING DEAD

ROGER MA

ILLUSTRATIONS BY Y. N. HELLER

BERKLEY BOOKS, NEW YORK

THE BERKLEY PUBLISHING GROUP
Published by the Penguin Group
Penguin Group (USA) Inc.
375 Hudson Street, New York, New York 10014, USA
Penguin Group (Canada), 90 Eglinton Avenue East, Suite 700, Toronto, Ontario M4P 2Y3, Canada
(a division of Pearson Penguin Canada Inc.)
Penguin Books Ltd., 80 Strand, London WC2R 0RL, England
Penguin Group Ireland, 25 St. Stephen's Green, Dublin 2, Ireland (a division of Penguin Books Ltd.)
Penguin Group (Australia), 250 Camberwell Road, Camberwell, Victoria 3124, Australia
(a division of Pearson Australia Group Pty. Ltd.)
Penguin Books India Pvt. Ltd., 11 Community Centre, Panchsheel Park, New Delhi—110 017, India
Penguin Group (NZ), 67 Apollo Drive, Rosedale, North Shore 0632, New Zealand
(a division of Pearson New Zealand Ltd.)
Penguin Books (South Africa) (Pty.) Ltd., 24 Sturdee Avenue, Rosebank, Johannesburg 2196,
South Africa

Penguin Books Ltd., Registered Offices: 80 Strand, London WC2R 0RL, England

This book is an original publication of The Berkley Publishing Group.

Cover design by Diana Kolsky.
Cover illustrations by Diana Kolsky and Y. N. Heller; "Zombie Combat Club" logo by John Fisk.
Interior illustrations by Y. N. Heller.
Text design by Georgia Rucker Design.

PRINTING HISTORY
Berkley trade paperback edition / April 2010

Library of Congress Cataloging-in-Publication Data

Ma, Roger.
The zombie combat manual / Roger Ma.—Berkley trade paperback ed.
p. cm.
ISBN 978-0-425-23254-5
1. Zombies—Humor. I. Title.
PN6231.Z65M3 2010
818'.607—dc22

2009043934

PRINTED IN THE UNITED STATES OF AMERICA

20 19 18 17 16 15 14 13

Most Berkley Books are available at special quantity discounts for bulk purchases for sales promotions, premiums, fund-raising, or educational use. Special books, or book excerpts, can also be created to fit specific needs. For details, write: Special Markets, The Berkley Publishing Group, 375 Hudson Street, New York, New York 10014.

To Zoe and Logan, forever under my protection.

To Mom, for her strength and discipline.

To Dad, for that fateful day in 1978.

CONTENTS

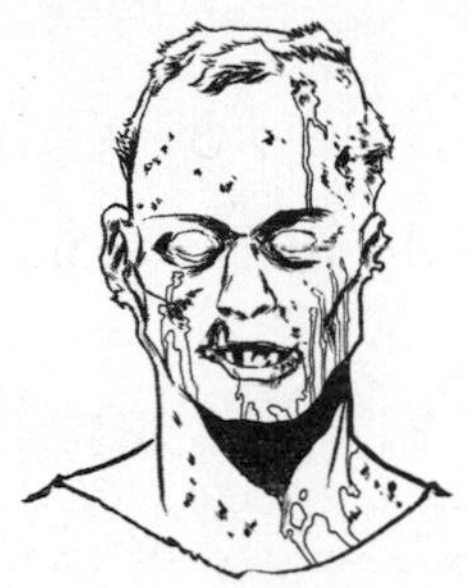

Introduction

I. Disinformation and Misconceptions

II. Anatomy

III. Conditioning and Preparation

IV. Weapon Selection

V. Combat Strategies and Techniques

THE ZOMBIE COMBAT MANUAL

INTRODUCTION

The first hand-to-hand zombie attack I saw lasted six seconds. The confrontation took place in Brooklyn, New York, during the Gravesend Riots. From the safety of the police barricades, I witnessed a man swagger down the middle of the street. He was muscular, probably in his midtwenties, and wore a white sleeveless undershirt; wiry strands of chest hair corkscrewed through the thin fabric. He brandished an aluminum baseball bat that was slung casually over his right shoulder. With a smirk on his face, he headed directly toward a ghoul shambling down the same street, her green housecoat streaked in crimson. The man reared back and swung. The curlers in her hair ricocheted in all directions from the impact of his blow, which rang off the top of her skull. I was close enough to see his eyes widen in disbelief when she didn't go down. Disbelief turned to terror when his second, panicked swing wildly struck the side of her neck as she closed the distance between them. His third and final strike landed harmlessly across her back, as she raked her manicured fingernails across his thick biceps. His screams twisted into high-pitched squeals when she tore out his throat with her teeth.

Unfortunately, this was not the last time I witnessed an attack where an individual with seemingly all the requisite skills to survive perished unnecessarily. In the hundreds of assaults I have seen or recorded from eyewitness accounts since that night in Brooklyn, I have noted that many of the victims held distinct similarities. Most of them had the strength, the means, and the tools. What they lacked was the knowledge. For far too long, many have made light of eliminating the undead, with tragic consequences.

This work seeks to accomplish a singular goal: to provide the scientific, technical, and combative knowledge to enable you to destroy a zombie in your immediate vicinity, perhaps seconds from ending your life and that of your loved ones. There will be no discussion of fortifications, firearms, supply rationing, or modes of transport, nor will we examine the origin and spread of the contagion that has caused the dead to reanimate and feed on the living. Other noteworthy works cover these subjects in great detail. The focus of this text is simple: to develop you into an effective warrior against the living dead. This book is not meant for the trained soldier or martial artist with years of experience, although they can certainly benefit from the information. It was written for you, the everyday civilian with no prior knowledge or skill in the combat arts.

The knowledge provided herein, however, should not be construed as either endorsement or encouragement to engage in unnecessary hand-to-hand combat with the undead. The safest method to defeat a zombie still remains to destroy its brain via a long-distance ballistic weapon, such as a firearm or crossbow. The fact is, however, that during a zombie outbreak, there is nearly a 100 percent chance you will have to engage in hand-to-hand combat. Perhaps you reside in a state where possession of a firearm is a legally difficult process. Perhaps you have run out of ammunition. Perhaps the sound of a discharged firearm will draw more walking corpses to your position. For those times when the only path to safety lies in the strength in your arms and the weapon in your hand, the knowledge in this book will prove most useful.

If you are reading this manual because you find yourself in the midst of an undead infestation and/or imminent attack, then heed these words carefully. The information contained within can be put to immediate use. If you are reading this during a time of relative peace and safety, good for you. You have taken the first step in obeying one of the oldest tenets of combat: "In times of peace, prepare for war." Learn the lessons in this manual well; it is my hope you will never have to use them.

CAUTION!

The methods and techniques described within this manual are meant solely for human-versus-zombie combat. Under no circumstances should they be used or attempted against other living human beings. Such action would be not only illegal and immoral, but ineffective, as the techniques take advantage of traits, behaviors, and anatomical vulnerabilities exhibited only by the living dead.

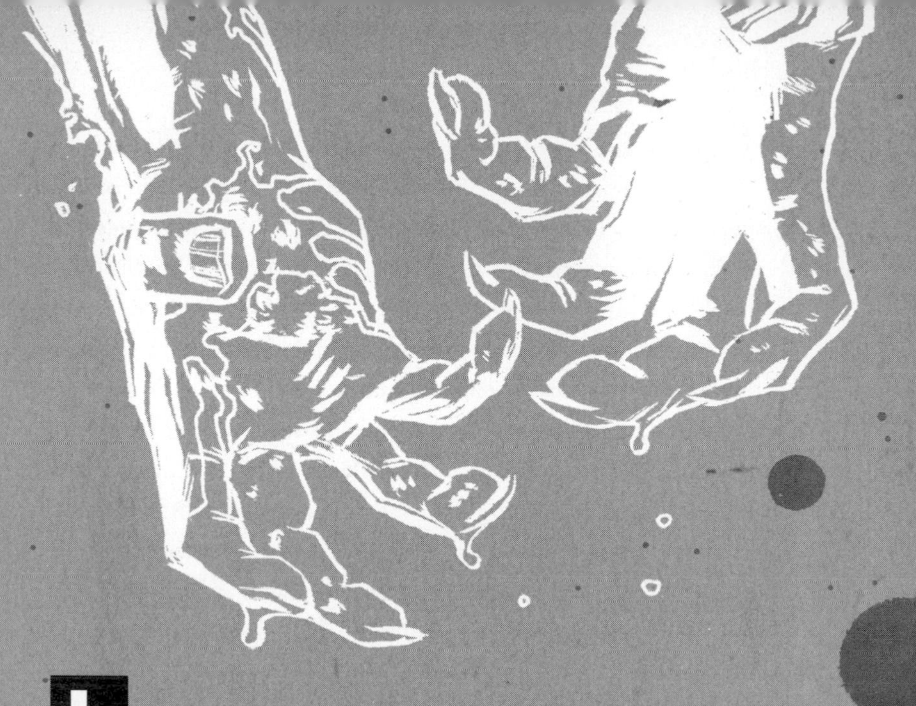

I.

DISINFORMATION AND MISCONCEPTIONS

. . . et resedit qui erat mortuus,
et coepit esurire.

—ORIGIN UNKNOWN

They are known to us by many names—Hell's minions, walking plague, the living dead. Despite the varying nomenclature, they all fall under the same scientific subspecies category, commonly known as the zombie. In case any confusion exists, let us take this moment to clarify—a zombie is a former human being that has become deceased and reanimated, and now seeks to devour the flesh of existing humans. Much has been written, fantasized, and manipulated regarding the zombie, so before delving into the specifics of undead physiology, it is important that we first dispel many popular, yet inaccurate, notions that exist about this unique adversary. Many of these misconceptions have led to the deaths of those who, believing them to be reality, met their unfortunate end. The source of these inaccuracies varies. Some believe their spread was due to an orchestrated campaign of disinformation by the powers that be to intentionally confuse and mislead the general public. Others believe that major news sources are responsible for spreading unsubstantiated reports of "living dead attacks" to mask outbreaks of public dissent.

Whether they were spread by media, myth, or word of mouth, how these inaccuracies developed into publicly believed truths is not important. What is important is that the spread of this disinformation ends with the following clarifications.

MISCONCEPTION #1: ZOMBIES CAN RUN

As we will examine in greater depth in the section on anatomy, an undead corpse with both legs intact moves at a maximum speed of just under three miles per hour, slightly slower than the average adult human walking pace. This pace seems to remain consistent regardless of weight, age, or build, with minor deviations depending on the height of the specimen being measured and whether it is in active pursuit of prey. Due to the transformation the infected specimen undergoes during the reanimation process, a zombie cannot exceed a speed that can outpace an ambulatory human being.

Individuals have claimed to have witnessed "zombies" running full speed after their victims. It has been determined that in these instances, the attackers were not in fact reanimated corpses. The specific affliction that caused this unruly behavior has not been determined, but it has been confirmed that these assailants were not, in the strictest scientific sense, the living dead.

MISCONCEPTION #2:
ZOMBIES FEED ONLY ON HUMAN BRAINS

The walking dead will devour any living flesh on a human being with which it comes into contact. Any exposed area of human tissue in the vicinity of a ghoul's open jaws is vulnerable to attack and subsequent infection. Do not trust that wearing a piece of protective headgear such as a military or sports helmet will effectively protect you from an undead attack.

Double-blind studies conducted by both public- and private-sector research groups have determined that a ghoul, when presented with both cranial tissue and other human flesh, will not select one sample over the other consistently. This is one of the primary reasons why close-quarters combat with a zombie is so hazardous—any part of the human body that comes within range of an undead attacker's clutches is literally up for grabs.

MISCONCEPTION #3: ZOMBIES RETAIN MEMORIES OF THEIR PAST HUMAN LIVES

Whoever the person was, be it your coworker, friend, or family member, ceases to be that individual once he or she has yielded to infection and reanimated into a walking corpse. Every connection to the victim's former existence—interests, hobbies, occupation, and relationships—is severed once that person rises from the dead, just as it would if said person had remained deceased.

In a distinguished study known as Project Recall conducted by IUCS, a U.S.-based bioresearch and policy institute, a thousand reanimated specimens of varying ages and states of reanimation were presented with artifacts that were a vital part of their human existence—photographs, toys, mobile phones, and laptop computers were among the sample objects. Additionally, these items were presented by volunteers who were known to the subjects in some capacity—either relatives or companions of the formerly human test subjects.

Of the one thousand trial cases, none showed any acknowledgment of the artifact itself or the presenting volunteer, even after repeated attempts at visual recognition. Even more unfortunate, fifteen of the volunteers were assaulted by their subjects during the course of the study. It was concluded that the use of personal effects in the hopes of triggering a past human memory has proven to be not only unsuccessful, but dangerous to the bearer.

MISCONCEPTION #4:
ZOMBIES CAN BE TRAINED

As poor as attempts at triggering a zombie's human recollections have fared, efforts to instruct the walking dead to obey a suggestion, request, or command, regardless of its simplicity, have proven equally futile. Early attempts to train ghouls to perform manual labor have been wholly unsuccessful. The region of the zombie brain that typically controls "executive functioning"—problem-solving and cognitive abilities—no longer functions as it would in a living human being. The undead do not seem to have the aptitude to execute even the most mundane or repetitive of tasks. Government projects aimed at controlling and weaponizing the walking dead have also failed, often with disastrous consequences (see Combat Report: Brent Taylor).

MISCONCEPTION #5:
ZOMBIES HAVE EVOLVING INTELLIGENCE

Once a person has been infected and turned from a human being into a living cadaver, all internal organs, including the brain, cease to function beyond the most rudimentary of operations required to accomplish three specific tasks: move, hunt, and feed. Once reanimated, all physical and mental development ends, regardless of the age of the human at the time of reanimation; infant zombies will not grow, teenage zombies will not mature. Research shows that the dexterity, motor skills, and mental capacity of ghouls that have been reanimated for years show no marked improvement over those that have been turned for less than twenty-four hours.

Zombies have shown no ability to communicate, assemble,

or leverage their considerable numbers in a cohesive manner. The only form of "communication" one could say they exhibit is the apparent recognition of a ghoul's moan as a potential signal that prey is within the immediate vicinity. These exchanges, however, are not intentional in nature. It has been determined that a zombie's moan is, for all intents and purposes, a Pavlovian response to sensory stimuli that a victim is near, rather than a transmission to other ghouls of that fact.

MISCONCEPTION #6:
THE MOST PRACTICAL WAY TO NEUTRALIZE A ZOMBIE IS WITH A FIREARM

The most *effective* way to neutralize a zombie is with a firearm shot into the braincase, but it is not the most practical. The fact that ammunition is always a finite resource means that every discharge of your weapon brings you one step closer to rendering it completely useless, not to mention the skill required to consistently fire an accurate headshot at a moving, albeit slow, target. Silent, easily mastered, and requiring no additional resources, the most practical method of eliminating a ghoul is via a hand-based weapon.

MISCONCEPTION #7:
ONLY SUPERIOR ATHLETES/MARTIAL ARTISTS/ SOLDIERS CAN SURVIVE A ZOMBIE ATTACK

All regular civilians, young or old, male or female, inactive or fit, can defend themselves quite successfully against the undead without any special equipment, extensive training, or exotic weapons. In fact, some of the most successful living dead fighters have been those who had no previous combat experience. Although this may seem inconceivable, it actually makes a great deal of sense.

Those who have spent prolonged amounts of time on the mat, in the ring, or on the field of battle often have preconceived notions of what is required to bring down an opponent in combat. When facing the living dead, however, nearly all typical rules of combat are ineffective. It is precisely why this text needed to be written, and why those who enter into zombie combat with a completely blank slate often are those who experience the greatest success.

You need not be in exceptional shape, knowledgeable in combat, or skilled with firearms. What you do need is the appropriate information and preparation *before* you find yourself in the midst of an undead outbreak. You alone are responsible for your own survival.

COMBAT REPORT:[1] BRENT TAYLOR[2]

Sergeant, 22nd British Special Air Service Credenhill, England

BT: People think of the SAS as this supersoldier, James Bond bollocks, but when everything went tits up, we were soiling our trousers just like everyone else. Especially after the nightmare at Piccadilly, that was a right balls-up. Some of the lads lost it after that. One of them swallowed the end of his Sig outside the Criterion after he had to knife two deadheads probably no older than twelve years combined. It was after that action that the commanding officers decided they needed to run the squadrons through another evaluation, one that focused on getting the Regiment used to dealing with this particular threat. Despite the whinging, I know that a lot of us were relieved. We thought we were trained to handle nearly any combat situation. Nothing we had seen or done had prepared us for this. Although no trooper would ever ask for help, we knew we needed it.

I'm not sure how much you know about Selection, the process of how a soldier is chosen for the Regiment. It's not a walk in the park, especially the longer exercises like the Fan Dance and the Long Drag. Even current members who decide to run through them again as a challenge have a tough

---

1 The combat reports presented throughout this text are for informational purposes only, and are not meant to be construed as additional instruction. The reports were recorded during the period known as the The Healing Years, after the official conclusion of major undead combat operations on most of the seven continents. As of this writing, outbreaks continue to be reported throughout the world, but major commerce has resumed, consumer travel has been officially reauthorized, and safety nexuses exist throughout North and South America, Europe, Antarctica, and Asia. Contact has not yet been reestablished with Australia and Africa.

2 Author's note: This name is a pseudonym. Additional details concerning the location of this interview have been removed, per the interviewee's request.

go. A few years back, one trooper decided to try one of the exercises again for a laugh. The poor bloke died of exposure in the field. There's a saying that goes, "Death is God's way of telling you that you have failed Selection." That was not what the COs wanted. This wasn't about stamina, or skill, or being able to tab forty kilometers with a three-stone bergen. They didn't want to bin perfectly good troopers; Christ knows we needed every able body we could get. This was more of a mental exercise—making sure our heads were prepared for what we were going to face and setting up a smaller troop to specifically deal with DAs—dead actions.

Modified Selection was made up of two exercises. The first was called the Dead Drag, a variation on the final stamina course we all run through during Selection; you're given a map and compass and required to reach a set number of checkpoints in a certain period of time. This version was different from the original course—shorter routes and less kit to carry. There was also another modification. Zombies were seeded throughout the Beacons, tagged and tracked to monitor their movement and proximity to every man on the course. Varying in age, weight, and decomposition level, the dead outnumbered the living five to one. The plan was that throughout the Drag, every soldier would encounter at least that many attackers by the end of the course. A lot of us joked that this was going to be easy-peasy. We were wrong.

The Dead Drag was the first sign that some of the best of us were not ready for this type of conflict. Keith, one of my mates and in the Regiment for years, was originally from the area around Hereford. Growing up around SAS headquarters, as a kid he dreamed of being a part of the squadrons. On his turn through the course, he ran up behind a ghoul and staked it through the back of the head with his dagger. Turns out it was his cousin from Glasbury. Like a good trooper, he didn't quit. He ended up completing the Drag, but he pulled himself out of the process after that. I couldn't believe the bloody coincidence. That story still circulates among the squadrons. If I hadn't known him, I'd have thought it was one of those Selection myths. Part of me wonders if it was intentional on the part of the DS,[3] that they wanted to see what he'd do. I wonder how many other dead relatives were part of the process.

The second exercise was the Haunted House. This was also a modification of a typical Selection exercise, where teams would run through a Kill House—a building designed to simulate close-quarters room clearing. The difference here was, just like on the Drag, the house was scattered with the dead. We also weren't allowed to use firearms, which was to be expected. We were already trained to double-tap targets with rounds to the noggin. What we had to learn was how to deal with those things in close. And the smell. That blasted smell. After all the squadrons were finished, a select group of us were picked for Grey Troop. It was only after graduation that I learned the facts.

ZCM: The facts?

BT: Jimmy, one of the DS officers, told us this story at a pub in Swainshill after the Grey Troop graduation. At first I thought he was just lagered, but when I realized he was serious, I was gobsmacked. Turns out he was a member of Task Force 68, a joint special-operations team operating along the Afghanistan/Pakistan border. Unit 68 evolved out of the other TF teams whose missions were to conduct snatch-and-grab operations on high-value targets in the Afghan. They received intel that several HVTs were meeting at a training camp in Waziristan for a three-day planning session. Their mission was to drop in, tab to the location with specialized cargo, release the cargo, and rendezvous back at the LZ.

3 DS: directing staff, instructors.

ZCM: Why not just use military air strikes on the site?

BT: I wasn't there giving orders, but it's pretty evident why not. We're not talking about a questionable border clash along the Khyber Pass. Air power may have been used previously on targets like this, right up until the time when one of your armed drones mistakenly destroyed that schoolhouse in Chitral. After that, as Jimmy put it, "Foreigners had officially overstayed their welcome in Pakistan." The targets were in an area where we definitely were not supposed to be *full stop*, much less carrying out offensive operations. Not to mention that the Fourteenth Infantry Division of the Paki army was already stationed in the region. As far as black operations were concerned, Jimmy's op sounded like it was ten shades past midnight.

A six-man team was assembled for what was called "Operation Appleseed"—two Americans, a couple of Fritz's from KSK, Jimmy and his mate from the Regiment. All were equally qualified, but it sounded like the multinational aspect was less about capability than culpability. A coalition of willing hands needed to be soiled on this job. As usual, the team did not get the official go-ahead until about six hours before execution, so there wasn't much time to prep and rehearse. Jimmy said that it was supposed to be a piece of cake. No direct action, no engagement, "one step above a recce,"[4] he was told. The only missing element was the cargo they were supposed to deliver. He figured it might be some new type of ordnance or perhaps a tracking device they would activate after extraction, but when the team was led to the containment room, Jimmy said his jaw hit the floor at the same time his goolies tucked themselves back up inside him.

Inside the room, he said, were six cargo "specimens" dressed in ragtag Pakistan infantry dress, their hands zip-

4 *recce:* reconnaissance mission.

tied and mouths secured with ball gags. The creatures became agitated when they entered the room, struggling against their bindings and gnashing their jaws. Although their skin was gray and their hair dyed a laughable shoe-polish black, it was obvious to Jimmy that these things never called South Asia their home. Once they were in country, the team was to meet up with their cargo, which was to be air-dropped in a separate container tank. Each man was to control one specimen and tab twenty kilometers to the training camp. Once in position, they were to release all six cargo into various locations in the camp—two into the sleeping quarters, two into the underground tunnel entrances, and the final duo into the area where the HVTs were supposed to be convening. Once all hell broke loose, they were to withdraw to the RV for immediate extraction.

The initial part of the mission was gravy. The team landed in the target area; uncrated their cargo, each of which had a black bag knotted around its head; and arrived at the encampment, positioning themselves around the release targets. It was then that things started to go pear shaped. As soon as the bags were removed from their heads, the things began to twist and squirm violently. When the gags were unbuckled, their mouths began biting and snapping. Jimmy said that one of the creatures writhed so violently, it knocked off his mate's nose clips, which were part of the nonstandard equipment the team was issued for the mission. When he took in a gob full of air surrounding the corpse, Jimmy said that he looked as if he'd just been tear-gassed. He fought through it, and both of them managed to force their specimens into the camp's underground tunnels. The Americans also had difficulty with their cargo. Once released, they shambled around and started heading back toward their keepers, but they managed to get them turned back around and into the sleeping quarters. The Germans unfortunately fared the worst. Everyone heard a bloodcurdling scream and one of the Fritzes broke radio silence, saying his mate had been bitten. Jimmy flicked on his night vision just in time to see the German wrestling with his corpse.

Things really went sideways after that bite. The camp started to light up. Shrieks could be heard from the caverns and the bunks where the cargo began to feed. Jimmy and his mate tried to reach the Germans, but the bitten soldier was already gone. The other Fritz had released his corpse and was being pinned down by small-arms fire. The Americans also arrived, and they all began laying down covering fire to give him time to escape. That's when Jimmy saw something he said still makes him wake up in cold sweats. The bitten German sat up, saw his teammate returning fire, and sank one of its thumbs into the soldier's eye socket. It proceeded to twist and pull at his head, eventually wrenching it right off the neck. It then began devouring the tendrils of flesh that hung down from the torn-off cranium.

At that point, Jimmy said that the camp was in complete chaos. Men were running out of tents and clambering out of the tunnels holding bite wounds. There was so much madness going on that they barely noticed the four of them as they called in a helo extract to the alternate RV, much closer to the camp than desired.

As the helo took off, Jimmy said he could see some of those bitten starting to turn. The German had finished with his teammate and was wandering around the camp looking for other targets. One of the last things Jimmy said he saw was the German and the other fresh deadheads being set upon by the terrorists, who bound their mouths and hands with keffiyeh head scarves and carted them off back into the tunnels.

ZCM: What do you think happened to those specimens?

BT: I would tell you to ask Jimmy that question, if I knew where he was. Shortly after that night at the pub, Jimmy went missing. His flat was completely cleared out. I tried looking him up in the database, but his record's been expunged. Queen and country, eh?

It doesn't take a genius to figure out what happened. Look at the timing, what happened afterward in Saudi Arabia and Iran. Just look around you, mate. What do you think happened?

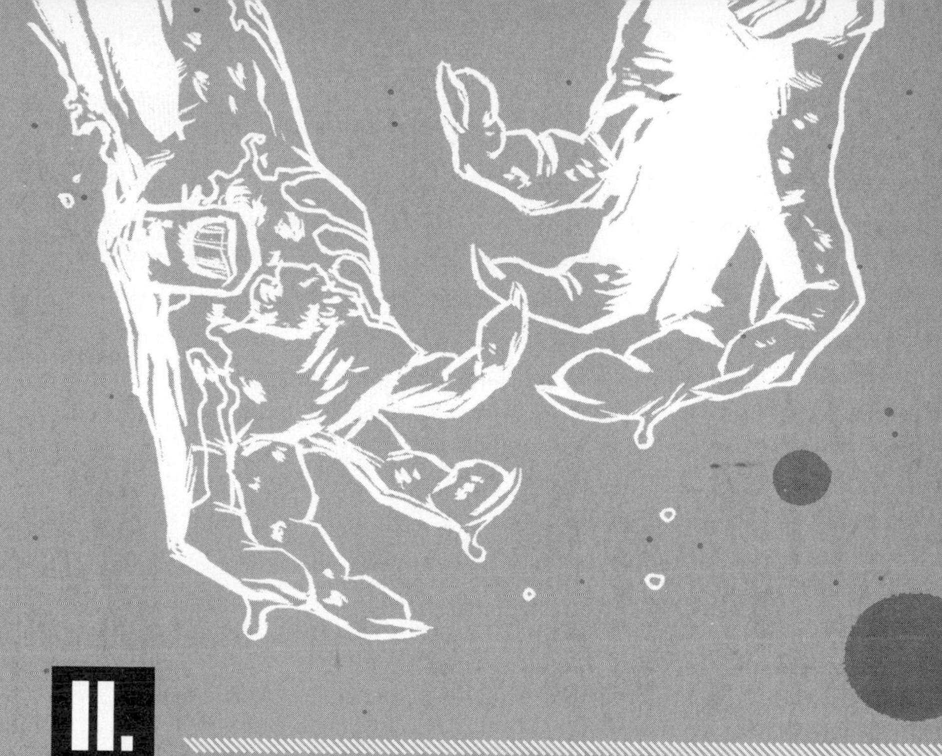

II.

ANATOMY

If you know both yourself and your enemy, you can come out of hundreds of battles without danger.

—SUN TZU

Having clarified some common misconceptions about the living dead, we can move forward with an in-depth examination of your undead opponent's anatomy. This assessment can provide you with an advantage in combat that may mean the difference between success and reanimation. In order to effectively defeat a zombie in hand-to-hand battle, it is essential that you first have a complete understanding of all its potential attack methods and vulnerabilities. This includes a review of its biological strengths and weaknesses, as obvious as this may seem. It is precisely the lack of a complete understanding of zombie traits and characteristics that has resulted in many unnecessary deaths. Thus, it is recommended that you review this section in its entirety, regardless of how much you believe you already know about the living dead.

STRENGTHS

Every undead specimen has three primary offensive weapons at its disposal: its mouth, its left hand, and its right hand. It also has a number of secondary strengths that can provide a combative advantage and contribute to its lethality. We will address each of these strengths individually, starting with the most common.

Mouth/Teeth

The bite is the primary mode of attack for the living dead. Research has discovered that during the reanimation sequence, the teeth undergo a radical transformation, and are not identical to those of its formerly human self (see Combat Report: Joseph Gartner). It is for this reason that, after years of weathering nature's elements, a zombie showing considerable decomposition throughout the rest of its physical structure will still have most of its teeth intact. Analysis has shown, however, that the bite strength of the zombie is the same as that of a normal human being—approximately 170 pounds of pressure per square inch. Attempts at developing chemical or biological countermeasures to specifically address the zombie's primary attack method have thus far been unsuccessful. As such, the mouth of a zombie is clearly its most dangerous threat. Once within an effective attack range, a ghoul will attempt to ingest any human flesh in closest proximity to its open maw. Any wound from a zombie's bite, regardless of size or severity, will result in infection and eventually transform a human being into a member of the living dead.

Fingers/Grip

Bloodied, corroded, and teeming with infection from tiny cuts and lacerations, the hands and fingers of the undead are nearly as lethal as its teeth, and some believe even more so. Often overlooked, a ghoul's fingers are a leading cause of human blood contamination, second only to that of a bite. It is for this reason that close combat with the living dead has an extremely high probability of viral transmission, even if the human avoids being bitten entirely. A single scratch that comes in contact with undead fluids will ultimately result in infection, death, and reanimation. It is this characteristic that makes some female zombies potentially more dangerous than males. Long, polished fingernails, like the claws of a feral animal, can tear swiftly through exposed, unprotected flesh.

The grip of a zombie is a commonly misunderstood element of its attack. Victims who have survived the clutches of the living dead have described their attacker as having a "viselike hold" of seemingly superhuman strength. Does this mean that a zombie's strength is far greater than that of a normal human? Studies that have measured the pound-for-pound compressive force of the undead have found that, like its bite, a zombie's grasp is no stronger than that of its average human counterpart.

There is, however, one difference in undead physiology that may explain this phenomenon. The muscles in our hands and forearms behave like all fast-twitch muscle fibers in the body—they contract powerfully but quickly tire, causing our grip to eventually fail. In the living dead, these same muscle fibers contract, but do not fatigue, and will continue to grip with the same level of intensity and power as when first grasped. Whereas a clench from the hands of a human being, even a powerfully built one, may pinch and aggravate the skin, an ordinary zombie has been known to rend chunks of flesh from soft-tissue areas on the human body with ease. In greater numbers, this grip becomes even more lethal. Anecdotal records show that as few as three specimens can pull a human being limb from limb in a matter of minutes.

Endurance

From a certain perspective, the zombie can be considered the ultimate endurance athlete. It requires no sustenance, no recovery period, and no sleep. It will incessantly carry on whatever activity it deems necessary to achieve its only goal: feeding on the living. Studies have shown that a zombie will cover hundreds of miles without pause in pursuit of prey if it is able to maintain a tracking scent. As such, it should never be taken for granted that our speed is much greater than that of the undead. What the zombie lacks in velocity it more than makes up for in stamina and persistence.

A ghoul's activity is also not limited to tracking. Whether it is breaking through a locked door, pulling down a steel fence, or forcing open a wooden crate, a zombie will continue unceasingly until one of four things occurs: (1) It is destroyed, (2) it loses the scent, (3) it is distracted by a more accessible target, or (4) it reaches its victim.

Sensory Perception

IUCS research studies and other published works have already established that the senses of the undead are highly developed and more fully utilized than they are in humans. Although a zombie does not possess any elevated or enhanced perception in any of its five senses, it uses all of them to maximum effect for the sole purpose of hunting prey. Therefore, it is nearly impossible to take the undead by surprise. As silent as you believe your movements are, trust that the ghoul is aware of you often before you are of it. A zombie chooses to ignore a human target for two primary reasons: Either (1) it is focused on a more available target or (2) it is feeding.

Durability

As we will examine in more detail later in the section on vulnerabilities, it is fairly common knowledge that the only way to neutralize a walking corpse is to inflict massive trauma to its brain tissue. Some have incorrectly extrapolated that because the brain is a ghoul's greatest vulnerability, it is then also susceptible to knockout blows to the head from the fists or feet like a normal human being. In fact, the exact opposite is true.

Any strike to a zombie's skull that does not penetrate

into brain matter is largely dismissed by an attacking ghoul. Concussive blows, punches, and kicks that would knock a large human opponent unconscious have proven to be ineffective to even the feeblest specimens of walking dead. In addition, any blows that attack nerve clusters or any technique designed to elicit an involuntary pain reaction are completely useless against the undead. Those who have attempted such maneuvers against a zombie have not only been frustrated by their futility, but have also suffered psychological trauma at the ghoul's seemingly invulnerable nature. This has contributed to the myth that zombies are an unstoppable, insurmountable force. They are not. The key is to remember that your opponent, despite its humanoid appearance, does not exhibit the same human vulnerabilities once it has reanimated. This being the case, most traditional rules of human combat do not apply.

Odor

The stench of a decaying body is one of the most disagreeable odors a person can experience. Now imagine that offensive scent creeping toward you, persistently following your every step, and you begin to understand the power the living dead possess simply in their physical presence. This particular strength is another element of a zombie's defenses that is often underrated by the general public. A ghoul's stench is nothing less than an all-out assault on the human olfactory system, and may cause nausea, light-headedness, vomiting, and epiphora (excessively watery eyes.) This effect is magnified substantially when encountering the living dead in greater numbers. On a scale of one to ten, one being the equivalent of a riot control device such as CS/CN tear gas and ten being a Schedule 1 chemical nerve agent such as sarin, a ghoul's malodor ranks at a five: nonlethal, but with severe incapacitating potential.

A deceased infected human typically begins its reanimation cycle anywhere from several minutes to three hours postmortem, during which time the decaying process is most severe. Analysis has shown that during this period between death and reanimation, decomposition seems to accelerate appreciably beyond the normal human decaying process. Although still scientifically unproven, this accelerated putrification seems to be a direct result of the transformation that turns a human being into a walking cadaver.

Upon reanimation, decomposition appears to slow dramatically, enabling the corpse to avoid complete cellular disintegration for years. Although the subject's atrophy has decelerated, the affecting odor is still very powerful. The scent of decay is overwhelmingly unpleasant to many, especially in close quarters. The effect on the senses can be so severe as to be completely debilitating and can impede the ability to defend yourself or mount a successful counterattack.

The dramatic effect this emanating odor can have on a group of humans was described to the author in the following interview, the larger recorded account of which has come to be known as "Survival in the Spire":

> . . . did you know it takes forty-three seconds for the elevator to get from the bottom to the top of the Needle? That round trip, waiting for those doors to slide open again, was the longest eighty-six seconds of people's lives. One of the defenders, this grizzled old Marine named Edgar, was helping shepherd the children into the elevators and guiding others toward the stairs. That's when we started to smell it. Faint at

first, like someone with terrible indigestion had just passed gas. Then it got much worse.

As the last of us were trying to make our way up the stairs, Edgar and the others blocked off all the entrances except one and closed rank, hoping to thin the oncoming mass. Even before they came within twenty feet of our group, our eyes started tearing. Some passed out. As they started to engage the mob, the dry-heaving kicked in. Some started vomiting onto the attackers. I saw this one poor guy, he was in the middle of an uncontrollable heave when one of them took a chunk out of the back of his neck while he was bent over.

Edgar, a crowbar in each leathery fist, stepped out in front and started swinging wildly at the attacking mob. It looked like he was fighting through tears, as he kept wiping his eyes with his forearm sleeve in between swings. Between the tearing and the dry-heaves, he still managed to bring twenty of those things down. Finally, the group broke rank and Edgar pulled two of the men who fainted clear of the horde, making their way back for that final elevator ride to the top with the last of us.

It wasn't until they were all cleaned up and settled in that I noticed the jagged scratch on Ed's forearm. He didn't say a word to anyone. He just smiled, handed me his crowbars, and walked out to the observation deck. I never saw him again.

—Joseph, Seattle, WA

Although we can classify odor as a general strength of the living dead, this trait can also be an undead liability. One of the first indications that a zombie is near, before even taking sight of your opponent or hearing its lamenting moan, is the unmistakable waft of death in the air. This is especially pronounced when you are away from a metropolitan area, where the concentrations of living dead may be high. On the open road with the wind in your favor, one of the best ways to monitor the proximity of an undead threat is through your sense of smell.

Ferocity

A common misjudgment committed when fighting the living dead is the underestimation of its combat abilities. Nowhere is this more evident than during a ghoul's transition from pursuit to attack. As we will examine shortly in the section on weaknesses, a zombie maintains a relatively slow, regulated speed during its hunting phase. Many individuals mistakenly assume that this seemingly casual, laissez-faire attitude is sustained once a ghoul is within arm's reach of prey. Those who have never seen an actual undead attack believe it is similar to a human being picking a sandwich up from his plate and taking a leisurely bite.

In actuality, the assault is more like that of a crazed animal—snarling, vicious, and unrelenting. Whether this is a result of the close proximity of human flesh or some instinctive attack response mechanism remains unclear. What has been observed is that once within grabbing distance of its victim, a zombie can attack with a brutality that belies its previously dawdling pursuit. This is why grappling with a ghoul has a high incidence of infection and death and should be avoided if at all possible.

WEAKNESSES

Just as the undead possess certain strengths in battle, they possess comparably important weaknesses that we will analyze and exploit in order to develop the most effective combat countermeasures.

Intellect

A zombie's greatest weakness is by far its lack of intelligence. Nearly every living species possesses the most primitive level of intuition in order to survive its environment. The walking dead, on the other hand, do not exhibit even the slightest instinct for self-preservation. They will walk straight into the path of an oncoming train without pause or directly into the metal teeth of a whirling buzz saw while in pursuit of a victim. This disadvantage also has major ramifications on the field of combat. A zombie is unable to strategize, outwit, or outthink its opponent. It will fall into every trap that is set for it, as will every other ghoul that follows in its identical path. As explained in the opening chapter on misconceptions, a zombie's aptitude does not increase, develop, or evolve as it continues its existence as a member of the living dead. Evidence has shown that it is not a trainable entity, nor does it learn from its mistakes.

Coordination

Besides basic ambulatory functions, reaching and grasping, and pushing or pulling of objects, the zombie is an uncoordinated creature. It cannot use primitive offensive weapons such as stones or clubs or defensive equipment such as helmets or shields. Nor is a ghoul able to position its limbs to protect against an oncoming attack, such as by blocking strikes or disarming opponents of their weapons. Should a zombie manage to grab hold of a weapon and pull it away from its bearer, it is doing so not to disarm, but to gain proximity to its target.

A zombie will not kick or punch its victim, and its attack is limited to a predictable sequence: grabbing the target, pulling it in close, and finishing with a bite to the flesh nearest to its mouth. Although most humans can outmaneuver one or several undead attackers with no special training, this weakness should never be taken lightly. We will address strategies for taking advantage of a zombie's limited coordination later in the chapter on combat strategies and techniques.

Skeletal Structure

A zombie's physical composition, like our own bodies, is a fragile assembly of organs, muscle, and bone. You only need to look at your own anatomy to discern the key areas of weakness on an undead creature. The brain, however, is the single most important target on a zombie. This fact should be common knowledge, but it merits repeating: **The only proven method of stopping an advancing undead attacker is to sufficiently destroy its brain.** Sufficient destruction of the brain can be defined as any attack that results in deep structural damage to the organ itself. Although the fine degree of damage has not been extensively tested (will a pinprick to the

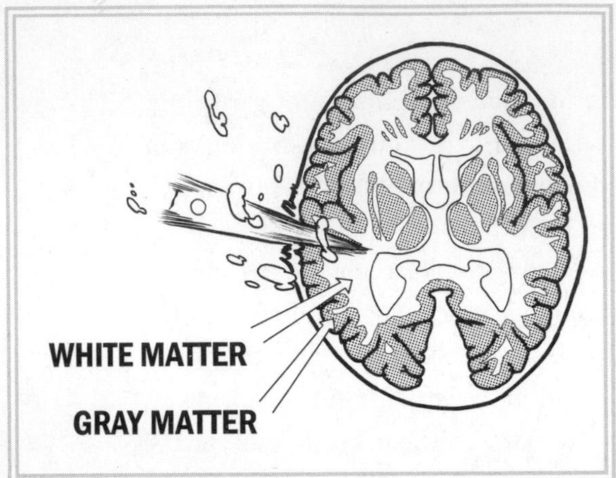

brain halt a zombie?), it is safe to say that any penetration into the skull, past the dura mater, through the gray matter, and into the white matter will stop a walking corpse.

Speed

The steady cadence of a living corpse is one of its greatest weaknesses, second only to its lack of intelligence and reasoning ability. In extensive research studies that timed the movements of a large sampling of undead specimens, experts calculated that the average zombie moves at a relatively consistent forward pace of twenty-three minutes per mile. Its stride does seem to increase slightly during its active hunting phase, but research has shown that this pace will never exceed twenty minutes per mile. To date, the undead contagion has not mutated to a stage at which the living dead can maintain a slow jog, much less a sprinting run. Pay close attention to the rates of speed in the following chart, which has been developed based on actual timed distance evaluations. These figures may assist you in judging approximate time to targets if you are being pursued by the undead:

UNDEAD CONDITION	AVERAGE PACE
Upright, no damage	23 minutes/mile
Upright, slight limp	25 minutes/mile
Upright, severe limp	30 minutes/mile

UNDEAD CONDITION	AVERAGE PACE
Crawling, one leg missing 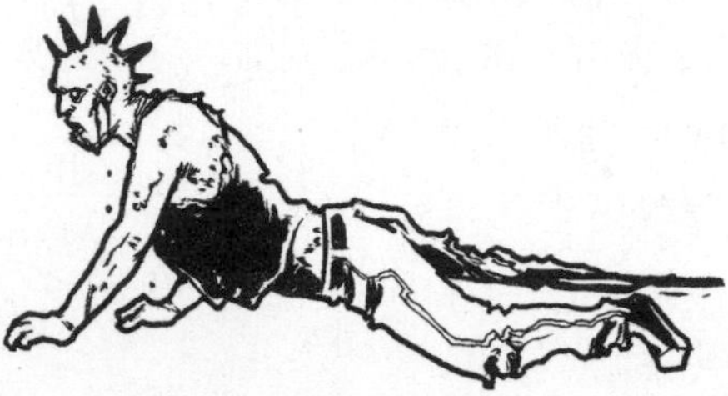	45 minutes/mile
Crawling, both legs missing 	60 minutes/mile

VULNERABILITIES/ REGIONS OF ATTACK

Having reviewed a zombie's various strengths and weaknesses, we can now detail the specific vulnerable targets on an undead specimen to exploit in combat, in order to develop tactics that tilt the odds in your favor during any engagement with a walking corpse.

The Zombie Skull

Although the majority of the populace is aware that destruction of the brain is the only known method to terminate an undead attacker, most are confused as how to actually accomplish this task. Many people mistakenly believe that it is "just like cracking an egg." Nothing could be further from the truth. The protective case known as the skull is one of the hardiest structures on the human body and can withstand a significant amount of abuse. The hair, muscles, and scalp covering the skull all provide additional insulation for the brain, which is itself covered by a fibrous, protective layer known as the dura mater. Many victims have engaged in undead combat believing that destroying the brain would require only a slight rap on the head, only to have the attacking ghoul finish the battle.

In order to inflict a wound severe enough to stop a zombie in its undead tracks, you need to strike with enough force that your blow cracks the skull and penetrates the brain. This act is much easier said than done. Not only must you fracture the skull, you need to cause a severe depressed or compound fracture, in which shattered pieces of bone are driven into the cranial tissue. Ideally, your strike should be powerful enough that the weapon itself penetrates the dura mater and enters the brain cavity. A follow-up blow to the same target area is often required to ensure adequate brain trauma.

Never assume that simply because your blow has landed and penetrated the skull, your strike has incapacitated your attacker. Numerous accounts of combat engagements have involved zombies who had been dealt a seemingly terminal blow but continued their assault, much to the shock and dismay of their human opponent. This can be attributed to a strike that has inadequately penetrated the braincase. Incidents such as this are not unique to zombie altercations. A well-known historical example of such an occurrence is the assassination attempt of Bolshevik revolutionary Leon Trotsky.

On August 4, 1940, a Soviet assassin infiltrated Trotsky's home in Mexico, where he was in exile. The assassin buried the tip of an ice axe into Trotsky's skull. Unfortunately for the attacker, his poorly executed blow failed to penetrate the brain, enabling Trotsky to continue struggling with the assassin, who was subsequently captured by Trotsky's bodyguards. Trotsky died a day later in the hospital. In relation to living dead combat, the lesson to be learned in this example is that even if all external factors seem to align in your favor, never assume that your undead opponent is finished until you watch it collapse to the ground in an unmoving heap.

Primary Targets

Delivering a terminating blow is more easily accomplished on certain regions of the skull than others. We define these areas as *primary targets*, and they should be your first choice of attack in any undead combat engagement:

TEMPORAL REGION (TEMPLE): This region is one of the thinnest areas of bone on the skull and is represented by the sections along the sides of the head, above the ears and just beyond the eyebrows. A blow of sufficient force with an appropriate weapon can fracture this fragile area and penetrate the brain.

NASAL/ORBITAL REGION (BRIDGE OF NOSE/EYES): The area surrounding the eyes and the nasal cavity is especially vulnerable, as it is composed of seven smaller bones that form the orbital socket. An aggressive, cleaving strike to this area can splinter these bones and drive your weapon straight through to the braincase.

OCCIPITAL REGION (BASE OF SKULL): The area on the back of the head where the spinal cord enters the brain cavity is another point of vulnerability on the zombie, and can be targeted for a blunt-force attack. The difficulty lies in pinpointing this area, as ghouls will confront you face forward most of the time during their initial attack sequence.

MIDDLE CRANIAL FOSSA REGION (MCF) (UNDERSIDE OF SKULL): This area is the thinnest part of the entire skull, directly above the back of the mouth, known as the soft palate. Above the MCF is the underside of the brain. Although it is the thinnest area, its location makes it difficult to target, save for one particular attack method, which we will describe later in the chapter on combat strategies and techniques.

Secondary Targets

Secondary targets on the living dead are those that are non-lethal, in that they will not permanently neutralize a zombie. Attacking these targets can, however, severely diminish the lethality of an attacking corpse during a confrontation.

MANDIBLE: A blow to the mandible, commonly referred to as the jawbone, will not keep a zombie from advancing on your position. However, if you eliminate a ghoul's ability to bite, you have significantly reduced the threat it poses. A powerful enough strike can shatter the jaw and possibly detach the lower half of the creature's mouth from its body. The strike should focus on the weak temporo-mandibular joint, where the jaw socket connects with the temporal bone. (See the following illustration.)

NECK: Not technically part of the skull, the neck is still a vulnerable target on a zombie, and is susceptible to a strike that detaches the head from its torso, isolating the risk of the specimen's bite. Though secondary in nature, this target is most effective if you are wielding an edged weapon. Because the brain remains intact, the mouth of a decapitated zombie continues to pose a mortal threat and will snap at any human that unwisely comes into contact with it. After decapitation, you can completely neutralize your target with an appropriate strike to the braincase.

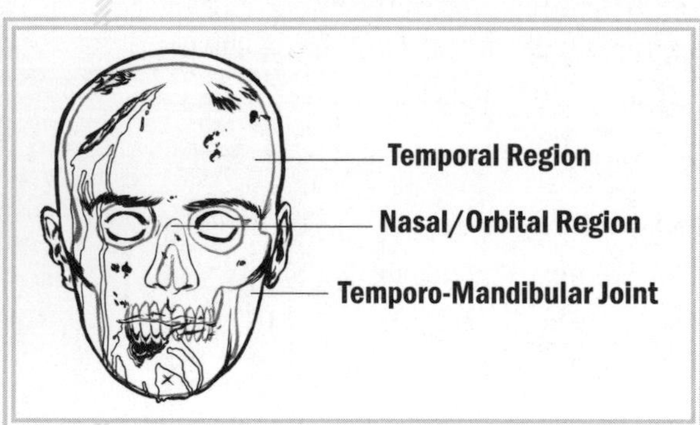

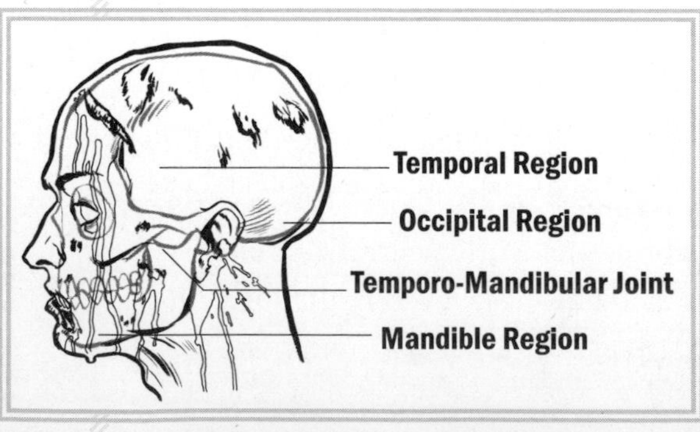

Tertiary Targets

If both primary and secondary targets on a zombie are unavailable, which should rarely be the case, there exist several *tertiary targets* on a zombie that can be targeted. These areas are mostly not recommended, as they only delay an imminent zombie attack. The energy spent focusing on these regions could be better spent to pinpoint areas that would fully incapacitate your opponent. There are special situations when attacking these alternative targets makes sense (if your opponent is wearing a helmet or face mask, for example). In these instances, striking these targets may provide you additional time to either escape or expose another vulnerable region.

Tertiary targets are areas on the zombie frame that, when struck and disabled, appreciably affect the rate of speed by which it can track its prey. The logic for these targets is that if you are unable to neutralize a zombie, you should at the very least prevent it from maintaining its pursuit. This is why these targets focus exclusively on the lower half of the body.

PATELLA: A strike to the patella, otherwise known as the kneecap, can seriously debilitate an advancing ghoul. This area is composed of not only the fragile patella bone, but also a series of muscles, tendons, and ligaments that serve as a pulley to connect the upper and lower leg and work in unison to propel the leg forward. Destroying this area can prevent a zombie from straightening its leg completely. Either blade or bludgeon can be used to attack the patella, turning an upright corpse moving at a steady pace into one that limps along at a much slower rate.

CALCANEAL TENDON: Commonly referred to as the Achilles tendon, the calcaneal tendon connects the muscles of the lower leg to the calcaneus, or heel bone. The vulnerability of this region is well known to those who engage in recreational sports that require sudden bursts of speed. Obliterating this area, evident from the snap you will hear of the tendon rupturing, will also prevent a zombie from walking properly. Be aware that this is not an easy target—not only is the calcaneal tendon the strongest in the entire body, it requires that you navigate around your attacker and strike at the area closest to the heel.

Keep in mind that the goal in any undead combat engagement is to terminate your opponent. Should a blow to one of the aforementioned tertiary targets cause your challenger to stumble and collapse, it is highly recommended that you spend the time to finish the encounter with a concluding strike to the brain. Simply because a zombie can no longer walk upright does not mean that it has lost interest in feeding on human flesh. Several undead engagements have been recorded in which a zombie was left hobbled from a tertiary strike, only to resume its attack later by dragging itself toward its intended victim. Leaving a zombie in a crippled state is also hazardous to other humans who may come upon it, as it will be low to the ground and out of the upright field of vision.

Targets to Avoid

Some regions on the zombie physique should be avoided entirely during your attack. Normally these areas would fare well as targets on a human opponent. Do not be confused in believing that these same areas are just as vulnerable on the living dead.

TORSO: Broken ribs or a punctured lung mean nothing to a walking corpse. Witnesses have seen ghouls with their entire midsections blown open from artillery fire continuing to amble forward as if undamaged. The only reason for targeting this area is to gain additional distance between yourself and your undead opponent for you to mount an escape or a counterattack.

HANDS: As mentioned at the beginning of this section, the hands comprise two of a ghoul's three primary means of attack. It may seem logical, then, to debilitate these appendages in order to limit a ghoul's offensive capability, which in turn should improve your safety. In actuality, targeting a ghoul's hands is contradictory to increasing your level of security. Strikes to the hands will cause additional cuts, gashes, and lacerations, all of which will be rife with infectious matter. As your opponent continues its attack, it will be extending and waving its hands toward you, resulting in a higher risk of infection.

GENITALS: Although a strike to this sensitive area can quickly incapacitate a human being, a blow to the genitals has shown to be completely ineffective against both male and female specimens of the living dead.

External Factors

Several other vulnerability factors can help influence your attack strategy prior to engaging an undead adversary.

AGE: Estimating the age of the human before it reanimated into a living corpse can help you determine the difficulty of delivering a finishing blow. The skin of the elderly tends to be thinner and their bones more fragile than an individual who was reanimated during the prime of his life. Likewise, children and teenage zombies tend to have skulls that are more delicate because of a lack of completed osteopathic development.

APPAREL: Just as your own clothing may serve as a defensive barrier to a ghoul's attack, the garments an individual was wearing just before reanimation may unwittingly serve it well in its undead existence. This serviceability is most evident in infected professional soldiers who have reanimated wearing full combat gear, or civilians who, in looking to protect their brains, donned bicycle or skateboarding headgear before they expired. These types of attackers will be difficult to quickly dispatch, so plan your combat strategy accordingly.

DECOMPOSITION: Zombies that have been reanimated for an extended length of time will be easier to eliminate than those that have not been exposed to nature's elements for longer durations. If disintegration has reached the point where areas of the scalp have dissolved, exposing the bare skull underneath, these uncovered areas become particularly fragile targets and are key indicators of where you should pinpoint your strikes.

HAIR LENGTH/QUANTITY: Does the zombie have a full head of hair, or a short, cropped buzz cut, or is it completely bald? As minor a consideration as this may seem, studies have shown that it is ten times more difficult to fracture a skull covered in scalp than an exposed skull.[5] Add to that a full head of long, matted hair, and it may take formidable strength to deliver a single destructive blow.

---

5 Cantu RC. Head and spine injuries in youth sports. *Clinics in Sports Medicine*, July 1995.

COMBAT REPORT: JOSEPH GARTNER

Dentist, 7th Combat Sciences Group McLean, Virginia

A secretary seats me in a conference room on the floor of the Biological Analysis Division, where I'm to meet Joseph Gartner, Team Leader of the 7th Combat Sciences Group. She apologizes and tells me that, as is typical of his scheduling, Dr. Gartner is running late. When he does arrive fifteen minutes later carrying a thick manila folder, he apologizes profusely and explains that he was gathering the file for our discussion. "Not sure how geeky you wanted to get with this stuff," Gartner says. He is an unassuming man, balding, and wears thick, dark-rimmed glasses. His demeanor is gentle, with an underlying hint of sadness in his voice.

JG: To tell the truth, I ignored the e-mail when I first received it. This was when the Net was still operating on a sporadic basis, and I assumed it was either a prank from one of my associates or some new variation of the Botswanan scam. Even though the age-modified draft had been in effect for more than six months, I thought my specialization would keep me 4-F, and, well, you can see that I'm hardly built for the front-line effort.

Gartner pats his paunchy belly.

It was only after receiving the second certified notice that said, "Failure to comply constitutes a violation of the Federal Emergency Health Powers Act and will result in immediate suspension of medical licenses and/or possible imprisonment," that I figured I should show up. Still, I couldn't believe that I would be of any use to them, given my subspecialty.

ZCM: And what was your subspecialty?

JG: Pedodontics—pediatric dentistry. One week I was knee-deep in baby teeth and anxious parents, the next I'm sitting in front of the director of the CDC and the Health and Human Services Secretary discussing this new division of the Combat Sciences Group. I'd heard of the CSG from what I read in the papers, mostly about the work done to analyze the virus's pathology and its neurological pathways, but the more they discussed the concept of the new division, the more it made sense.

He unfolds the manila envelope and removes several x-rays.

JG: Working with the teeth of children, you're privy to their chronological dental development—how the molars are forming, the developmental relationship of the maxilla and mandible and any associated pathologies. One of the issues the team realized with the virus was that when a human is first infected, the brain isn't the only human tissue that undergoes an evolution. The fundamental cellular composition of an undead specimen is altered after infection, including the teeth. See here, this is a panoramic x-ray of a normal noncontaminated adult. Now take a look at this one, six hours after infection. Here . . .

Gartner pulls out an enlarged scan of the infected specimen's upper teeth. Using the tip of a pencil, he points to a series of minute fibers protruding from the root of each tooth.

JG: Notice these tiny, cilialike projections? Remarkable. What do they look like to you?

ZCM: They almost look like . . . tiny hooks?

JG: Precisely. Or anchors, if you will. Even before the victim has fully turned, this transformation is already taking place. What this x-ray doesn't show you are the transformations of the supporting structures—the periodontal ligament, the gingival fibers, the alveolar bone. The entire infrastructure responsible for the retention and reinforcement of our teeth undergoes a rapid evolution. We realized that whatever mutations this virus causes, it isn't as rudimentary as bringing a dead body back to life. It alters the infected's anatomy to withstand cellular destruction in arctic temperatures, resist decomposition at sea, and reinforce its fundamental weapon: its teeth. The only way this transformation could be worse is if the infection caused the victims to become polyphyodontal—growing new sets of teeth to replace the lost ones, like a shark. Thankfully, we haven't seen any variants of that sort, yet. It is for this reason that our division was formed: to determine if we could approach the conflict from a different angle, by fighting the enemy's primary means of attack and infection.

ZCM: What ideas were you expected to develop?

JG: What weren't we expected to develop? If I could tell you some of the esoteric, exotic, and straight-up crazy ideas we kicked around, I tell you, feeding them candy wasn't too far off the mark. Our marching orders were to attempt to do the opposite of what I was educated to do and have done all my life. Instead of protecting and nurturing enamel and dentin, we were now attempting to reverse-engineer and potentially accelerate their decay.

ZCM: The government wanted to rot the zombies' teeth?

JG: Don't laugh, it isn't as crazy as it sounds. At the point when our group was developed, large-scale outbreaks were reported on all seven continents; analyses were making their way into the President's Daily Brief showing that for every one zombie that was destroyed, four were created. The brass thought that if we really got our heads underwater on eliminating existing specimens outright, we should try to see if there was any way to minimize the risk of new infections. This was just one of many tactics.

It was all about analysis in the beginning: what happens two hours, six hours, twelve hours after infection. After we determined that post-reanimation, cellular evolution seems to cease, we went on the offensive. We worked closely with the Chemical Weapons Division, on what was called the Methuselah Project. We labored for months, trying to develop an airborne accelerant that could be dropped on a hot zone and defang an entire colony of specimens within thirty days. We never really got it to work right—either the gas would be ineffective, or the dispersal agent would fail to dissipate quickly enough and drift into neighboring safe regions. Any isolated human survivors in the area would also be affected. That's when the brass drew the line. "Fighting a living corpse is bad enough, but subjecting innocent civilians to tooth loss is too much for anyone to bear," is what the defense secretary said. The only compound we created that seemed to work was a topical agent that caused extremely rapid decay within forty-eight hours. The Infected Subjects Research Division used it for a while on their cases. I hate to think of the research assistant whose job it was to apply the stuff. This is before we developed the "Tommy."

ZCM: The Tommy?

JG: Short for TME, or Tactical Mandible Extractor. Once the higher-ups put the thumbscrews to us about our "unacceptable failure rate" on chemical initiatives, our department head decided to change direction and had the team work closer with the manufacturing division. In hindsight, it was the right move, particularly because of the extensive use of tools like the Tommy. It's probably easier if I just show you.

We walk down the corridor through a set of lab doors that opens up to a hallway with a thick glass partition, separating us from a large, open examination room. Contained within the room are five zombies, positioned several feet apart. A steel cable runs from the wall and connects to a carabiner latched to a leather harness around the torso of each specimen.

JG: Put these on.

He hands me a packet containing a disposable lab coat, a pair of blue nitrile gloves, and plastic goggles. We don the safety wear and enter the room. The subjects immediately begin to stir. Gartner picks up a long, fiberglass staff with what looks like a miniature bear trap on one end and pruning shears on the other.

JG: The trickiest part is getting the timing right.

Gartner steps closer to one of the subjects. The zombie extends its hands and moans. Using the pruning end of the device, he snaps off all four fingers of the creature's left hand. The digits scatter to the ground like bloated caterpillars. With another snap, the fingers on the right hand fall to the floor. As the ghoul continues to moan, Gartner jams the bear trap end of the device into its mouth. He pulls a lever on the handle, which releases a spike through the bottom of the subject's jaw. With a single yank, Gartner pulls the ghoul's jawbone clean off the skull. It skitters across the floor. Gartner casually picks up the mandible with the trap end of the device and tosses it into a red plastic-lined bin marked Biohazard, *followed by its detached fingers. I look back at the creature. The remainder of what was once its tongue now lolls out of its mouth, quivering back and forth.*

JG: No muss, no fuss.

ZCM: Who uses this tool?

JG: Research groups mostly—any division of the CDC that conducts regular experimentation on undead subjects. I also heard that Special Forces uses it when they conduct live-fire room-clearing or mob-control exercises. There was a plan at one point to start dropping them into compromised security zones for use by the defending population. I guess the logic was, if we couldn't completely eliminate the threat, could we at least make them less dangerous? I couldn't imagine how that would work—people walking around town, going about their normal, everyday lives, with jawless, fingerless specimens meandering about. That idea got zeroed pretty quickly, but some of the Tommys did make it into civilian hands through some black-market channels.

He sets the contraption down quietly and sighs.

JG: My wife put me through dental school. Worked as an executive secretary for this private equity bastard for years while I finished my residency. If she were alive to see this, I don't know what she'd think. I was supposed to use my knowledge to help people, not to do this kind of work.

They tell me I'll be cycled out soon, given the safety declaration in the States and all, and that they'll call me back if additional projects "require my expertise." At this point, I'm not sure what I'll be going back to. I guess there's my practice. But I have to wonder, what are the people in my town going to benefit from more: my skills working with children, or my experience with the living dead?

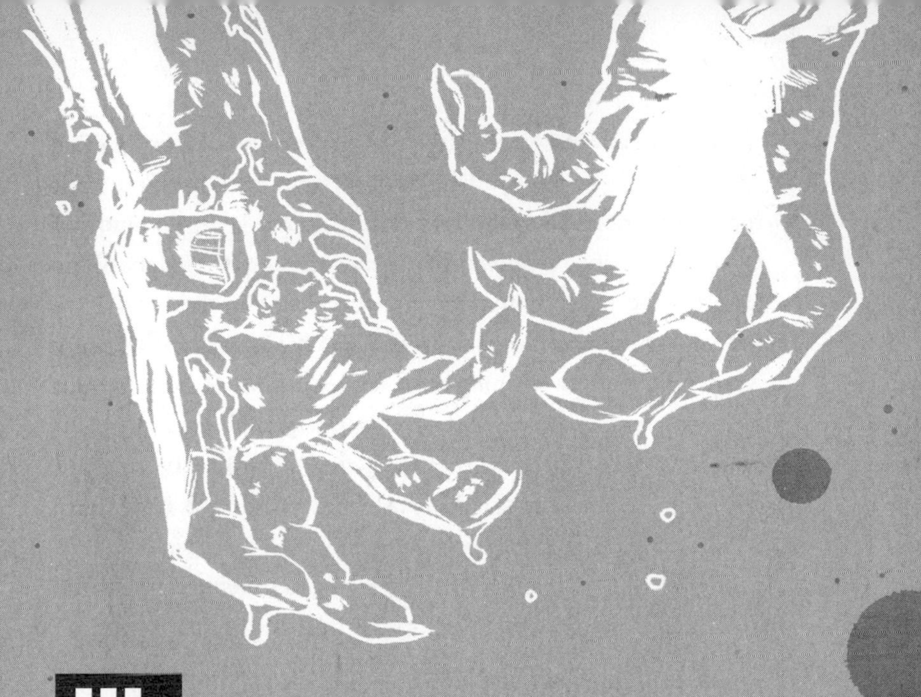

III.

CONDITIONING AND PREPARATION

Lack of activity destroys the good condition of every human being, while movement and methodical physical exercise save it and preserve it.

—PLATO

An often miscalculated aspect of preparing for a zombie assault is the rigorous toll it takes on both the body and mind. Many individuals plan for every other factor in an undead outbreak—weapons, supplies, fortifications, and transport—while ignoring the most fundamental element: the body's condition. Research has shown that during a zombie infestation, the first wave of casualties is composed largely of those who are just physically unable to weather the onslaught. Regardless of the strength of your fortification or the resilience of your weapon, if you are not mentally and physically hardened to contend with a walking corpse, your chances of survival will be poor. Do not, however, interpret conditioning to mean that you must be in elite-caliber physical shape. As we will explore shortly, individuals with a wide variety of physical characteristics and body types can successfully defend against an undead attack.

PHYSICAL SELF-ASSESSMENT

Just as there is no single weapon appropriate for all combat situations, there is no one ideal zombie-neutralizing physique. Every individual has unique attributes that translate into strengths or liabilities when confronting the living dead. In order to properly tailor your conditioning regimen, you must first objectively assess your own physical build and understand both the benefits and limitations that it may present in undead combat. In the 1940s, psychologist William Sheldon developed three classes of human physique, called *somatotypes*, based on the corporeal qualities of the human body. To assist you in your self-assessment, we have developed three combatant categories based on Sheldon's somatotypes—the ectocombatant, the mesocombatant, and the endocombatant.

The Ectocombatant

TRAITS: **THIN, LIGHT MUSCULATURE**
STRENGTHS: **ENDURANCE, SPEED, STEALTH**
LIABILITIES: **LACK OF STRENGTH AND POWER; EXTREMELY LOW BODY FAT**

With a wiry frame and lean physique, the ectocombatant's greatest assets are his or her speed and endurance—two of the most important physical benefits during an undead siege. Surviving during a zombie outbreak has often been likened to a marathon race, so what better physique to have than that of a long-distance runner? With an abundance of energy and stamina, the ectocombatant is able to constantly stay a step ahead of his or her hungry predators. Because of their narrow build, ectos with superior dexterity have been known to effectively navigate through a room packed with zombies and still avoid being mauled.

In offensive maneuvers, ectocombatants need to be more cautious. Their lighter frames often do not pack a large quantity of muscle, making it more difficult to execute combat techniques that require a greater amount of strength or momentum. Long-distance techniques generally do not work as well for the ectocombatant, as these weapons are often heavier and require some degree of centrifugal force. Engaging multiple attackers is also discouraged, as the ectocombatant may not be able to execute a long series of consecutive, neutralizing blows repeatedly without becoming exhausted. Interestingly, combat statistics reveal that ectos are often more successful in close-quarters engagements against the undead, perhaps because of their speed and their thinner appendages, which may be more difficult for a ghoul to grasp.

The ectocombatant also needs to be almost neurotically vigilant with his or her food supply during large-scale zombie infestations. The lack of adipose tissue on the body means that without a consistent supply of energy, individuals with this physical type will rapidly begin cannibalizing muscle tissue for fuel, leaving the ecto dizzy, light-headed, and in a weaker and more vulnerable state. It is difficult enough facing attackers that seek to devour your flesh; there's no need to prompt one's own body to do so as well.

The Mesocombatant

TRAITS: **ATHLETIC, SOLID MUSCULATURE**
STRENGTHS: **BALANCED LEVELS OF STRENGTH AND SPEED**
LIABILITIES: **LOWER BODY FAT LEVELS**

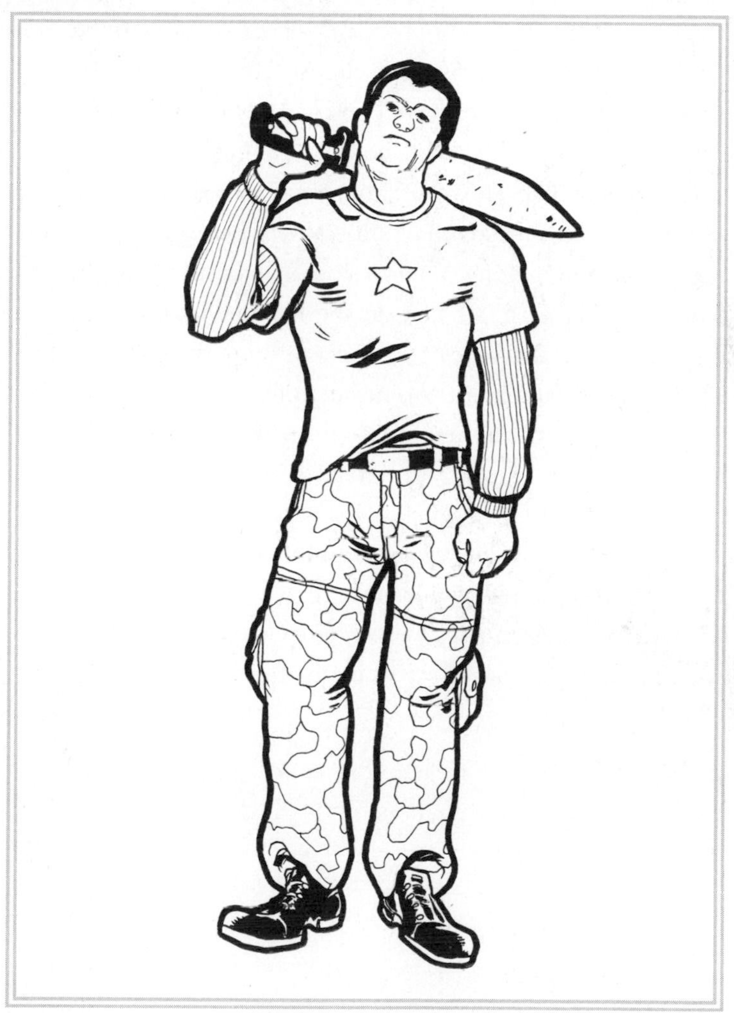

The mesocombatant has the benefit of being the most adaptable body type to all forms of zombie combat. This physique has the strength and weight to execute techniques that require greater amounts of power, as well as the stamina to endure extended evasive maneuvers. It is no wonder that individuals involved in various types of combat activities—boxers, soldiers, and martial artists—often exhibit this type of body structure.

Given the balanced nature of the mesocombatant, individuals with this body type can choose from a variety of offensive techniques to suit their personal style. Mesos typically perform equally well at all combat ranges—long, medium, and close combat. However, this equal physical distribution also means that mesos may suffer from being a "jack-of-all-trades, master of none" when it comes to battling the undead. They may never be as fast as the lithe ectocombatant, nor will they have the weight to execute long-range techniques that the endocombatant can perform flawlessly.

Like ectocombatants, mesos need to be keenly aware of their food supply during an outbreak, given their lower body fat levels. This may be an even greater concern for the mesocombatant, as the larger amount of muscle on the frame means that the body requires a greater caloric intake simply to maintain weight. Any loss of muscle due to lack of nourishment means a less effective combatant.

The Endocombatant

TRAITS: **HEAVIER BUILD, ROUND PHYSIQUE**
STRENGTHS: **ENERGY STORAGE, POWER, LEVERAGE**
LIABILITIES: **LACK OF SPEED AND ENDURANCE**

With a larger build and ample energy stores, the endocombatant is well suited to survive a supply shortage during an undead plague. Athletes in the endocombatant class include sumo wrestlers, football linemen, and some professional wrestlers.

Unlike the other two combatant types, the endocombatant can draw upon his or her larger adipose reserves should sources of food become scarce. In fact, studies have determined that well-trained endos have the highest survivability rate of all three body classifications during long-term zombie outbreaks because they can sustain themselves for the protracted duration. After extended sieges, many observed mesocombatants were in fact former endos whose body fat stores were depleted during the lengthy episode.

Because of their larger size, endocombatants are better suited to using weapons and techniques that take advantage of their heavier weight. Endos seem to fare particularly well with long-range tactics, where they can put the full force of their girth behind the weapon. Stronger endos also have the ability to burst through hordes of undead attackers, much the same way a football linebacker can breach the crush of several opponents.

Their larger size and slower speed, however, makes the endocombatant more vulnerable in close-combat situations, as more flesh is available to grab and attack. It is advised that endocombatants avoid close-quarters engagements if at all possible. Endos also need to develop their endurance to the levels of their ecto and meso counterparts, as they do not want to be responsible for slowing down an entire group with the dead in hot pursuit.

Although the specific types of combatant physiques outlined here are quite distinct from one another, rarely do individuals fall completely into one of these three categories. Most combatants straddle the line between two of the types described. You may be a mesocombatant with endo tendencies to gain weight, or an endocombatant with excellent endurance as a result of long-distance training runs.

Falling into one of these physical categories also does not imply that you inherit the strengths of that body type by default. This is particularly true of the ectocombatant class, as society often equates thinness with a superior level of health and fitness. Despite his leanness, an ectocombatant that smokes two packs of cigarettes a day will most likely not have the lung capacity and endurance level of a larger, nonsmoking endocombatant who jogs consistently. What is most vital is that you perform an honest and thorough self-assessment, noting your shortcomings as well as emphasizing your assets. With time and persistence, you can then work toward turning those liabilities into strengths to use against your cadaverous opponent.

FITNESS TRAITS AND CHARACTERISTICS

Make no mistake: Defending yourself against a walking corpse can be an exhausting endeavor. Facing two or three simultaneous undead opponents armed with a makeshift weapon can drain even a well-conditioned athlete. In order to protect yourself and others in your care, you need to maintain a certain level of physical fitness. Exceptional athleticism is not required, but a foundation of health needs to be maintained, particularly during large-scale outbreaks when attacks may be more frequent and resources slim.

What is considered a base level of fitness? As a general benchmark of the endurance level required for a zombie infestation, an individual should be able complete the following sequence in its entirety without feeling substantially spent:

- Cover 5 miles in 60 minutes
- 30 standard push ups or 50 easy push-ups
- 5 unassisted pull-ups or 10 assisted pull-ups
- 50 jumping jacks

For active individuals who already have a moderate level of fitness, this may seem like a relatively easy circuit to complete. This is also the bare minimum recommended for all civilians, regardless of age or weight. There is a great difference, however, between "base" and "combat-ready" fitness. Without a sufficient level of health and stamina, having to fend off multiple undead attacks during a full-blown outbreak can reduce an unprepared individual to a worn out shell of a human being within hours. To become a truly effective warrior against the undead, you must maintain a consistent fitness routine. When the desire to forgo your regular training regimen arises, let this be your motivation: Every session you skip makes you that much more vulnerable to being devoured alive.

With a combat-ready build, you enhance several traits in your physique that will be essential to your survival during a zombie attack:

STRENGTH: Without adequate strength, you will not only be unable to reinforce your fortification and forage for supplies, you will lack the ability to defend yourself from an untold number of undead attackers, especially if you need to do so without a firearm. It takes a considerable amount of power to deliver a finishing blow to the skull of a zombie; imagine having to do it dozens of times a day. Strength will be a key factor in your level of survivability.

ENDURANCE: During an undead assault, your objective should always be to eliminate only those attackers that pose an imminent threat to your existence. Many incidents have been recorded in which an overzealous combatant attempted to muscle his way through a large mob of ghouls, only to exhaust himself halfway through his attack, losing the ability to both eradicate the threat and escape with his life intact. You may also be required to travel long distances to a potential safety outpost, most likely on foot. Your endurance level will be critical in such situations.

ACCURACY: When fighting the living dead, the goal is to work smarter, not harder. It may require five blows to destroy a zombie, or it may take only one. The difference depends not only on your strength, but on the precision of your strikes. Having excellent hand-eye coordination can end every confrontation that much more quickly. As you develop your fighting abilities, you will expend less energy during each successive combat engagement.

AGILITY: One of the key advantages humans possess over our reanimated selves is the ability to synchronize our muscles and execute complex actions to outmaneuver our uncoordinated opponents. Do not let this agility go to waste or take it for granted. Not only will a good sense of balance and coordination improve your combat abilities, these traits are essential during an escape, when you may have to scale obstacles, traverse narrow passageways, and weave between lunging attackers.

An example of the influence agility can play in facing the living dead was described to the author in the following incident:

> . . . there were eight of us holed up in this apartment complex. We were able to rest and resupply for two days before enough of them finally pulled open the electric gates. We should have done more to secure the stairwells, but we were all so damn tired.
>
> We tried to bring down as many as we could and we tossed the bodies down the stairwells to slow their ascent, but by the time we made it to the roof, they were pouring out of the fire exits like ants from a sand hill. We managed to find this narrow plank of wood, and thank Christ it was long enough to reach the building next door. It was too flimsy for the weight of more than a single person at a time, so we had to cross one by one. Six of us made it across. Tom—we knew he was nervous, so Julie coached him from behind while the rest of us encouraged him from the other side. He couldn't walk across fast enough, so he had to start crawling along the board. Crawling. Dammit.
>
> He finally made it. Julie did a good job beating them back before getting on the board, but by the time she was halfway across, one of them had reached the plank and placed its weight on it. The board snapped in two. She didn't even have a chance to make a jump for it.
>
> —*Samantha, Chicago, IL*

EXERCISE REGIMEN

Disregard specialized workouts that overdevelop particular muscle groups for the sake of vanity, as well as exercises that require any unwieldy equipment. Your fitness routine should be practical and portable, and should replicate the functional movements you may be required to accomplish during evasion or defensive action against the living dead.

Think about what may be required of you in any given day during an outbreak. In a matter of hours, you may have to run from attackers, scramble over abandoned vehicles, crawl under fencing, and dispatch a group of zombies with several skull-crushing blows. It's no surprise that those employed in "blue-collar" jobs involving a high degree of manual labor exhibit some of the best survival rates during an undead siege. These individuals work their muscles almost daily in practical application.

Most of the primary muscle groups on the human body are stressed during a zombie attack:

- **Deltoids, pectorals**—pushing attackers, thrusting swords or spears
- **Latissimus dorsi**—pulling/extracting weapons, swinging bludgeons
- **Quadriceps, hamstrings**—running, climbing, kicking, and stomping
- **Abdominals, obliques, core**—every action previously listed

Although these are the major muscle groups on which you should focus in your fitness routine, you should also employ movements that require coordinating several of these muscle groups in unison. Straightforward, compound movements should be emphasized. Minimize exercises such as calf raises, concentration curls, and triceps extensions that work minor muscle groups. Develop the larger muscles aggressively, and the smaller ones will adapt accordingly.

You need to be able to accomplish your routine with minimal to no equipment (weights, mats, DVD player), silently (given your particular security situation), and in a confined area. This will replicate a possible scenario during a zombie outbreak in which you must remain quiet in a restricted space. Jogging becomes a luxury exercise during the course of an undead infestation. Given this unique situation, focusing on calisthenics and body-weight exercises is ideal. If you perform these movements regularly at an appropriate intensity level, you will become fit enough to defend yourself quite effectively for any duration.

Here are some foundational exercises to start your routine.

PUSH-UPS: The standard of upper-body-strength exercises. Even after decades of exercise fads, machines, and electronic "pulse" muscle developers, this exercise has stood the test of time and will build your shoulders, chest, and arms in addition to the complementary joints and ligaments that work in coordination with these muscles. Start with your palms and feet on the floor and your back straight. With your arms shoulder-width apart, bend at the elbows and lower your body until it nearly touches the floor. Press your body back up until your elbows are almost locked. For those who find this movement difficult, start with the easy version of this exercise, with your knees on the floor and legs crossed at the ankles. You can add variety to this movement and target complementary muscles more intensely by varying your hand positions so that your palms are closer or farther apart.

PULL-UPS: Coupled with push-ups, these two exercises form an excellent foundation for building a ghoul-destroying upper body. Pull-ups are infamously challenging for many people, so do not let the difficulty of this exercise dissuade you from including it in your routine. This exercise also requires use of a bar or overhang, but you can use any extended pipe, bar, or tree branch for this purpose. You can also purchase a removeable, door-mounted pull-up device, which has the advantage of being portable so that it can be taken with you should you need to abandon your shelter.

Burpees

BURPEES: A simple yet intense exercise that has been used extensively in military physical training. Starting in a standing position, crouch down in a ball with your knees to your chest and hands on the ground. Extend both feet backward explosively while keeping your hands on the floor, ending in a push-up position. Do one complete push-up. Bring both feet back to your previous position, knees to chest. Explode upright and jump upward.

SQUATS: What push-ups are to your upper body, squats are for the lower half. Many are familiar with this exercise using heavy barbells. Body-weight squats, however, can be just as effective in building strength and stamina. Standing with legs shoulder width apart, bend at the knees and lower your hips until your thighs are parallel to the floor, and push yourself back up to standing position. Holding on to any accessible weight (logs, bricks, a small child) will increase the difficulty of this movement.

JUMPING JACKS: You may remember these from your high school physical education class. As simplistic as this movement may seem, jacks can build endurance when performed rapidly and in substantial quantity. Starting in a standing position with your arms at your sides, jump straight up and open your arms and legs apart in midair. Land with your hands clapped over your head and your feet wide apart, then jump back into the air and reverse your movement for one complete jack. In addition to improving your conditioning level, this exercise can stabilize and strengthen the joints in your lower legs. By building up the tendons and ligaments, jacks can help prevent one of the worst injuries you can suffer during an unanticipated evacuation—a twisted ankle.

BOX JUMPS: This exercise will build explosive strength in your legs, but does require a box or platform eighteen to twenty-four inches high. Simply jump up on the box and jump down for a set number of repetitions. Land with your knees bent when jumping both on and off the platform to absorb the shock of the landings.

Linking these exercises in sequence can form the structure of your zombie fitness routine. Following a circuit such as this will enable you to build and maintain strength and endurance in a short amount of time without the need for a large space or unique equipment. The following Zombie Basic Fitness Circuit (ZBFC) can be accomplished in a single room smaller than the size of the average U.S. prison cell (eight by twelve feet).

Zombie Basic Fitness Circuit

- 20 push-ups
- 10 pull-ups
- 20 burpees
- 10 box jumps (or 20 jumping jacks, should a box be unavailable)
- 20 squats

Remember to move quickly between exercises with no rest in between. Keep track of the time required for you to complete the sequence in its entirety. Once you can accomplish this circuit easily, increase the repetitions for each exercise as appropriate. Log your time and repetitions and always try to best your previous numbers. Not only will this meticulous record keeping help increase your fitness levels, it can help preoccupy your mind while the living dead pound against the exteriors of your fortification.

Combat Exercises

You can also incorporate several exercises into your routine that both build overall fitness and simulate actions that you may have to execute during a combat scenario.

BLASTERS: A modification of the standard push-up; instead of raising your body to an elbows-locked position, thrust your body upward, attempting to lift your upper torso completely off the ground. The forceful movement will help build explosive power in your upper body. Training your body to initiate bursts of strength is also critical in close combat with the undead. This exercise can help build the strength to shove an attacking corpse away from you as far and as fast as possible. Imagine at the bottom of each repetition that rather than pushing off the floor, you are pushing a ravenous ghoul away from your body.

KICKOUTS: This technique has the same power-building premise as blasters, except for your lower body. Similar to a karate-style front-thrust kick, this exercise develops strength in your thighs and calves so that you can launch an attacker away from you with your feet. When using this type of movement on the living dead, the goal is to push the zombie's torso forcefully away from your body, while at the same time avoiding its grasp. In a standing position, raise your knee to your chest and push outward with the ball of your foot, imagining that you are pushing a zombie away from you. After your leg is fully extended, retract your foot quickly to avoid being caught by an undead hand.

WOODCHOPPERS: Ideally this exercise would involve the actual splitting of lumber (as the adage goes, the person who chops the wood warms himself twice). Place a mark on a tree or any solid, freestanding object and try to strike that mark repeatedly with one-handed and two-handed swings. If an actual ax is not available, any long, heavy object such as a tree branch or sledgehammer will do. This exercise not only will help build strength in your upper body and core muscles, but it also develops the coordination required to strike a small target, such as the temporal area on the skull, accurately and repeatedly. Mentally picture the mark you are striking as the cranium of an attacking corpse.

SKULLPOPPERS: Another exercise that simulates an action that may be required of you in undead combat. Place a car tire on a stable surface. Mark a spot on the tire. Raise your knee to your chest, then stomp on the mark as forcefully as you can.

Execute a number of repetitions, making sure you complete an equal number of stomps with each leg to ensure balanced development. Building strength in this exercise will help when you must finish fallen or decapitated zombies with the heel of your boot.

Just as with the previous ZBFC routine, you can link the combat-oriented exercises listed earlier into one Zombie Combat Fitness Circuit (ZCFC):

Zombie Combat Fitness Circuit

- 25 blasters
- 25 kickouts (each leg)
- 25 woodchoppers (two-handed)
- 25 skullpoppers (each leg)

Ideally, you should create a unique circuit incorporating a variety of all the exercises previously listed to avoid the boredom that comes with repeating monotonous fitness routines. The more varied and persistently challenging you make your workouts, the more likely you are to look forward to completing them, and the fitter you will be against the undead.

People used to always ask me, "With all the science, technology, and research available, why is everyone still so fat?" What no one understood or accepted back then was that being fat did not necessarily mean not being fit. When the dead began to walk, that's when everybody figured it out. As much as fitness professionals like to say they emphasize health, many just gave the public what it wanted—and it wanted six-pack abs, even if it meant getting them in the unhealthiest ways possible. They didn't realize that having your body fat level so low may be nice eye candy, but if you need to walk fifty miles with a mob of inexhaustible creatures on your ass and the only food you've eaten in days is a wedge of moldy bread, a single-digit body fat percentage could be a death sentence.

I saw it happen to a lot of my colleagues. Sure, many were educated, learned professionals, but there were just as many in the business because they looked good with their shirts off. Shredded glutes, ripped obliques, rectus abdominis muscles so cut that you could insert a quarter between each muscle. "He looks diesel; he must know what he's talking about." Turns out a lot of them didn't, at least when it came to having a body that helps you survive the living dead rather than attract a mate.

There was this one trainer I knew from my gym—Billy. Everyone called him "Mr. Anatomy" because he looked like one of those science posters that display all the muscles on the body. I lost touch with him after the initial outbreaks. Then, by sheer coincidence, I saw him in the infirmary of a rescue station months afterward. Stroke of luck that I recognized him, really, because he barely looked like the man I knew. Billy wasn't infected, but he didn't

> look much better than a lot of those things. He must've lost a quarter of his body weight and was suffering from rhabdomyolysis, where the muscle breaks down so fast that the kidneys start failing. His hospital gown hung from his shoulders like it was on a wire hanger.
>
> To be fair, no one could have expected or planned for something like this; instead of dialing up for takeout or passing through the drive-through, now we all have to work for our food. We've returned to being a hunter-gatherer society. People also realize that you damn well better have some meat on your bones. Because now, we're not the only ones out there hunting.
>
> —*Jim, Personal Trainer, Los Angeles, CA*

Diet warrants only the briefest of discussions. This is because during a zombie outbreak, you will most likely not have the luxury of eating properly. Depending on the length of infestation and availability of supplies in your region, you may not be able to consume a balanced diet for very long, and may soon be eating for survival, not balanced nutrition. This is particularly true if commerce and commercial shipping are disrupted as a result of the rising number of walking dead.

During instances of minor infestation, your pantry supplies hopefully can sustain you with an adequate quantity of carbohydrates, proteins, and calories. One food item that may be beneficial to store in quantity is a high-calorie nutrition bar. Typically eaten by endurance athletes, mountain climbers, and soldiers, these nutrient-dense bars supply vitamins, minerals, and calories for active individuals. Food purists may argue that this type of product is merely a highly processed, glorified candy bar. Although this may be true of some brands, many are nutritionally complex and, more important, conveniently portable, a beneficial asset should you have to quickly abandon your fortification with your food supply in tow.

During a modest undead epidemic, you should consume a normal quantity of food as long as you possibly can while monitoring your overall food supply. Do not ration yourself too strictly, particularly at the outset of an infestation. Remember, your body will need to expend a considerable amount of energy to sustain your muscle mass and endurance while you are fending off attackers, reinforcing your stronghold, and evacuating the area if necessary. In fact, it is to your advantage if you carry a few added pounds on your frame, which your body can use as stored energy if supplies run low. Without an adequate amount of fat on the body and minimal food intake, your system will burn the only energy source available—muscle mass, leaving you weaker and more vulnerable. This is especially dangerous for the ectocombatant body type. Although it may be attractive during peacetime, an extremely low body fat level and a "ripped" physique during a zombie attack could potentially cost you your life. This does not, however, give you an excuse to overindulge in order to shore up your fat reserves. An unconditioned, overweight physique is just as dangerous as one that is too lean.

During large-scale outbreaks that last for a significant duration (more than twelve months), you will most likely be limited to "survival subsistence," which means ingesting anything edible in order to keep your body functioning. This type of diet is not conducive to long-term health, but may be required given your specific circumstances. In the most dire of outbreak scenarios, you may need to survive on the poorest of food choices—soda, candy bars, and snack foods—because these items are generally plentiful and contain enough preservatives to prevent them from turning rancid for years. You should resort to this type of consumption only if you have no other alternative, and only as a stopgap measure until the time comes when you can forage for healthier food sources. Fighting the living dead on this type of diet may help you reach the next rescue station, but it will not sustain your combat abilities for long.

During times of peace, you are encouraged to maintain a healthy diet composed mainly of whole grains, fruits, vegetables, and lean protein. You should avoid meals consisting entirely of simple or processed carbohydrates such as white flour and sugar, which cause excessive spikes in energy levels followed by spiraling lows. To reiterate, this is peacetime eating; during an outbreak, you should consume whatever nutrients are available to stay alive. Do not be overly obsessive on your actual weight, but focus instead on your overall fitness level. The healthier you are during times of tranquility, the longer you will survive during a time of undead chaos.

MENTAL PREPARATION

Many warriors have acknowledged that the most difficult part of preparing for and winning in battle is not the physical exertion, but the mental challenge. Nowhere is this truer than when fighting the living dead. Not only must you overcome the psychological absurdity of defending yourself against a walking corpse, but you may also face the unfortunate situation of having to do so against a ghoul that was once someone to whom you had a close, personal connection.

As a result, it has often been stated that in order to survive in a zombie-infested world, you have to become somewhat of a zombie yourself. It is vital that you detach your feelings and emotions from the threat you face. Zombies are not friends, not family, not serene, otherworldly creatures. The only thing the undead should represent is a violent threat to your life and the lives of any remaining humans in your care. You cannot afford the time or the luxury of waxing philosophic about zombies in your proximity: who they were, how they were infected, how they ended up in front of you reaching for your throat. Your only objective should be to either evade or eliminate the threat.

This detachment, however, can be mentally taxing, particularly if you had an emotional attachment to your opponent. Perhaps the zombie is a young child or teenager, a neighbor, a teammate, even a member of your own family. It takes tremendous mental fortitude to look past the association you had with the formerly human individual lurching toward you and eliminate the oncoming threat to your life. Here are some techniques that may help you in this task:

- **Ignore superficial appearances.** The more time you spend examining the personal effects of what connected the zombie with his or her former living existence, the more vulnerable you are, both physically and emotionally. It does you no good to notice that she's wearing designer earrings or that you like the band on his T-shirt. Look past clothing, jewelry, eyewear, and any other trinket that would make the specimen seem more human in your eyes.

- **Pinpoint attack targets.** Once you confirm that the individual in front of you is indeed a zombie and presents an impending risk, focus on how you will eliminate this threat. Zero in on the most vulnerable targets. Concentrate on key weaknesses such as the strike points described earlier—neck, temple region, and occipital area: Which of these targets is the most exposed and ripe for attack?

- **Avoid eye contact.** A living human's eyes have often been described as the windows to the soul. Similarly, peering too intently into a ghoul's pupils may cause you to believe that you have witnessed a flash of their former humanity: intelligence, fear, sadness. **You have not.** Many victims have psyched themselves into becoming zombie fodder by making this mistake. Do not do the same. Target a vulnerable area, eliminate the threat, and move along.

Post-Undead Combat Trauma

Hand-to-hand fighting of any kind is one of the most unsettling types of combat any human can experience. Trained soldiers who have had to terminate opponents in non-ghoul-related warfare have stated that the most traumatic of all events were incidents where they needed to do so with a hand-based weapon, such as a bayonet or a truncheon. Zombie combat can be even more distressing, given that it occurs not just between professional warriors, but among the civilian population as well. Combat with the living dead is also the type of conflict in which only one combatant is left standing at the conclusion of an engagement—ideally the living one.

An entire manual can be devoted just to dealing with the emotional stress of fighting the undead. For untrained citizens required to eliminate a walking corpse to survive, the range of emotions felt after a successful combat engagement can be overwhelming, and similar to the posttraumatic stress experienced by warriors after human combat. During an extended outbreak, individuals may find themselves isolated, their only interaction being with the undead. Cases have been documented of individuals who faced these circumstances and, upon rescue, launched into unprovoked attacks toward anyone with whom they come into contact, living or undead. A diagnosis has emerged from the medical community specifically pinpointing these unique types of maladies—PUCT, or Post-Undead Combat Trauma.

As much as we try to detach ourselves from the human element of our attackers, there may be times when you experience feelings of extreme remorse, regret, and unhappiness for having to eliminate an undead attacker. **These feelings are completely normal** and do not imply weakness, cowardice, or lack of nerve. It is recommended that you confront these feelings honestly and allow yourself to work through them when the opportunity and safety of the situation allows. Discussing these feelings with others who have shared similar experiences can help dissipate these painful thoughts. If the mental trauma does not subside and becomes increasingly unbearable, it is advised that you seek professional medical assistance from a physician expressly qualified to treat victims of PUCT.

COMBAT REPORT: THOMAS DONNER

Store Manager, ShopMaxx Super Stores Bedford, Ohio

Tom Donner and I speak at the Paterson rescue station where he's been residing for the past six months. He is a young, prematurely graying man, wearing what looks to be the same uniform he wore on his last day of work, the day he is describing to me. Like many survivors I speak to, I attribute his detachment to Post-Undead Combat Trauma, but I come to realize that perhaps it is not shock, but acceptance behind his hazel eyes—acceptance of both the living dead and the lengths humanity will reach to survive them.

TD: It's a logical thought, so I don't blame anyone for trying what they did. Find a place that has plenty of food, fresh water, and supplies. A place that could become a potential long-term stronghold—somewhere accessible and familiar—and stay put until the cavalry arrives. It's a great plan for five people, or fifty. Maybe even five hundred. But five thousand? There was just no way. I remember that day like it was yesterday. Al was working the gates as our hospitality greeter. He always arrived at work a half hour before everyone else. I used to razz him about gunning for my job, and he'd just grunt at me. It was late afternoon when we received a message from corporate that we were going to be closing early. That was the first sign that something wasn't right. Corporate never closed us early. Then we noticed the emergency broadcasts that started flashing on the plasmas in the electronics section.

We started to direct shoppers out of the store so we could begin shutting down, but once people saw what was happening, they just refused to leave. They ran around stacking their carts with soda, canned fruit cocktail, and beef jerky, even though we had already closed all the registers. We finally gave up and just let whoever was in, stay in, and began locking down the gates. Al and a couple of others managed to get them closed, but through the metal slats we saw more and more people headed for our entrance. They were screaming, begging for us to open up. Behind them, I saw at least seven fire trucks and ambulances speed past. Al wanted us to open the gates, saying that we had plenty of room on the floor, but I nixed that idea quick. An hour passed, and the crowd outside just kept growing larger and more frantic. Some held up their babies, pleading for us to just take their children, if not them. That's also when we started hearing the moans in the distance.

The pounding on the gate became more frenzied as people tried desperately to get us to open up. I saw Al's hands ball into fists. He screamed that we couldn't just leave them out there. I shouted back that we couldn't do it, that management ordered us not to open up, but I'm not sure if he could or wanted to hear me. The people already in the store started backing away from the entrance to get away from the screaming and crying outside. I went upstairs to the office to ring the district manager and ask what we should do when I glanced at the parking lot security cameras. From across the lot, what looked to be a large, heaving mass was moving slowly toward the crowd of people pressed up against the entrance. My call had just connected with the DM when I heard the whir of the gates rolling up.

I dropped the phone and screamed to Al, but when I looked down toward the entrance, he was giving me the finger as he opened up the gates. His extended hand was the last I saw of him before he was trampled by the crowd.

The desperate mob that scrambled in under the half-opened gates was so crazed, they made a Black Friday sale look like a quiet Sunday morning. A couple of assistant managers and I fought our way back toward the entrance and managed to bring the gates back down. That's when I saw Al's sad, broken body a few feet from the entrance. We got a picnic tablecloth and carried him back toward the storage area. I thought to myself, "Well, at least we're all safe again."

That feeling lasted exactly ten minutes. Just as the crowd began to settle and things quieted down, a pair of high beams lit up the entrance. Seconds later, a yellow Suburban crashed through the gates and buried itself in a vitamin display. Behind it, the same gray mass I saw earlier on the security cam—now much clearer, and much more terrifying.

Pandemonium erupted on the shopping floor. ShopMaxx is basically just one big warehouse space, with pallets of merchandise and scaffolding providing the only means of escape. I saw everything from the second-floor office. The image of a kid's smashed ant farm flashed in my mind. I watched as the decisions people made in those few seconds determined if they stayed alive or were pulled apart by the dead. Whether you turned left or right, if you paused to pick up a purse or a child: These became grave choices.

The most critical decision was the choice of elevation—some people chose sensibly and stationed themselves on solid, heavy merchandise. Others clearly didn't give it as much thought. They positioned themselves on items that were more fragile—laundry detergent, boxes of diapers, rolls of paper towels. When the dead started going after these folks, reaching and pulling down items on their foundation, it looked like some nightmarish game of Jenga. It was only a matter of time before the whole structure came tumbling down, along with the victims. The only thing worse to see was people fighting for space, pushing others down closer to groping, rotted hands so that they themselves could survive. Ironically, one of the best places to stay was on top of the crashed Suburban. I'm not sure what the driver was trying to do, probably a smash-and-grab of supplies. He was beaten to death by the survivors even before the dead could get hold of him. After seeing victim after victim tumble down into the mouths of waiting dead, I couldn't stand it any longer.

ZCM: What did you do?
TD: What else could I do? I escaped through an office window on the second floor.

ZCM: You didn't try to help them?
TD: No.

ZCM: Didn't you feel guilty for leaving those people?
TD: I was just a company employee for ShopMaxx, and I had to comply with the company's policy. If Al had listened, maybe he'd be alive today, too. If you're looking to blame someone, blame those customers. They're the ones who acted like animals, and they made their choices. They chose to stay. They chose to rush in and ransack the place. They chose to throw others to their death while saving themselves. I had already done more than enough.

It could have been a nice setup there. We might have been able to ride it out for at least a month, maybe more. But it's always the same thing, no different than when we have a "limit two per customer" sale. There's always a selfish asshat that ruins it for everyone.

Donner looks down at his grimy, stained ShopMaxx vest. It is dotted with a variety of ornamental pins and badges. He unclasps one exceptionally glossy button and casually tosses it onto his cot. It reads "Employee of the Year."

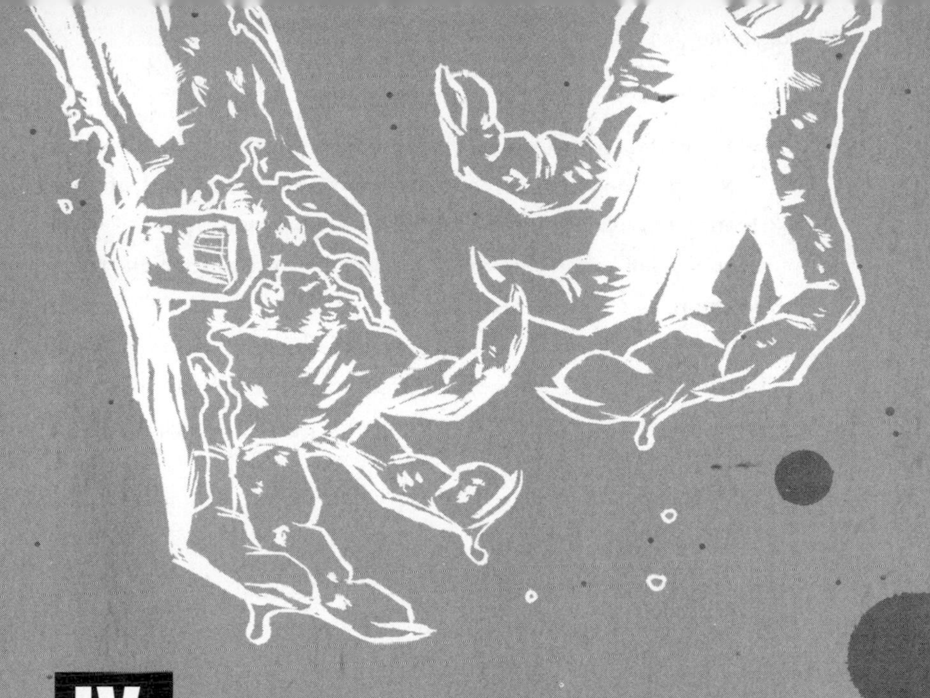

IV. WEAPON SELECTION

You don't want to go into battle with anything that feels less than perfect.

—LOU BROCK

Facing the living dead in combat is, first and foremost, a weapon-based art. Although we will later address strategies to face a walking corpse completely unarmed, most of your engagements should involve the use of an appropriate hand weapon.

Finding the ideal weapon and technique to use against the living dead requires a personalized approach. As you continue to train and develop your fighting skills, you will find yourself more proficient at certain tactics than others. Your preferences for particular combat ranges and techniques will also become apparent. Because of the inevitability that you will have to engage in zombie combat at a distance that is not your preferred method, and because one weapon will never be appropriate for all situations, it is advised that you gain moderate competency in all ranges covered, and equip yourself with at least one weapon to cover each designated combat distance.

When assessing a weapon's adequacy in combat against the living dead, there is one specific factor by which all armaments need to be judged: the effectiveness of neutralizing a ghoul in as few blows as possible. What this means is that any weapon, modern or historical, Asian or Western, needs to be judged under a set of parameters specific to undead combat. Many traditional armaments that have serviced warriors for centuries may not perform as acceptably when your opponent is an ambling corpse. Simply because a weapon has fared well against the living is no reason to assume that it will function just as well against the dead.

SOURCING YOUR ARMAMENTS

Regardless of the type of weapon you choose, it is critical that you rely on a reputable supplier when assembling your arsenal. When selecting a weapon, your first thought may be to venture to your local flea market martial arts supply stand and pick up one of many swords, axes, or spears on fanciful display. In reality, you would be better off heading to your neighborhood toy shop, as many of the weapons you'll find in such establishments are little more than that. A majority of mass-produced weapons are cheaply made and poorly crafted. There is also the other mistake of choosing a weapon reproduction intended to mimic those from an alternate time period, television program, or galaxy. It is strongly recommended that you avoid these facsimile weapons at all costs, regardless of any personal connection or affinity you may have toward them.

True battle-ready weapons are available from custom craftsmen and weaponsmiths but are notably more expensive than those found at mass merchants. There are also reputable large manufacturers who produce quality armaments (see Combat Report: Kenjiro Itto). Use price as an initial indicator of superiority as well as the reputation of the producer. In undead combat, the phrase "You get what you pay for" takes on a much more critical meaning, and could result in having your weapon shatter into fragments against a zombie skull, as described to the author in this firsthand account of the Tragedy at Hever:

> If I could take back that message, I would. I didn't mean any harm. It was only supposed to be our small group, the circle of friends that regularly came together and had some fun in the fields just beyond Hever Castle. But I reckon my note was forwarded,

and reforwarded, and reforwarded. When I arrived at the clearing, there was what looked to be more than a hundred people, none of whom I knew from Adam.

I was a medieval role player. All of my kit was based on authentic historical context. There were a few like me there, one guy in a full suit of armor. He looked well hard, even though I thought he'd overdone it a bit. These other types, I haven't a clue as to what they were thinking. They came dressed in all sorts of genres—high fantasy, cosplayers, goth—all of them happy as Larry, and all of them carrying bizarre weapons. Some of the items, they certainly looked menacing, but how they'd hold up in actual combat they hadn't the faintest idea. I guess that's what they were hoping to find out. I wondered to myself if any of them had any experience with the weapons they carried. This one bloke, I remember, was waving around this double-hooked scythelike thing. How anyone could possibly use it in a real battle was a mystery to me. That didn't stop him from trying when we saw a large horde rising over the low hills to the east. That was our first blunder, waiting in the bottom of a valley for them to come to us. I take that back; the first blunder was ever thinking to do something this daft in the first place.

It was a bloody horror show. In the first attack wave alone, I saw four swords splinter on impact. I watched another blade fly right out of its handle through the air and stick itself into the chest of a man dressed as an elf, who let out a ghastly scream. Many other weapons didn't hold up much better than that. I'd be lying if I said those wielding the medieval arms fared better than the others. Even I was shocked at how terribly many of the so-called fighting-ready weaponry fared against the dead. Most of those who saw their weapons come apart in their hands were smart enough to scamper off. Others weren't that wise. By the time they tried to pull out some backup dagger, it was too late. Screams echoed across the open valley as they tore through us. Even those with armor managed poorly. I remember seeing this one unlucky sod wearing a chain-mail top; I thought he'd be alright. A zombie grabbed him by the collar with both hands and ripped it apart like it was a T-shirt. A shower of chain rings scattered to the ground, followed by the man's innards. Right after seeing that, I figured I'd had enough and took off running. One of the last sights I caught was that bloke in the armor plate, at least what was left of him. His headless body was seated on the grass. Three ghouls were squatting around him, pulling flesh out from around his steel collar like he was an open tin of baked beans.

—*Derek, Highbrook Reenactment Society, Sussex, UK*

LONG-RANGE WEAPONS

Long-range armaments vary anywhere from four to eight feet in length and are used to engage undead assailants at distances of at least five feet between opponents. Though long-range weapons afford you the greatest level of safety during zombie combat, they can also be among the most difficult weapons to master. Depending on the weapon, these arms may also be difficult to acquire for the everyday civilian.

Weapons used at this distance fall into one of two categories: obstructive or destructive.

Obstructive Weapons

The category of obstructive weapons is defined by the concept that it would be exceedingly difficult to deliver a ghoul-stopping blow with the weapon given its weight, length, and physical structure. As such, obstructive weapons are meant largely to delay the incoming onslaught of a walking corpse. The most primal of weapons in the obstructive category, and the foundation for many other long-range weapons, is the simple fighting staff.

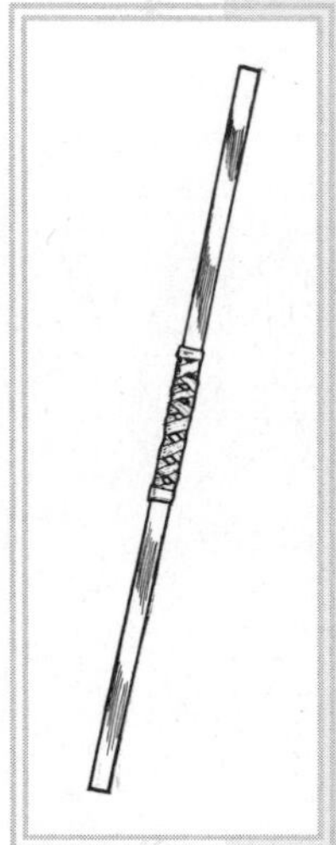

Staff: This weapon has a long history in both Asian and Western combat arts. Known as the *bo* in Japan, the *guin* in China, and the quarterstaff in Europe, it is generally made of hardwood and anywhere from six to eight feet long.

With no sharp edges to cut, nor weighted ends to increase striking damage or penetration, the staff is primarily considered a nonlethal weapon popular with individuals, such as monks or friars, who would typically show mercy toward their attackers. Mercy, however, is a trait that cannot be afforded to the living dead.

The proficiency required to deliver a single incapacitating blow to a zombie with a staff, with its wooden structure and lack of an aggressive point, is very high. Individuals who can do so consistently have typically trained with this weapon for years. Given the staff's weight and dimensions and the skill necessary to wield it effectively, thrusting attacks to the cranium have limited effect on the undead. It is highly difficult to penetrate a ghoul's braincase with a thrust from a staff even if directed toward vulnerable areas, such as the ocular socket. The circumference of the weapon is typically larger than that of the average eyeball, not to mention the precision required to deliver such a blow. Centrifugal attacks will also do minimal damage on the undead skull, resulting in wounds that are mostly superficial in nature depending on your strength and ability to generate momentum with the weapon.

Staff Combat Strategies

With a limited ability to quickly deliver a neutralizing blow, how practical is this weapon in undead combat? The most effective application of the staff or any stafflike implement (broom handles, mops, painting rods) is to take advantage of the weapon's length and keep the ghoul at bay, thereby obstructing its attack. This can be done by grasping one end of the staff with both hands and forcing the other end into the midsection of the zombie. In executing this technique, there is a slight chance of the ghoul grabbing or pushing the weapon out of the way. Most zombies will be too focused on reaching their prey to execute such a maneuver, but should this occur, reset your weapon and force the end of the staff back into the corpse.

Using this strategy, you can keep a zombie at a moderately safe distance indefinitely, provided you have the energy to do so. Do not dismiss the usefulness of this tactic, as it may provide a small window of time for you or your party to escape. This technique can also be used in coordination with another human to pin the ghoul down while your teammate delivers a finishing blow. If you have a sufficient strength and weight advantage over your attacker, you can also use this technique to maneuver the zombie backward and drive it over a ledge or embankment.

Given its limited destructive power, the staff should be a weapon of last resort, used only if no other choices are available. It does provide some advantage over being completely unarmed, and can be used effectively in a team-based operation.

Destructive Weapons

All other weapons in the long-range category fall under the destructive class, as they have the sufficient mass, weight, and structural properties to deliver incapacitating blows to the undead. Destructive long-range weapons fall roughly into three categories:

Polearms: This class of weapon incorporates the length of a staff with the neutralizing power of a cutting or piercing head. Weapons in this category include the Swiss halberd, the Roman *pilum*, and the Japanese *naginata.* Although they are somewhat heavier at the blade/point end, they are generally more evenly balanced than long-range bludgeoning weapons with a large, heavy steel blade, such as the battle-axe.

Battle-axes: A special class of axe developed specifically for combat, the battle-axe differs from a utilitarian axe by its extended length and wider blade structure. Like all common axes, battle-axes are heavier at the blade end, generating considerable momentum when swinging the weapon and landing on target with a great deal of force. People commonly associate the battle-axe with European medieval arms, but examples of this type of weapon can also be seen in the Chinese *guan dao* and the Greek *labrys.*

Great swords: Longer and heavier than your average sword, great swords, also known as long swords, typically need to be brandished with both hands. Living up to their name, swords in this category can be up to six feet in length. Examples of this type of weapon include the Scottish claymore, the Japanese *nodachi*, and the German *zweihänder*.

Although there are a number of different weapons to choose from as your primary long-range protection, the following are evaluations on some specific armaments. We will also provide analysis for armaments that fall into the other combat ranges later in this text. Before we begin, let us take a moment to explain the various categories for each evaluation:

Effectiveness: How quickly can the weapon neutralize the ghoul? The easier it is to end the engagement with a single blow, the higher the effectiveness rating.

Life span: How many combat situations can the weapon endure before it needs to be repaired or replaced? The figures provided are average life spans for the weapons evaluated.

Skill level: How skilled a combatant must you be to wield the weapon? Armaments that require little to no training would rate low, while weapons with a steep learning curve would rate very high.

Availability: How easy is it to procure the weapon? If it is a matter of a pickup at the hardware store, the weapon is common. Arms that are custom forged or special ordered are very limited.

Cost: How expensive is the weapon to purchase? A tool that costs a few dollars qualifies as very inexpensive, while those that run upwards of several hundred dollars fall on the opposite spectrum.

WEAPON EVALUATION: SPEAR

EFFECTIVENESS: **MODERATE**
LIFE SPAN: **100+ ZOMBIE ENGAGEMENTS**
SKILL LEVEL: **VERY HIGH**
AVAILABILITY: **VERY LIMITED**
COST: **MODERATE**

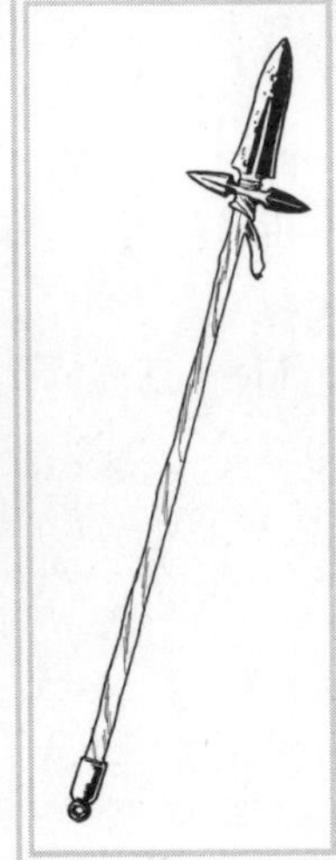

OVERVIEW: The spear has an illustrious history across many cultures as the quintessential long-distance combat weapon. Its extended reach and pointed tip, often made of iron or steel, have been used to effectively keep both man and beast at bay. Against an enemy that does not fear its sharpened spire, however, this weapon loses all of its deterrent capabilities.

Although the spear's length provides the bearer a considerable level of safety against the living dead, the skill required to deliver a felling blow with this weapon is one of the highest among long-range arms. Stabs to the limbs and torso of an attacking ghoul are useless in thwarting its attack. Stories exist of those who have seen spears used ineffectively against the living dead, with several ghouls impaled on a single pike, each continuing to writhe and snap at its prey.

Using this weapon against a walking corpse requires a precise, thrusting strike to the skull in order to penetrate the brain. Targeting the eyes of an oncoming zombie, though effective, also necessitates an unwavering hand. Unskilled spear fighters often execute many ineffective thrusts, which can glance harmlessly off the sides of the corpse's moving head as it closes in. The life span of the spear can also be somewhat finite depending on the number and severity of combat engagements. The shaft of the weapon is almost always made from wood, which makes it vulnerable to rot and splintering during undead combat.

WEAPON EVALUATION: VIKING AXE

EFFECTIVENESS: **HIGH**
LIFE SPAN: **200+ ZOMBIE ENGAGEMENTS**
SKILL LEVEL: **HIGH**
AVAILABILITY: **VERY LIMITED**
COST: **EXPENSIVE**

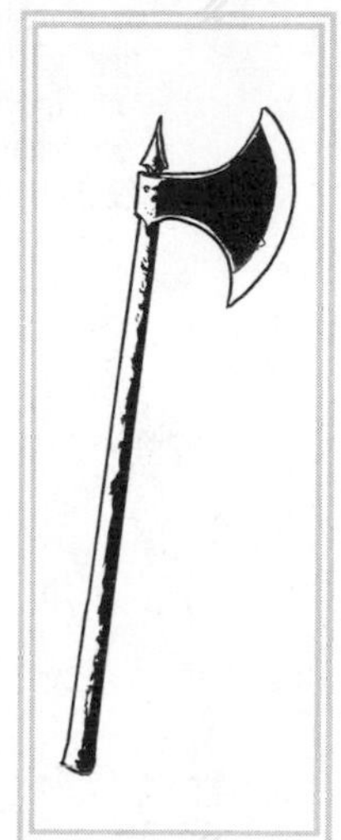

OVERVIEW: Combining the striking power of a hand axe with the length of a short staff, the Viking axe makes a formidable weapon against the living dead. As with all axes, the damage inflicted by this weapon comes primarily from its broad cutting edge, which is secured to a shaft more than three feet long. This two-handed weapon was made famous at the Battle of Hastings, where the Saxons used a version of this axe to cut down the horses of the Norman cavalry.

The most effective use of this particular weapon against the undead is for the bearer to swing it in a wide, circular arc and crash the blade down upon the skull of an attacking ghoul. As we discussed earlier in the section on anatomy, the primary attack target with any weapon should be the skull. As tempting as it may be, attacking areas on the torso with this weapon is not advised. Not only are those types of strikes ineffective, you run the risk of having the weapon lodge itself in the ghoul's body cavity, making weapon extraction difficult. A forceful blow with the Viking axe to the neck, however, has the potential to separate the zombie's head from its torso, which then must be followed up by a finishing blow to the brain.

As with the spear, the Viking axe's greatest liability is its wooden handle, which may crack or splinter after extensive combat. Under normal circumstances, it would be a simple task to replace a damaged handle. During a large-scale undead outbreak, however, most natural resources, including axe handles, will most likely be in short supply.

WEAPON EVALUATION: *ZWEIHÄNDER*

EFFECTIVENESS: **HIGH**
LIFE SPAN: **150+ ZOMBIE ENGAGEMENTS**
SKILL LEVEL: **HIGH**
AVAILABILITY: **VERY LIMITED**
COST: **VERY EXPENSIVE**

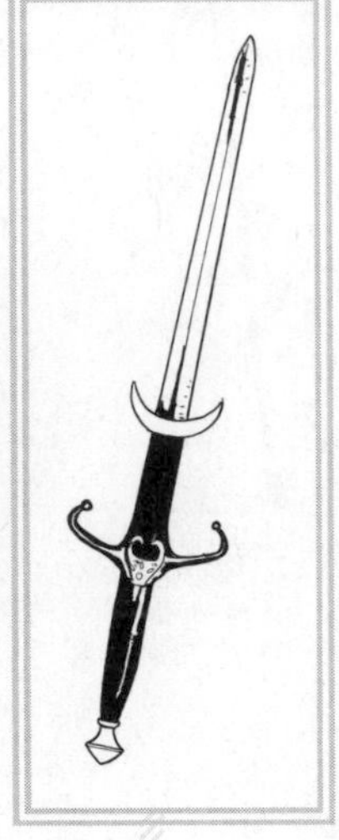

OVERVIEW: German for "two-handed," the *zweihänder* is a powerful sword that was allegedly used to break through the pikes and spears wielded by soldiers at the front lines of battle. Its most famous (or infamous) use was by Frisian warrior Pier Gerlofs Donia, whose mythic strength and stature enabled him to behead several opponents simultaneously with a single swipe of this weapon.

Swung by a stout and capable fighter, a properly-forged *zweihänder*, with a blade between four and five feet long, can cut down a pack of living dead. Crafted almost entirely of steel, this two-handed sword has an excellent life span, provided it is well maintained after each zombie engagement. Its heavier weight provides the ability to smash through bone and can swiftly decapitate undead opponents in combat. Certain models of this weapon also have a grasping ring at the crossguard, so that the sword can be more comfortably held by the combatant to punch through the skull of an attacking corpse.

A weapon of this size, however, requires extensive practice to brandish with consistent skill. Battle-ready *zweihänders* are also difficult to find and can be quite expensive. Do not err on the side of frugality by purchasing an inexpensive version of this weapon. Ensure that you patronize a reputable armaments dealer if your weapon's intended use is against the living dead.

WEAPON EVALUATION: *NAGINATA*

EFFECTIVENESS: **MODERATE**
LIFE SPAN: **100+ ZOMBIE ENGAGEMENTS**
SKILL LEVEL: **VERY HIGH**
AVAILABILITY: **VERY LIMITED**
COST: **EXPENSIVE**

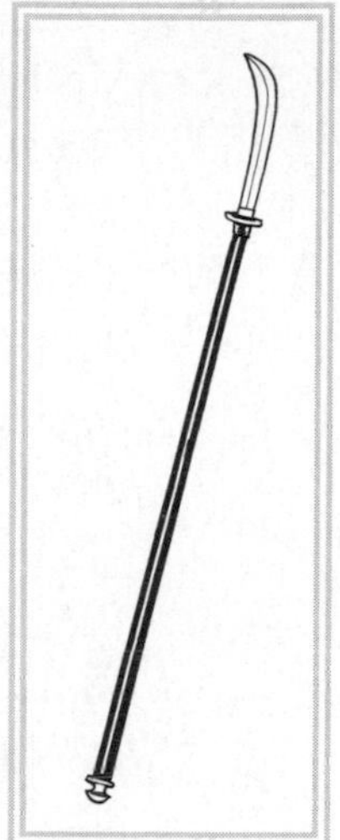

OVERVIEW: Many are familiar with a samurai's two primary weapons: the longer *katana* and the shorter *wakizashi* swords. Few are familiar with the Japanese polearm, the *naginata*. Much like all polearms across cultures, the *naginata* was used primarily by foot soldiers against cavalry, where its longer reach could attack samurai on horseback. It is composed of a curved blade approximately three feet long mounted atop a shaft up to seven feet long, creating a weapon that is potentially ten feet in total length. Interestingly, the *naginata* was often wielded by female samurai and was popular among Japanese women in general, who used the weapon's length to neutralize any advantage an attacker had in weight, height, or strength.

Like all long-range weapons, the *naginata* can be awkward to wield against the living dead. The traditional curvature of the blade makes it difficult to thrust straight into the skull. The *naginata* is more effective as a slashing weapon; decapitation of an oncoming ghoul is an appropriate tactic for this particular armament. You can also use special combat techniques with a long-distance weapon of this type; they will be explored later in this text.

With the rise in popularity of the samurai legend in film and pop culture, many unscrupulous makers have tried to take advantage of the public's interest in Japanese weaponry by creating replica weapons. Thus, it may be easy to purchase a *naginata* blade that looks ready for battle but in reality would not last a single encounter with a zombie. Beware of flimsy imitations.

Fire as a Weapon Against the Undead

Much has already been written on the effectiveness of fire as a weapon against the living dead, so much so that we believed the subject required no further clarification. However, research polls indicate that much confusion still exists about the use of flame against a walking corpse. Therefore, we hope to clarify once and for all the efficacy of neutralizing a ghoul via incineration.

In a study conducted by IUCS researchers, dubbed "The Prometheus Sessions," fifty undead test subjects were ignited with a variety of ordinary combustible compounds, including gasoline, lighter fluid, and alcohol (100 proof). Each of the immolated specimens was then timed to determine how long it would be before the subject fully succumbed to the flames. Forty percent did not yield to the combustion before the flames extinguished themselves and the specimen required reignition. The remaining sixty percent survived an average of fifteen minutes before finally collapsing. Additional testing showed figures consistent with these results, regardless of the flammable substance used or whether the initial detonation point was applied directly to the specimen's head or to another part of the body.

Based on this research, let us assume a best-case scenario in which a zombie does indeed yield to the flames. It still would require an average of fifteen minutes before this occurred. Recall the information in the section on anatomy regarding the ambulatory pace of the average zombie. In fifteen minutes, an ignited ghoul could cover a distance of more than half a mile before falling. Should the corpse remain ignited the entire time, it could set everything it contacts ablaze, including your fortification, or even worse, other humans. The noxious fumes created from incinerated, infected flesh must also be taken into account when using fire as an offensive undead tactic.

As a result of these findings, the only recommended use of fire as a weapon against an attacking ghoul is at long range in an outdoor environment, where you have the time, safety, and surroundings to allow the inferno to do its work. There is also the possibility of combining fire with another long-range weapon that enables you to keep the ignited ghoul contained and at bay.

MEDIUM-RANGE/ MELEE WEAPONS

Just because you can pick it up and swing it doesn't mean you should fight with it. I've seen weapons go flying from hands in the middle of a fight because they were too large, too unwieldy, or just plain wrong for the fighter. It may look like what I do is just pounding pieces of metal together until they look nasty enough to do damage. It's actually more like designing a custom-made suit. No two people are the same, and no personal trait is taken for granted.

Your weapon should feel like an extension of your body. Reach, build, hand size, strength; these are only some of the things I consider when forging one of my creations. I don't want it to sound mystical or ethereal, because it's not. When it comes down to it, the tailor comparison is most appropriate. Sure, you can grab something off the rack, and it may fit just fine, but it's nothing like having something designed for you. I've got it so that the minute someone walks through my doors, I can almost instinctively tell what's going to work for them.

Most of the time, the choice is not so clear to the customer. There was this one woman who came

> to see me; she was about five foot three and couldn't have weighed more than a hundred and ten pounds. Never picked up a weapon in her life, unless you count a kitchen knife. She walked out of my shop with an eight-pound war hammer. Last I heard, she's racked up about two hundred notches on it. Both she and the hammer are still going strong.
>
> —*Simon, Weaponsmith, Cody, TX*

Weapons within the melee class are typically between two and three feet long and are used to engage undead attackers at a distance of approximately four feet between opponents. At this combat range, you will most likely employ a melee weapon that falls into one of two categories.

Blunt instruments

Arms in this category include any object that can be used to cause a compound or depressive fracture on the skull and penetrate the brain cavity. They include but are not limited to formal weapons such as maces, war hammers, and cudgels, in addition to any number of improvised blunt-trauma tools.

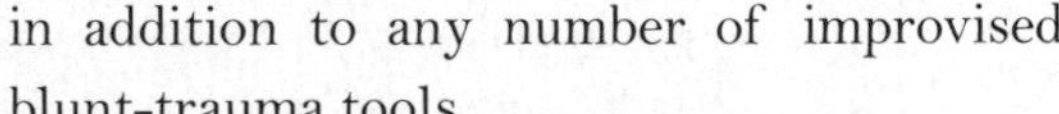

Cutting implements

Any weapon with a sharpened single or double cutting edge falls into this weapon class, which includes swords, machetes, hand axes, and tomahawks. Bladed weapons of sufficient weight can be used to strike and penetrate the skull. Lighter weapons made of thinner steel may have difficulty penetrating the cranium and thus should focus on strike points around the neck area.

Given the choice of blade or bludgeon, which is the preferred medium-range weapon? We believe that blunt-trauma weapons hold a slight advantage at melee range. This conclusion has been drawn based on several reasons:

1. **Durability:** All bladed weapons require regular maintenance and sharpening, most frequently after prolonged combat operations. Even the reputable Japanese *katana*, an excellent weapon when properly crafted, requires several swipes over a sharpening stone after battle. An ordinary blunt instrument requires much less tending, and a well-crafted bludgeon even less so.

2. **Reliability:** Any weapon, regardless of its resilience, will eventually need to be replaced. This can happen over the course of days, months, or years depending on the weapon and extent of its use. Bladed weapons, on average, seem to depreciate much more quickly than bludgeons. This is mostly attributed to the fact that the primary attack area is always the undead skull. Even the thinnest, most delicate areas of bone will wear down the sharpness of an edged weapon after a modest number of strikes. A battle club, on the other hand, is typically crafted out of a single piece of iron or steel. Even bludgeons that are not of the highest quality will most likely outlast all but the most exceptionally crafted (and expensive) bladed weapons.

3. **Flexibility:** In order to extend the life of a bladed weapon for the reasons mentioned previously, it benefits you to focus attacks specifically on the softer muscles in the neck for a decapitation attack. With a bludgeon, it is the opposite. The neck will not be an appropriate target, but you have many more assault points on the ghoul at your disposal. This makes the bludgeon a much more flexible weapon in terms of target opportunity and weapon maintenance. In addition, bludgeons can be studded with spikes, knobs, or flanges that make brain penetration much easier.

Despite this recommendation, it is important to reiterate that weapons are still very much a matter of personal preference. Using a bludgeon may also require greater strength than an edged weapon, and therefore it may not be the preferred choice for more feeble individuals. It is recommended that you train with a wide assortment of implements and discover what works best for your specific physique.

The following are evaluations of specific melee combat tools you may consider as possible choices for your arsenal:

WEAPON EVALUATION: MACE

EFFECTIVENESS: **VERY HIGH**
LIFE SPAN: **150+ ZOMBIE ENGAGEMENTS**
SKILL LEVEL: **LOW**
AVAILABILITY: **LIMITED**
COST: **INEXPENSIVE**

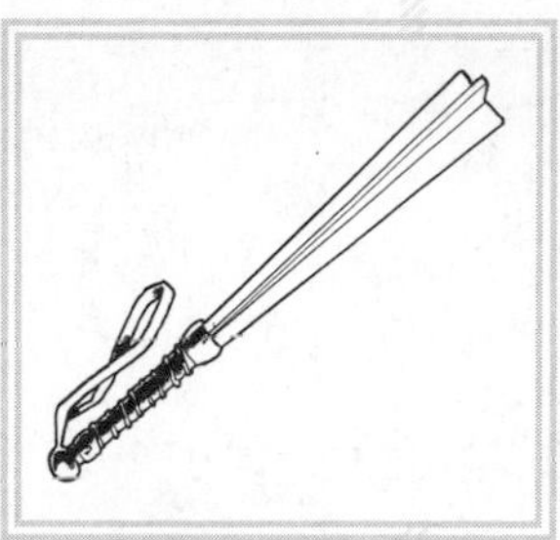

OVERVIEW: With a combat history that spans over several millennia, the mace is one of the most ancient weapons known to humankind. Some of the earliest evidence of such a weapon has been found in Egypt, where stone heads were affixed to wooden clubs. The weapon's destructive might increased dramatically with the advent of the Bronze Age, where the weapon's vicious striking head could be crafted from metal rather than stone. During the Middle Ages, the mace became a popular weapon for its devastating power against the plate armor worn by knights and soldiers.

As an implement to defend against the living dead, the medieval mace is a nearly ideal weapon. Crafted to inflict severe trauma against an individual encased in a suit of armor, the mace can do outstanding damage to the comparatively fragile skull of a zombie. The cost of this weapon is low, as is the skill required to wield it, which explains its popularity throughout history as a weapon of the proletariat. The learning curve to master this weapon is also quite manageable—any individual who has swung a hammering tool of any sort can be effective with this armament in short order.

The greatest liability of this particular weapon is its availability, as the quantity of high-quality maces is somewhat low and poorly made replicas abound. This liability is also somewhat minimized because even a lower-quality mace, provided that it is maintained well and inspected regularly, can be serviceable for several dozen combat sorties.

WEAPON EVALUATION: KUKRI

EFFECTIVENESS: **MODERATE**
LIFE SPAN: **50+ ZOMBIE ENGAGEMENTS**
SKILL LEVEL: **HIGH**
AVAILABILITY: **LIMITED**
COST: **EXPENSIVE**

OVERVIEW: One part camp hatchet and two parts combat blade, the kukri knife, also known as the Gurkha Blade, is the national knife of Nepal and the traditional weapon of the legendary Nepalese Gurkhas, where boys receive their own kukri blade when they are barely out of diapers. The expertise with which the Gurkha warrior wielded this weapon gave rise to the false myth that blood must be drawn every time a kukri was removed from its sheath.

Although the design of the blade enables its multifunctional use in agricultural activities such as splitting wood and clearing brush, it is most effective as a tool for combat. The blade's shape may look similar to that of a boomerang, but the kukri was not crafted as a throwing weapon. The length and deep belly at the front of the blade place additional weight at the forefront of the weapon, enabling a fighter to generate a great deal of chopping force with each swing.

As a weapon against the living dead, the kukri is at its deadliest when targeting the zombie's vulnerable neck region. Primarily a hacking weapon, the kukri can decapitate a ghoul almost as effectively as any heavy-bladed polearm. The notch at the base of the blade can also help prevent infectious fluid from trickling down onto the bearer's hand. Given its unusual shape and shorter length, there can be a marked learning curve for those with no prior experience to wield the kukri successfully against an attacking ghoul.

WEAPON EVALUATION: EXPANDABLE BATON

EFFECTIVENESS: LOW
LIFE SPAN: 5+ ZOMBIE ENGAGEMENTS
SKILL LEVEL: LOW
AVAILABILITY: LIMITED
COST: MODERATE

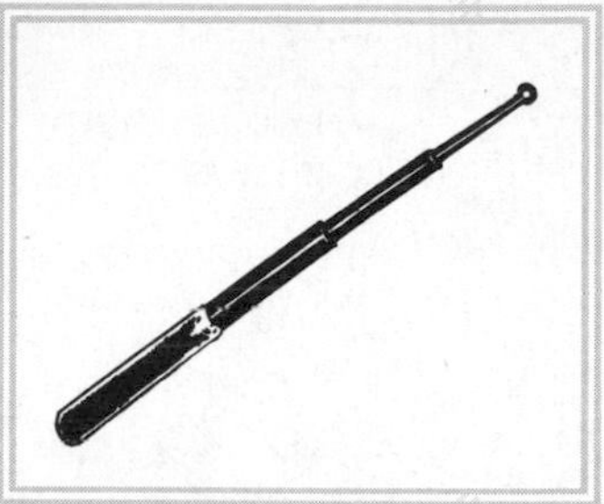

OVERVIEW: A modern weapon made popular as standard equipment among many law enforcement organizations, the expandable baton may seem like an ideal weapon against a walking corpse. It is crafted entirely of aluminum or steel, made with a comfortable handle, expands to a respectable melee range, and retracts to a fraction of its size when not in use.

Unfortunately, the baton suffers many liabilities in undead combat. As a weapon made for keepers of the peace, it is specifically classified as a nonlethal weapon. Thus, it was not made to withstand constant and repeated blows to an individual's skull. It was intentionally designed without any severe edges that could potentially lacerate an assailant. The most common attack points for this weapon are typically on the arms and legs in order to temporarily incapacitate or disarm a threatening human. Its segmented, collapsible rods also make the weapon structurally weaker than one made from a single bar of metal.

Tests show that when subjected to the incessant battering that occurs in an undead attack, the structural integrity of the expandable baton becomes seriously compromised, and suffers from warping and irrevocable damage. Although it can be used temporarily and may be found in the duty belts of law enforcement officers who were felled in a zombie attack, it is recommended that a more reliable weapon be sought quickly as a replacement, as the expandable baton may not even last a single undead combat encounter.

WEAPON EVALUATION: TOMAHAWK

EFFECTIVENESS: **HIGH**
LIFE SPAN: **150+ ZOMBIE ENGAGEMENTS**
SKILL LEVEL: **MODERATE**
AVAILABILITY: **LIMITED**
COST: **EXPENSIVE**

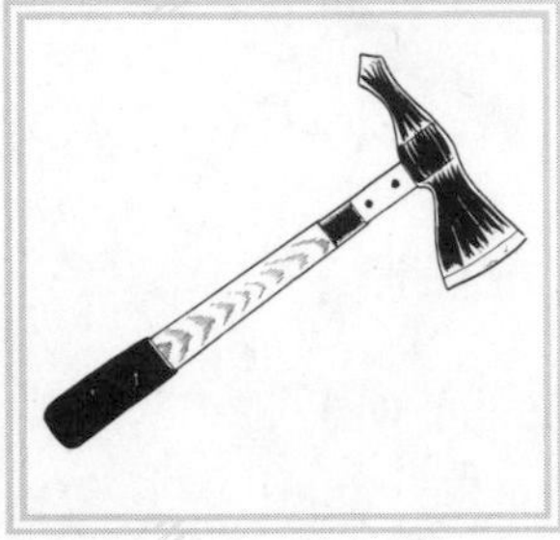

OVERVIEW: An implement with a long heritage on North American plains of battle, the tomahawk is a particular type of hatchet originally used by Native Americans in hand-to-hand fighting. As with the mace, the earliest incarnations of the weapon's striking face were made of stone, with steel being the more durable choice as it became more readily available. This weapon experienced a resurgence during the twentieth and twenty-first centuries when it was modernized and distributed in limited numbers during conflicts in Asia and the Middle East. The contemporary version of the tomahawk radically improves on the historical model by replacing wood with modern polymers and heat-treating specific regions of the blade to reduce shock from heavy striking while still retaining a keen edge.

As a zombie-neutralizing tool, the tomahawk fares nearly as well as the medieval mace. The weapon can penetrate bony skull plates using either end of its wedge-shaped blade, and the modernized upgrade of this historical tool has addressed its traditional shortcomings. It does, however, suffer from several minor liabilities of which you should be mindful. The tomahawk is a rather short weapon for a melee engagement, having an average length of fifteen inches. The weapon's sweet spot is also concentrated in a small area on the striking head, requiring a greater level of precision for each blow.

Although this weapon can be and has been accurately thrown in battle, it takes a great many hours of consistent practice to successfully perform such a maneuver. The probability that you will be able to strike a bobbing target with the tomahawk's blade is low. Even if you are able, by luck or talent, to accomplish this feat, you must then walk the distance thrown to retrieve your weapon from the ghoul's head, leaving you weaponless and vulnerable in the interim. Do not perform this maneuver unless you find yourself with no other choice. We will address the viability of throwing weapons at living dead attackers later in this text.

Using Hooked Armaments

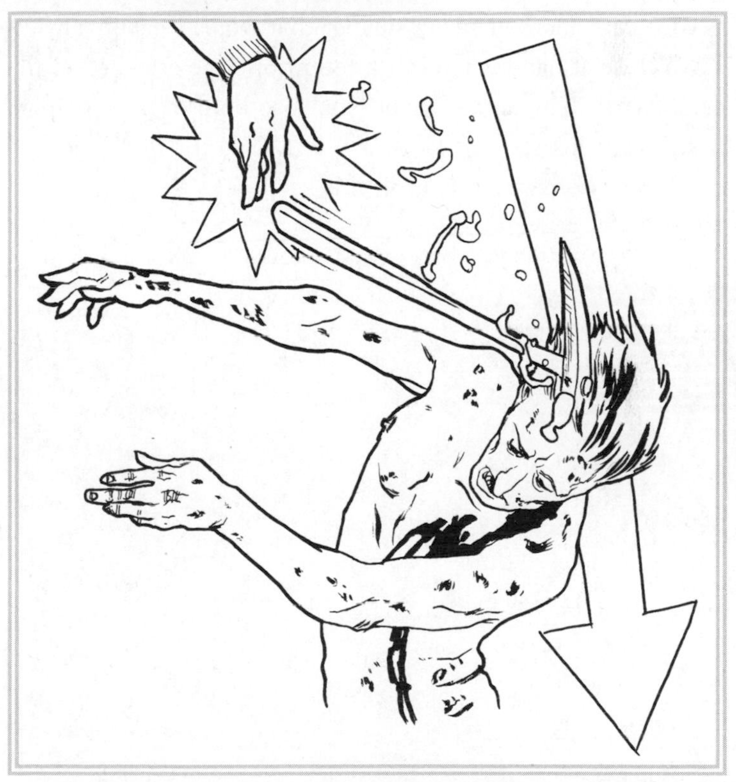

When selecting a melee weapon, be wary of bludgeons that have extended hooks or long, narrow bolts, such as the claw end of a hammer, a longshoreman's hook, or the point of a pickaxe. Although these protrusions provide excellent penetrating power into the skull, they also tend to lodge in the brain cavity. Remember that once a zombie's brain is destroyed, its entire body instantly becomes dead weight. There have been many recorded cases of a weapon being pulled out of a fighter's hand after becoming wedged in the ghoul's cranial vault, leaving the individual unarmed for several crucial seconds. The time required to pull your weapon free could be crucial to your survival, particularly if engaging simultaneous attackers. This is not to say that you should not select this type of weapon, but be aware of its shortcomings during battle. One method of ensuring that your weapon always stays close at hand is to craft a retention loop attached to the armament's handle, so that if you lose hold of the weapon, it still remains secured to your wrist. (See the discussion of weapon customization later in this section.)

COMBAT REPORT: KENJIRO ITTO

Chief Operating Officer Kusanagi Enterprises, Sakai, Japan

I'm escorted from the helicopter pad atop Hikosaburo Plaza by four heavily armed security personnel and led down to the reception area of Kenjiro "Kenny" Itto, chairman and COO of Kusanagi Enterprises. The company is currently the world's largest producer and exporter of modern Japanese combat arms. It was also founded by the Kishida-kai organization, one of the oldest Yakuza syndicates in Japan. The company has been instrumental in revitalizing the country's financial system, so much so that it has been said by its detractors that post-undead Japan has effectively become a "RICO-economy," one that is governed by what was formerly considered the criminal underworld. Kusanagi Enterprises exports its products to every country with functioning safe regions and provides training to military and civilian groups on four of the seven continents.

Mr. Itto greets me with a slight bow followed by a firm handshake. As we make idle chatter before starting the formal interview, he asks if I am aware of the reinstatement status of the higher education system in the United States. "As a former Illini, I'm hoping for the best," he states. We begin the interview in his office, but he decides that he would rather talk while taking me on a tour of the factory several floors below.

KI: Even before the first Japanese citizen rose from the dead, ours was a nation in free fall—economically, emotionally, and spiritually. I am a student of business, not psychology, but I know enough to realize that a man often judges himself in two very fundamental ways—as a warrior or as a provider. Our country had a rich, illustrious history as a warrior nation;

one that was nearly devastated by Fat Man and Little Boy.[6] After that humiliating defeat culminating on the deck of the USS *Missouri*, many in our society felt that it was better to relinquish our combative ways to more powerful nations, lest we suffer additional disgrace at the hands of *gaijin*.

Many also believed we would not recover, that we would forever be international pariahs, never again contributing to the world's significance. But the Japanese are an industrious people. After several decades, we managed to scratch and fight our way back to a place of esteem; this time, as providers to the global economy. We leveraged our growing dominance in the automotive, semiconductor, and electronics sectors to branch out into property, banking, even entertainment, which alarmed you in the United States the most. By the mid-eighties, we were such an economic force that American families were teaching their children Japanese in preparation to communicate with their future supervisors, just as they are fluent in Mandarin and Farsi today.

Then came the second demoralizing blow. Instead of the blast of an atomic cloud, it was the sound of our economy crumbling on itself like a controlled demolition. The financial collapse was too much tragedy within too short a historical time frame for our culture to bear. Now, we were defeated not only as warriors, but also as providers. What did we have left? Sociologically speaking, in a world of adults, we became pubescent children. Our society became obsessed with the juvenile, the prurient. Instead of exporting semiconductors and electronics, we were foisting Hello Kitty and Keroppi Hasunoue upon the world. What a travesty. Thousands of years of culture, and the best we could now offer society was cartoon characters and soft toys. Elements of a healthy social

6 *Fat Man* and *Little Boy*: military code names for the weapons of mass destruction detonated over Hiroshima and Nagasaki during World War II, effectively ending Japan's participation in the war.

order began toppling like domino tiles—rising obesity rates, dramatic increases in *otaku*[7] and *hikikomori*,[8] plummeting birthrates, and abandonment of religion. Even despite a mild economic recovery, the cultural damage that had been done was irreversible. By the time the dead began to walk, our populace was in no condition to fight back.

At the same time, the family business was doing well. Our primary industries are essentially recession-proof. The greatest losses we suffered were as a result of our diversification into so-called legitimate lines of business—the Internet, high finance, real estate. Therein lies the irony. All those bankers, executives, and politicians—the ones responsible for hollowing out our financial system—how many lives did they ruin? And we were the ones considered criminals.

Don't get me wrong. I am under no false illusions regarding the nature of our business. It was not something I was proud of—the extortion, the gambling, the pornography. This is the reason I left. As much disdain as I felt for our cultural woes, I wanted no part of this other life either. I wouldn't admit it then, but I sought to distance myself from the embarrassment of both my homeland and my family. I convinced myself that my travels were a way to explore the world, to take advantage of what other countries had to offer. And because there were few legitimate opportunities in my own country, I went to the place where there was—to America.

And so it was for almost fifteen years. I kept in touch with family, sent money regularly, even though I knew they didn't need it. I didn't want them to worry. I almost returned when Mother passed, but my father, in his typical stoic manner, told me it was unnecessary. As an investment banking drone putting

7 *otaku:* term used to describe individuals with obsessive interests, particularly in comic books and video games.

8 *hikikomori:* a sociological phenomenon describing individuals who have chosen to withdraw from society.

in hundred-hour weeks, I was in no position to argue. That all obviously changed when the first signs of outbreak began.

I'm still unsure what prompted my decision to return. It wasn't a question of safety; the reports coming from Asia were just as frantic as those in the West. It wasn't a question of protection; I knew that my family would not need my help in this respect. I curiously wondered, if the death of my mother could not drive me home, what could? It was then, facing my own fragile mortality, that I realized if I were to meet my end between the jaws of a shambling corpse, I would rather it be on my nation's soil. I arrived at Kansai International just before civilian air travel was grounded indefinitely.

This was our country's darkest moment. After Prime Minister Sato declared a national evacuation and all of the major islands were abandoned, many believed this to be the final nail in our nation's coffin. Our financial system failed us. Our government failed us. There was no one left to turn to for help. There were pockets of civilian resistance surviving on various islands, but no cohesiveness, no unification. The other syndicates were close to deserting the homeland and reestablishing businesses from their base of international networks. Father, however, was steadfast. "This is not the time to run," he declared. I mistakenly took this declaration as arising from an archaic sense of pride or nationalism. Though I'm certain there was an element of both in his decision, Father has always been a businessman first, and a patriot second. What he saw was the clear opportunity to take rightful control of a country that, in his eyes, had been utterly mismanaged. Where so many legitimate sources of power failed the people, he believed the families would not. Where many saw the end of days, he saw a beginning. No. A rebirth.

And like most beginnings, this one too would be painful. Before we could address our common external adversary, we needed to deal with the internal struggle among the syndicates. We anticipated much difficulty. There have been several attempts throughout history to consolidate power by various families, all of which ended badly. In order for Father's plan to work, the syndicates needed to unite. The Ohki-gumi clan had contacts with international militaries. Kobayashi-kai had resources in heavy manufacturing. We controlled the ports and shipyards. There was no question that the syndicates had to band together, and there could be no disrespecting of families or territorial disputes. Even in a land overtaken by walking dead, loss of face was of the highest concern.

ZCM: How did he bring them together?

KI: To paraphrase our Italian-American peers, he made offers they could not refuse. Not threats, mind you, but lucrative opportunities that would far exceed the wealth and power they could have achieved in pre-infested Japan. First, the syndicates would divide equally any profits derived from this new business venture. Second, any of the country's abandoned islands or regions would be available to any family who cleared the area and reestablished order. Much like your nineteenth-century western land rushes, syndicates could claim any territory they desired, so long as they dealt with the living dead. Of course, Father made certain that our family's strategic regions were secured before offering this arrangement.

Although the internal strife was being resolved, it still was not an easy process. Despite our connections with arms traffickers and gunrunners across the globe, we made a conscious decision not to pursue this route to secure our country. We knew that if we relied on firearms as our primary defensive source, we would be forever beholden to the networks that control the manufacturing and production of such firepower, and we would to continue to suckle the international teat. We wanted, we *needed* to be self-reliant in our attempt to rescue the homeland. Not only did we desire to take advantage of our indigenous knowledge and resources, we saw it as our way to right our cultural ship. And with a sword-making history that dates back more than five hundred years, we had the knowledge, as long as we could find living sensei to guide us.

We began by locating any surviving swordsmiths on the four major islands. There are only a few hundred to begin with at best, and we were able to tap a talented handful. I distinctly remember the recovery of one sensei in Kochi Prefecture; his apprentices were defending the perimeter of his village workshop around the clock when we arrived. The pile of bodies was so high, the extraction team needed to scramble over them like boulders to snatch him and his protégés out. Once the expertise was assembled, we began to scavenge for resources—namely steel—to begin production. This was extraordinarily difficult, as the government had begun stockpiling metals in anticipation of an ambitious retaliatory effort that of course never materialized. We knew that we would not have access to the traditional premium-grade metals that these swordsmiths were accustomed to using, but they understood the complexity of the situation. We began by salvaging steel from local kitchen supply shops, smelting down anything we could get our hands on—knives, forks, even pots and pans. The steel composition was very impure, but at that stage we had to make do, knowing that eventually our production lines would be able to refine their resources. We were able to produce a quantity of crude weapons to outfit our security forces as they continued to sweep the islands for survivors and materials.

As we began eradicating the zombie threats, our support from the remaining populace grew. Now, look how far we've come.

Itto pauses and gestures toward a wall of glass that provides a full view onto the factory floor. Rows of sophisticated-looking, miniature blast furnaces are visible, with forging tools and equipment alongside them. Two people work each station: one sensei, one apprentice. Each team seems oblivious to the other, concentrating on forging the blades that will become the weapons for which Itto's company is renowned. Slats filled with finished swords line both sides of the factory floor. A worker arrives alongside us, bows respectfully to Itto, and extends to him in both hands a finished katana *in its scabbard. We continue to walk.*

KI: As much as I resented our family business in my youth, the command of our family's industries was instrumental to our success. Because we controlled the harbors and shipping lanes, we were able to quickly establish both rescue and commercial routes to the major island ports, and our ability to fend off attacks enabled us to control many regions across the islands. We've been able to fully reclaim half of the previously inhabited lands and establish safety perimeters on the remaining half. We've even secured the routes and processes to produce the rare *tamahagane* steel, the finest sword steel on the planet, the entire quantity of which is shipped right to our storage facilities.

ZCM: Your entire inventory is produced at this one facility?
KI: Heavens, no, we could never manage the international volume we're required to produce daily in this setting. Most are manufactured in several automated factories in Shimane Prefecture.

ZCM: Isn't that a bit misleading?
KI: How so?

ZCM: Doesn't Kusanagi Enterprises state that it produces only traditionally crafted samurai weapons?

KI: We simply do not have the number of swordsmiths necessary to do that.

ZCM: Why not import resources from other countries?

KI: Like many foreigners who visit this facility, you have misunderstood our purpose here. This isn't merely about producing weapons and armor. We are restoring what was nearly lost by our country, lost at the hands of those who thought they knew what was better for our people. We lost, some believe renounced, our tradition of *bushido,* the way of the warrior, and foreign influence played no small part. It is why the country has made the recent decisions it has: closing foreign immigration, revoking Article 9, choosing not to participate in the restored UN Security Council. Until we re-instill a sense of honorable tradition to our people, we cannot afford to open our doors again to Western influence. We nearly sold our souls once in doing so; we must ensure that it does not happen again. In time, this nation will return to our historical preeminence and our rightful place as a warrior society.

Itto unsheathes the finished katana.

KI: Our country is much like this sword. For centuries, it represented the soul of our people. Then the world bastardized and abused it, ruining its edge. Like the master swordsmiths we now employ, we have taken it back, trued the blade, and restored its luster. Once again, it can be considered the most distinguished of weapons, rather than a cheap cinematic prop. And every individual on the planet who uses one in combat against the living dead can be considered not only a warrior, but an extended member of the Kishida-kai family.

Itto resheathes the sword, and like the worker who brought him the weapon, he extends it in both hands and offers me the katana.

KI: For you, to remember what you've seen. Now you are family as well.

CLOSE-QUARTERS WEAPONS

At a combat range of two feet or less between opponents, your weapon must be compact, fast, and easily accessible while simultaneously providing sufficient cranium-penetrating power. Your strike also needs to penetrate the zombie's skull without requiring a great deal of acceleration or momentum given the distance from your attacker and still cause an appropriate level of brain damage. Therefore, a bladed armament is your most logical choice when engaged in zombie combat at this precarious distance.

Not every knife, however, will work effectively in a close-combat situation against the undead. You should look for certain characteristics when selecting the optimal edged tool for close-range zombie encounters.

Weapon Characteristics

- **Length:** The length of the blade is the most important trait to consider when selecting your weapon. The blade needs to be long enough when thrust to the hilt to penetrate the brain from the farthest point of distance possible on the human skull—the underside of the chin. It is recommended that you choose a knife with an edge length of six to nine inches. If you are unsure of a weapon's adequacy, line up the base of the knife edge along your jawline. If the tip of the blade extends beyond the top of your ear, it is a sufficient length to tap into brain matter.

  Do not be tempted into choosing a weapon that is too long. With an aggressive thrust, you run the risk of penetrating the opposite side of the skull, possibly damaging the blade tip and making extraction from the skull cavity difficult. The thickness of the blade is another important consideration, as you will require a stout weapon that resists breakage, even after repeated thrusts through flesh and bone.

- **Edge type:** The edge of your knife should be completely straight, preferably devoid of serrations, to facilitate a quick thrust and a smooth, fast withdrawal. Though somewhat useful in a utilitarian situation, saw teeth on a knife used to battle the undead are completely inappropriate. Jagged indentations can catch on muscle, tendons, and sinew, increasing the likelihood that your weapon will become snagged within a ghoul's cranium.

  Should you choose a blade with a single or a double cutting edge? This is largely a combatant's preference, but for frequent zombie combat, we believe that a single-edged knife is slightly superior. A double-edged dagger may benefit from improved penetrating power, but this comes at the expense of a structurally weaker blade and more fragile point. In brutal combat situations in which you are repeatedly plunging the weapon through bone, a single-edged blade with a thick spine will hold up better under intense use. Some combat techniques also require you to wield the knife in close proximity to your opposite hand. A double-edged blade may increase the likelihood of accidentally nicking yourself in combat, escalating the risk of infection.

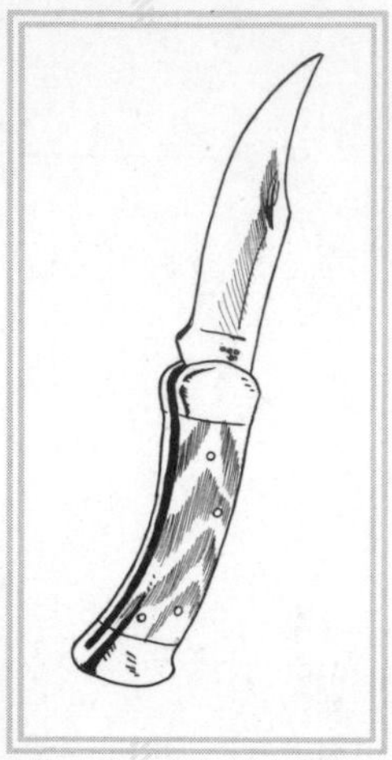

Fixed Blades versus Folding Knives

Knives fall under two general classes: fixed and folding blades. Fixed knives are those whose blade is attached to a handle and stored in a separate sheath when not in use. Folding knives have blades that pivot into the handle itself and often incorporate a locking mechanism to secure the blade in the open position. It is highly recommended that you choose a fixed blade over a folding knife as your undead close-quarters weapon for the following reasons:

- **Speed:** In close-range combat with the undead, speed is of the essence. The time it takes to extract your weapon and strike your target is critical to a successful neutralization. Every extra second required to draw your weapon makes you more vulnerable to a ghoul's attack. In noncombat situations, drawing a fixed blade knife is typically faster than drawing a folding knife. When your face is inches away from a rotting corpse, this speed differential becomes even more pronounced.

- **Dexterity:** Opening a folding knife requires greater fine-motor coordination in your fingers than pulling a fixed blade from its sheath. In a combat situation, stress levels peak and your body is flooded with a surge of adrenaline, known as the "fight or flight" reflex. This reflex can provide a temporary boost in strength, but it also causes major disruptions to your manual dexterity, making small movements, such as thumbing open the blade of a folding knife, nearly impossible to accomplish. This loss of precision can be somewhat controlled by constant practice and drills with your weapon, but why take the chance?

- **Construction:** A fixed blade knife is a very simple tool. At its most primal level, it is a single length of sharpened steel. A folding knife, though often more elegant in design, is a much more complex device with a folding pivot, locking mechanism, and the bolts that hold the components in place. Like any tool, the more complex in construction, the greater potential for failure in one or several of its elements. Additionally, a folding knife has many small crevices compared to a fixed blade—crevices that run the risk of retaining infectious residue during combat.

Knife Styles

Peruse the knife case of any hunting shop or cutlery store and you will note a broad variety of knife shapes and blade styles: hunter, spear point, Wharncliffe; the list is seemingly endless. Many of these styles can be adequate for your undead combat needs, as long as the previously detailed requirements are met. Make certain that whatever design you choose, the blade comes to a sharp, sturdy point. Avoid diving, sheepsfoot, and rescue-type knives, and any blade with a dull or rounded tip. In a safety situation in which a sharp point may unintentionally pierce delicate material, equipment, or flesh, this safety-tip style of knife is ideal. In an undead-combat scenario, it is nearly useless.

With so many different choices available, is there an optimal knife design to use against the living dead? Although there is no one ideal style, there are three particular blade variations that are worth a closer analysis.

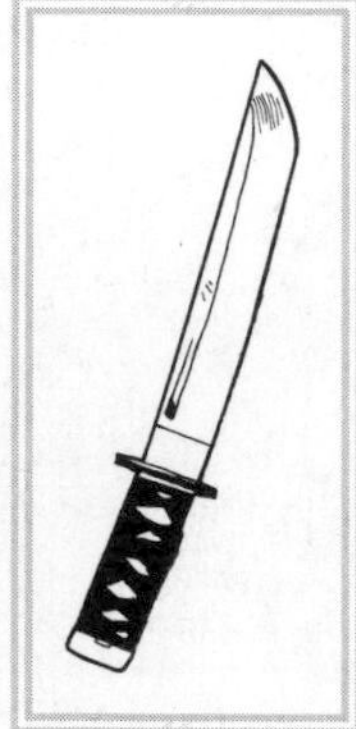

Tanto

Japanese in style and modeled after traditional *katana* blades, the *tanto* combines the benefits of its larger brethren in a smaller, close-combat package. Wielding one of these blades is akin to having a miniature samurai sword in your pocket. With a thick spine, unserrated edge, and aggressive point, the *tanto* blade possesses an almost ideal combination of characteristics for close-quarters zombie combat. The strongest feature of this blade style is its broad, chisel-like point, which can handily penetrate bone with negligible damage to the knife tip. This blade style is a popular choice for custom and production knife makers alike, making it relatively easy to find a high-quality, moderately priced weapon. Just as in your search for long-range and melee weapons, be skeptical of any "exotic" *tantos* that are designed more as showpieces than combat arms.

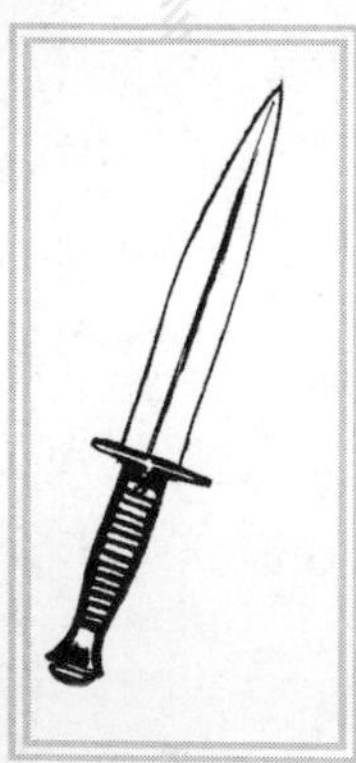

Stiletto

The root of its name originating from the Latin word *stilus,* literally meaning "pike" or "pointed tool," the stiletto has been used for centuries as a stabbing implement in close-combat situations. Throughout history, it was a stiletto-type blade that was used to deliver the coup de grâce, or mercy blow, to a fallen ally or enemy whose wounds were too grave to survive. It could be said that the use of this blade in undead combat parallels its historical context. This style of knife was also popular during World War I, in which soldiers often found themselves engaging opponents in violent trench warfare. The stiletto's long, thin blade slides effortlessly into flesh and penetrates soft targets with ease. This narrow profile also contributes to the weapon's greatest liability. Although nonzombie use of the stiletto targeted organs such as the heart and liver, ghoul neutralization necessitates penetration of the skull into the brain. Thus, the fragile stiletto blade may not endure prolonged zombie combat.

Bowie

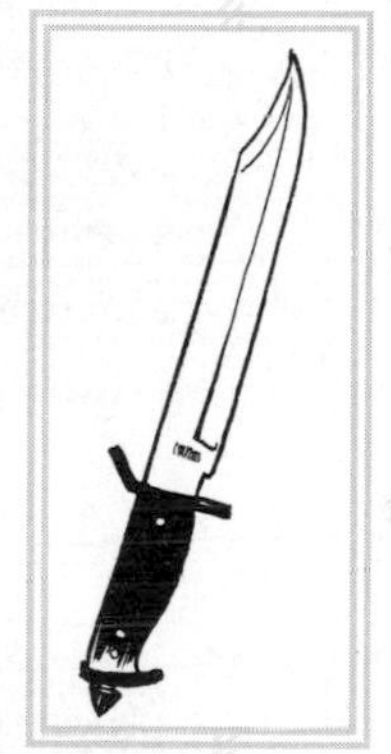

A legendary blade style made famous by its namesake, the bowie knife has an American history spanning nearly two hundred years. It grew into international prominence after the famed Sandbar Fight of 1827, in which Jim Bowie, having been bludgeoned, shot, and stabbed with a sword cane, still managed to impale one of his attackers, mutilate another, and run off the remaining group. This feat was related more to Bowie's deftness with the blade than the weapon itself. Nonetheless, the bowie knife gained a reputation for being a superior fighting implement. Wielded by a skilled combatant, the bowie knife can perform just as viciously against the living dead. Selecting the appropriate blade length is important for this particular design, as bowie blades can range anywhere from six to twelve inches, with some models that look more like small swords. The large, heavy blade can serve as both a stabbing and chopping tool against a zombie, the latter technique not encouraged given the close range between opponents.

WEAPON-CARRYING METHODS

Once you select your personal close-combat weapon, how will you store it so that it is available at a moment's notice, but out of the way during normal non-combat-related activity? A plethora of options are available—tucked into the waistband, wedged in the small of the back, strapped to a thigh or ankle—all of which have supporters and detractors.

Unlike long-range and melee combat, in which you will most likely be holding your weapon at the ready just before engagement, close-quarters battles with the undead often occur unexpectedly and in locations where your longer arsenal may not be practical. In our opinion, there is only one favorable carry position for undead close combat: the cross-draw position.

In this arrangement, your weapon is sheathed in a blade-up position, over the lapel opposite your dominant hand (if you are right-handed, it will be positioned over your left shoulder). This location provides several distinct advantages over other carry positions in close-quarters zombie attacks:

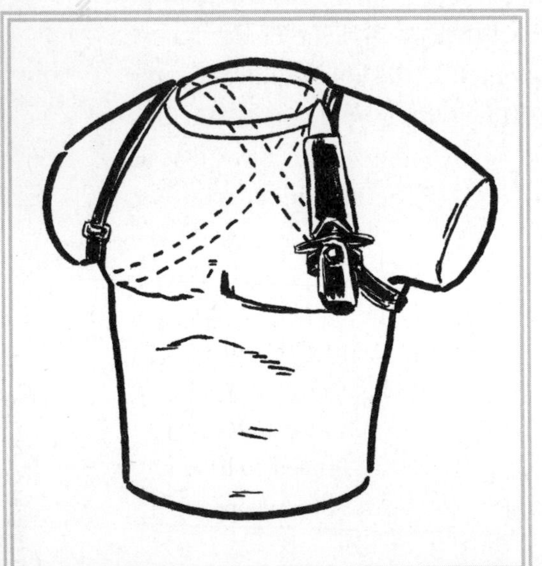

1. Accessibility: In the cross-draw position, the knife is stored near its ultimate target, the zombie's skull. Picture yourself in a boxer's stance, hands up in front of your torso in a fighting position. In this position, your weapon is inches away from your dominant hand, ready to be pulled at a moment's notice should you round a corner and find yourself staring into the lifeless eyes of the undead. There's no need to reach down into your waistband, behind your back, or down into your boot. As we will examine later in the chapter on combat strategies, this level of accessibility is integral to executing several techniques.

2. Position: Carrying your weapon in the cross-draw fashion not only enables close proximity to its target, but also positions it perfectly for an effective strike, with the blade tip pointing up and in front of your body. In comparison, carrying a weapon in your waistband requires that you drop your hand from a defensive posture down toward your belt to draw the blade. This leaves an entire side of your body exposed and defenseless when you lower your arm to reach the weapon. This same liability also occurs when you store your knife in the small of your back, and even more so if you carry it on your thigh or ankle. Remember, stealth is not a concern when battling the undead. There is no need to hide the weapon from your enemy's sight, as your opponent could not be any less concerned.

3. **Quickness:** Because of the easy accessibility and the optimal positioning of your weapon in cross-draw carry, this method enables you to engage your opponent, draw your weapon, and deliver a neutralizing blow in the shortest time possible. Veteran combatants have been able to end a close-quarters zombie engagement within three seconds of its initiation. It is your responsibility to frequently rehearse withdrawing your weapon. Regular drilling will also help you overcome the "fight or flight" reflex discussed earlier that may cause your hands to tremble, so that your movements eventually become instinctive and carried out without a moment's hesitation.

IMPROVISED WEAPONS

What is the most effective personal zombie combat weapon? Is it the Japanese *katana*? The medieval morning star? The Swiss halberd? This question has been argued time and again by soldiers and civilians alike. The answer is actually quite simple: The best weapon is the one you have at the ready during an undead attack. A handcrafted samurai sword worth thousands of dollars is useless if it is lying in your sleeping bag as a zombie rips at your throat. Likewise, a ten-dollar crowbar can provide years of faithful, defensive service if maintained well and used properly.

For an excellent historical example of weapon improvisation, look to Okinawa as a guide. In 1609, the island was captured and occupied by the Japanese Satsuma clan. Shortly thereafter, the Japanese banned possession of swords and firearms by all commoners and the peasant community. In order to defend themselves, the largely farming population of Okinawa turned to their everyday agricultural tools and developed them into the Okinawan weapons-based martial art known as *kobudo*.

Tools that were used to dig furrows (*sai*), carry baskets (*bo*), and harvest rice (*kama*) were transformed into the weapons that are still actively practiced hundreds of years later. Two of the most popular *kobudo* weapons seen in the West are the *nunchaku*, or nunchucks, and the *tonfa*, which has been modified for law enforcement use as the side-handled baton. Okinawan history shows us that it is not necessary or required to spend hundreds of dollars on custom-made weaponry. Take a walk around various locations in your local surroundings. With a combat mindset, chances are good that you will spot many common implements at your disposal that can provide excellent protection against the living dead.

Let us explore some of these possible locations.

The Farm

If you have the time and have planned far enough ahead to stock up on inexpensive yet effective weapons for your arsenal, head to your local farming supply store. There you will find a selection of solidly built tools that are meant for decades of hard service working the land, which can be put to equally good use in battling the walking dead. Improvised farming tools even provide several advantages over conventional combat weapons:

1. **Availability:** Unless you order your weapons in advance or raid the armory section of a museum, the chances of acquiring a high-quality, combat-ready battle-axe or halberd are slim. In contrast, gardening and farming implements are fairly commonplace and readily available.

2. **Materials:** The handles of traditional long-range weapons are often made of wood. Modern farming tool handles are often crafted from synthetic materials such as fiberglass, which can be lighter and sturdier than traditional wood handles. The metal used in farming equipment is typically hardened tool steel, made to withstand the rigors of moving earth and rock, and certainly able to tolerate the frequent beating against undead skulls.

3. **Cost:** In a price comparison with actual combat tools, farming implements win nearly every time. A moderately well-made long-range combat weapon, such as a poleaxe, will probably cost several hundred dollars. A stout gardening shovel will run you a fraction of that price.

Some common agricultural tools that can have an alternate life as an undead weapon include those on the following pages.

WEAPON EVALUATION: LANDSCAPING SHOVEL

EFFECTIVENESS: **HIGH**
LIFE SPAN: **100+ ZOMBIE ENGAGEMENTS**
SKILL LEVEL: **MODERATE**
AVAILABILITY: **COMMON**
COST: **VERY INEXPENSIVE**

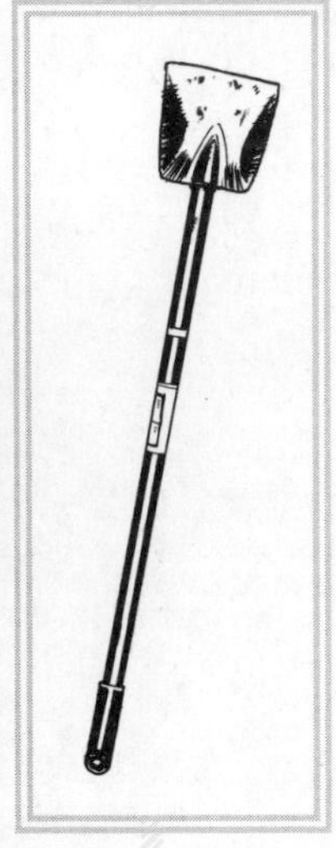

OVERVIEW: If there is any one implement that could be considered a modern-day combat spade, it's the landscaping shovel. Over five feet long with a blade made from heavy-gauge, tempered steel, the garden-variety shovel can be found in nearly every hardware store on the planet. Designed to endure years of hardscrabble labor, its low cost and sturdy construction make it a preferred choice of those who excel at long-range engagements but do not have the means to purchase a conventional long-distance weapon. Even models with a sturdy synthetic handle, preferred over the more fragile wooden type, can be found for less than $30.

Wielding this tool in undead combat is similar to using a weapon such as the battle-axe. It is best used to strike vulnerable areas of the zombie skull using the flat of the shovel or the pointed corners of the blade. Those who use this tool as their primary combat weapon have been known to file the edges down to a sharper angle, making this implement even more versatile at long range.

WEAPON EVALUATION: MACHETE

EFFECTIVENESS: MODERATE
LIFE SPAN: 25+ ZOMBIE ENGAGEMENTS
SKILL LEVEL: MODERATE
AVAILABILITY: COMMON
COST: VERY INEXPENSIVE

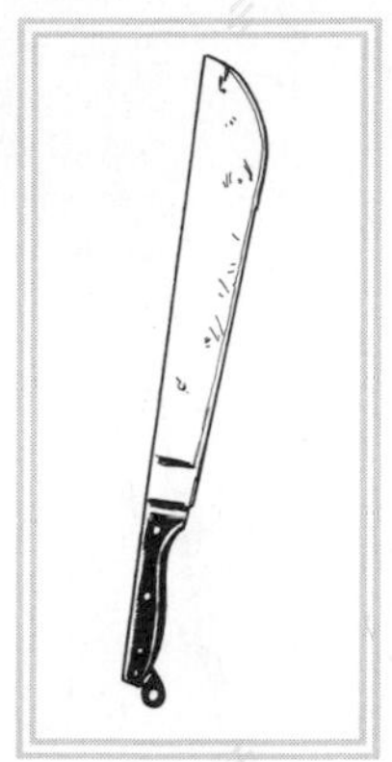

OVERVIEW: Popular around the world as a gardening and brush-clearing tool, the machete is already an infamous weapon used in conflicts throughout Africa and South America, where it instills dread in those who fear being hacked apart by its large, intimidating blade.

Because of its ubiquitous nature and low price point, the machete has become a common weapon in undead combat. Its most effective use against a walking corpse is via a decapitation attack rather than a blow to the head, where its thin blade may cause difficulty for those with inadequate strength to slice into the zombie skull.

The greatest liability of the machete, as with all edged weapons, is the tedium of keeping the blade honed and ready for action. Although this may be a simple maintenance task when using this tool exclusively to clear weeds and vegetation, you may find yourself in a never-ending cycle of slashing and sharpening during an undead outbreak. You would be surprised how quickly the edge of even a higher-quality machete dulls when having to hack through the necks of only a handful of undead combatants.

WEAPON EVALUATION: PITCHFORK

EFFECTIVENESS: **HIGH**
LIFE SPAN: **100+ ZOMBIE ENGAGEMENTS**
SKILL LEVEL: **HIGH**
AVAILABILITY: **COMMON**
COST: **INEXPENSIVE**

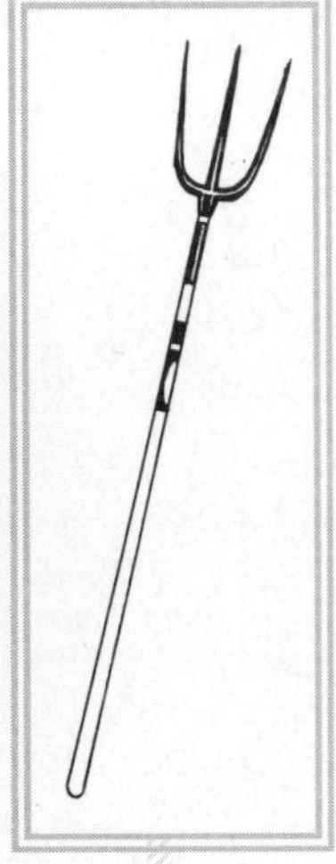

OVERVIEW: A common farm tool used for baling agricultural items such as hay, grass, or compost, the pitchfork can be an adequate counter-ghoul weapon in properly trained hands. It can function much like a spear, except with several sharp points at the ready rather than a single pike. Also, as with the spear, this tool is limited to a thrusting-type attack, as the pitchfork is not designed for a swinging, centrifugally driven blow against the zombie skull. Some have adapted this tool's original functionality to serve in undead combat by skewering ghouls and literally pitching them off the edges of high structures, such as cliffs or rooftops.

The pitchfork, like other stabbing weapons, is best used for a specific technique in which the tines of the fork are driven from the underside of the chin through the soft palate into the brain. We will describe this technique in specific detail later in this text. Striking the brain through the zombie's eye sockets may be another employable tactic. This technique, however, depends largely on the distance between fork tines, which often number anywhere from three to six. Targeting the eyes may be difficult to execute with a pitchfork that has narrow spacing between prongs and may cause the weapon to become lodged in the face of your undead opponent.

The Garage

Like farming implements, home maintenance tools are inexpensive and readily available and can prove highly effective in undead battle. You often need look only as far as your own garage to find several items that can double as outstanding improvised weapons. It is recommended that you steer away from powered devices as your primary weapon. As we will discuss later in more detail, power tools may indeed be effective weapons, but relying on external energy sources during an undead outbreak is not the most practical solution. Stick to tools that require only muscular energy; when the gas runs out or the electricity switches off, they will remain a trusted ally.

Some examples of construction tools that double as efficient zombie weapons include those on the following pages.

WEAPON EVALUATION: SIDEWALK SCRAPER

EFFECTIVENESS: **HIGH**
LIFE SPAN: **150+ ZOMBIE ENGAGEMENTS**
SKILL LEVEL: **HIGH**
AVAILABILITY: **COMMON**
COST: **VERY INEXPENSIVE**

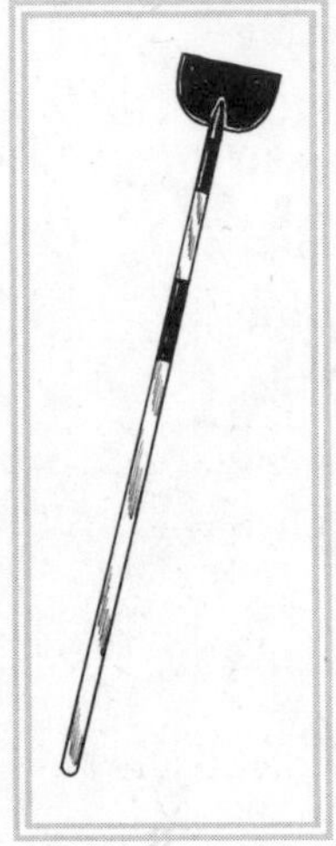

OVERVIEW: As good an improvised long-range weapon as the landscape shovel, if not better, the sidewalk scraper is composed of a wide, flat blade attached to a pole approximately four to five feet long. This implement is traditionally used by maintenance crews and building superintendents to scrape blemishes and sticky refuse such as chewing gum from the pavement. The potential lethality of the scraper is evident in frigid northern climates, where this tool is also used to break apart sheets of ice that form after a winter storm.

The forged, spadelike blade is thin and sharp, making it an excellent tool for targeting the fragile bone structure of the nasal/orbital region on the zombie skull. Warriors skilled with this weapon can cleave off the top of a ghoul's head cleanly with one well-placed thrust. The scraper can also be swung like an axe to attack the temporal or occipital regions of the skull.

Like many of the improvised pole-based weapons mentioned previously, the sidewalk scraper can be found with either a wooden or synthetic handle. Given a choice, it is recommended that you choose the latter. Although slightly more expensive, the durability of the synthetic handle far outweighs the added cost. Even given the added price, this weapon is still roughly a tenth of the cost of a professionally crafted polearm.

WEAPON EVALUATION: SLEDGEHAMMER

EFFECTIVENESS: **HIGH**
LIFE SPAN: **200+ ZOMBIE ENGAGEMENTS**
SKILL LEVEL: **VERY HIGH**
AVAILABILITY: **COMMON**
COST: **INEXPENSIVE**

OVERVIEW: A construction tool that needs no introduction, the sledgehammer is an implement frequently used for breaking concrete, driving spikes, and demolishing structures. Given its inherent use in destructive tasks, it is highly regarded as a powerful weapon against the living dead.

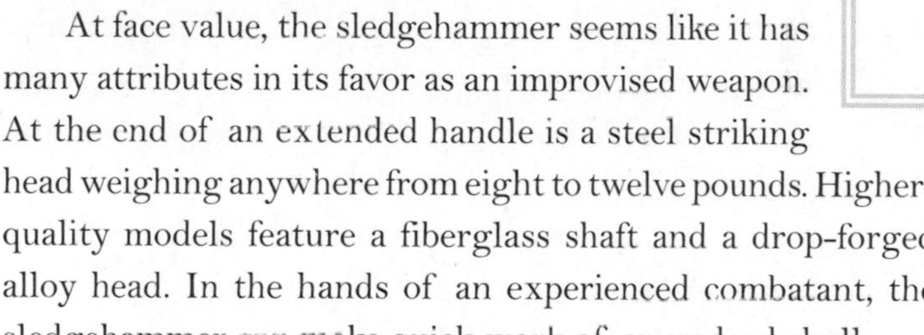

At face value, the sledgehammer seems like it has many attributes in its favor as an improvised weapon. At the end of an extended handle is a steel striking head weighing anywhere from eight to twelve pounds. Higher-quality models feature a fiberglass shaft and a drop-forged alloy head. In the hands of an experienced combatant, the sledgehammer can make quick work of an undead skull.

The liability of this weapon lies in the ability required to handle it effectively. The sledgehammer is considered a "commitment weapon," indicating that once you launch a strike with this tool, you are fully committed to executing it. Given the sledgehammer's weight and top-heavy structure, it is very difficult to change speed or direction midstrike. It is also a comparatively slow weapon and may be difficult to use against undead groups of five or more, where speed of elimination may be key to survival. Users of this weapon also need to be cautious of the "splatter effect." If a strike smashes into its target with a high degree of force, the zombie skull may fragment, scattering bits of contaminated bone and tissue outward, possibly toward unsuspecting humans in the surrounding perimeter.

WEAPON EVALUATION: CROWBAR

EFFECTIVENESS: **HIGH**
LIFE SPAN: **200+ ZOMBIE ENGAGEMENTS**
SKILL LEVEL: **MODERATE**
AVAILABILITY: **COMMON**
COST: **VERY INEXPENSIVE**

OVERVIEW: One of the most popular improvised weapons, second only to a baseball bat, the crowbar has a prominent standing as a solid, satisfying hunk of metal that can be swung with a high degree of force and accuracy. The crowbar's length, heft, and lethal hooked ends make it quite effective in medium-range zombie engagements. It is also a very practical improvised tool because of its low cost, its high availability, and its usefulness during a siege of walking cadavers. In the moments following an outbreak, you may indeed find the need to pry open boxes and force open doors in addition to caving in a revenant's skull.

Using this tool as you would any melee weapon, attack any vulnerable region of the cranium with the curved prongs on the crowbar. Just as with any hooked weapon, be watchful when using the arced tips so that it does not become jammed in an undead skull and pulled from your hand.

As the crowbar is little more than a dowel of steel with a curved edge, this improvised weapon benefits greatly from customization efforts. The smooth metal surface of this tool may make it difficult to grasp should it become coated with water, blood, or undead fluids. It is suggested that you wrap a more comfortable grip on the weapon, making it easier to wield in combat. See additional customization options later in this section.

The Toolbox

Though not everyone will have access to a farmhouse or a garage in their search for improvised weaponry, nearly every family unit has a collection of items in the home to tend to small repairs and domestic tasks. Look closely at your toolbox, and with a warrior's eye, you will note how many common household items can function as weapons against the living dead. Some of the more obvious examples include the following.

WEAPON EVALUATION: SCREWDRIVER

EFFECTIVENESS: **HIGH**
LIFE SPAN: **100+ ZOMBIE ENGAGEMENTS**
SKILL LEVEL: **VERY HIGH**
AVAILABILITY: **VERY COMMON**
COST: **VERY INEXPENSIVE**

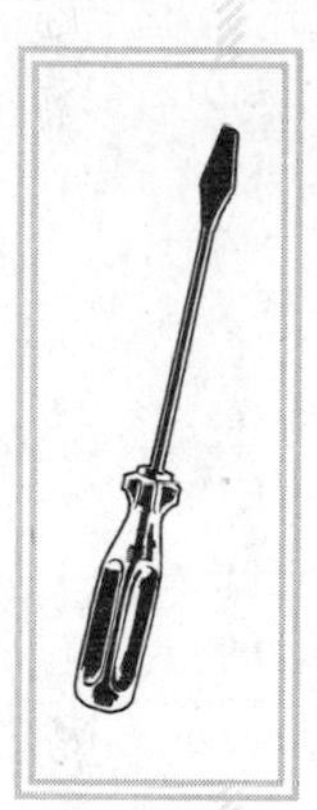

OVERVIEW: Perhaps the most mundane of all domestic tools, the ordinary screwdriver can be found in nearly every household. With proper training, however, this simple implement can function as a superior close-combat tool if a suitable edged weapon is not available. Because of its stout construction and piercing capabilities, it may be a preferable choice over an actual combat blade, and is certainly less expensive.

The same principles for choosing an edged weapon should also be applied when selecting an appropriate screwdriver for zombie combat. Ensure that the shaft is of adequate length to penetrate the skull and reach brain tissue if driven to the hilt under the zombie's chin. Find one that is of solid, single-piece construction that does not have an interchangeable or removable stem—the last thing you want to do is to extract the shank with your fingertips after it has remained embedded inside a ghoul's skull poststrike. It is also preferable to employ a flathead rather than a Phillips-head screwdriver in undead combat, as the level, angled blade supplies better penetrating power and can be sanded down to a sharper edge.

WEAPON EVALUATION: CLAW HAMMER

EFFECTIVENESS: **MODERATE**
LIFE SPAN: **100+ ZOMBIE ENGAGEMENTS**
SKILL LEVEL: **MODERATE**
AVAILABILITY: **VERY COMMON**
COST: **VERY INEXPENSIVE**

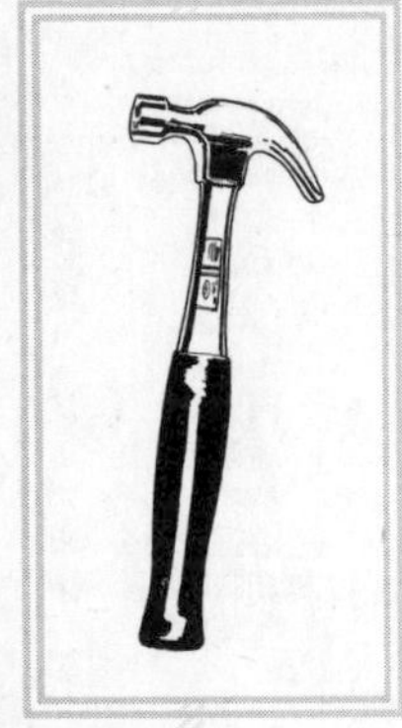

OVERVIEW: Like the everyday screwdriver, it is rare to find a toolbox that does not contain some type of hammering tool among its items. Typically used to pound nails or extricate them from wood, the claw hammer has a solid metal striking face that can do enormous damage from a blow of sufficient power, while the opposite prong ends can embed themselves deeply into the undead skull.

When it comes to selecting a claw hammer for undead defense, there are a wide number of variations to consider. Your best choice is a model whose head and shaft are both forged from a single piece of steel and whose handle grip is wrapped in a resilient, shock-absorbent material. Avoid variants with wooden handles where the metal head is affixed to a wooden shaft; after prolonged undead combat, the fragility of wood may succumb to splitting and cracking.

Exhibit caution when using this particular improvised weapon against an undead attacker. A claw hammer averages fifteen inches in length, shorter than your typical melee weapon. This requires you to draw in closer to your opponent than typical melee engagements, thus increasing the likelihood of being snared by ghoulish hands. The claw end of the hammer is also at risk of remaining trapped inside the skull cavity of your opponent.

WEAPON EVALUATION: CHISEL

EFFECTIVENESS: HIGH
LIFE SPAN: 100+ ZOMBIE ENGAGEMENTS
SKILL LEVEL: VERY HIGH
AVAILABILITY: COMMON
COST: VERY INEXPENSIVE

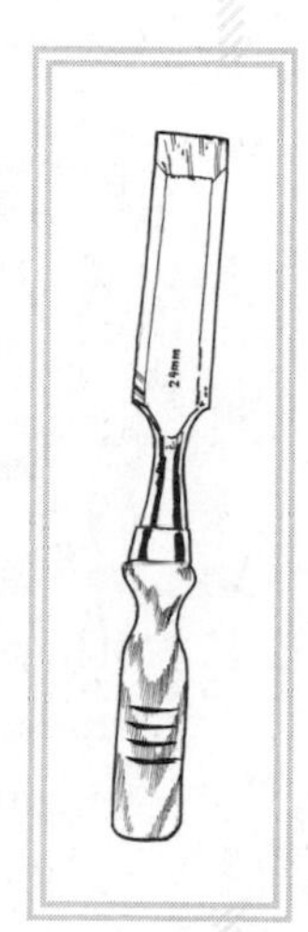

OVERVIEW: A specialty implement designed for a specific task, the chisel is most frequently used to carve wood, metal, or masonry. Its unique design also makes it a formidable weapon against the living dead, provided you adhere to particular selection guidelines.

The stout blade of the chisel is designed to chip away at its intended material when struck on the end with a mallet. This makes the fundamental structure of the tool extremely resilient, and ideal for undead combat encounters. A hammering blow to the skull with a chisel can easily penetrate bone with little accompanying damage to the blade. The design is so robust that custom knife makers often use a similar "chisel grind" to shape their combat blades. Higher-quality Japanese chisels are forged in a similar fashion to samurai swords, with a lamination of softer metal around a hard steel core.

The greatest caveat when selecting a chisel as your improvised zombie weapon is its length. Because of the nature of their intended purpose, chisel blades are often short and wide. Remember the parameters by which we selected a knife for close combat; the blade must be long enough to tap into the ghoul's brain from the farthest point on the skull possible. If the chisel blade is too short, you may strike with your weapon, only to have the zombie continue lashing out at you in a frenzied attack.

The Kitchen

Step into an ordinary domestic kitchen and you will find an assortment of utensils that can perform well as makeshift weapons. However, whatever tool you select from this area to serve as an undead weapon should remain a weapon from that point forward. It is highly recommended that you not multitask with these items and do not return them to their original task of cooking or preparing food. Ingesting even the smallest amount of virus-tainted blood or zombie tissue is a confirmed death sentence. Although the chance of infection from a properly cleaned and disinfected weapon is low, the risk is not worth the benefit. Either commit to using an item from your kitchen as an instrument against the undead for the remainder of its life span, or choose an alternative weapon.

The most logical choice of improvised weapons around the kitchen is the vast selection of edged tools at your disposal. You may not have the time, money, or inclination to purchase a custom-made, Damascus-steel combat knife, but with a knife block on your countertop, you have several possibilities at your disposal. As we covered earlier, there are specific criteria when selecting your close-combat edged weapon—you will need a weapon with a nonserrated blade long and sturdy enough to penetrate the zombie brain. Given these qualifications, you can immediately eliminate paring and utility knives as choices; these blades are generally too short to serve your combat needs. Bread knives are also a poor choice, as they have both rounded tips and serrated edges. The length of a boning or scaling knife is acceptable. However, its thin, flexible blade may have trouble piercing through several layers of flesh, cartilage, and bone. The popular Japanese *santoku* is a possibility, but its major disadvantage lies in the low, sheepsfoot sweep of the blade's point, which may hamper its ability to pierce the skull.

Given the aforementioned parameters required of all zombie weapons, you have a few choices from your knife block that can serve adequately in an undead encounter.

WEAPON EVALUATION: CHEF'S KNIFE

EFFECTIVENESS: **HIGH**
LIFE SPAN: **50+ ZOMBIE ENGAGEMENTS**
SKILL LEVEL: **VERY HIGH**
AVAILABILITY: **COMMON**
COST: **MODERATE**

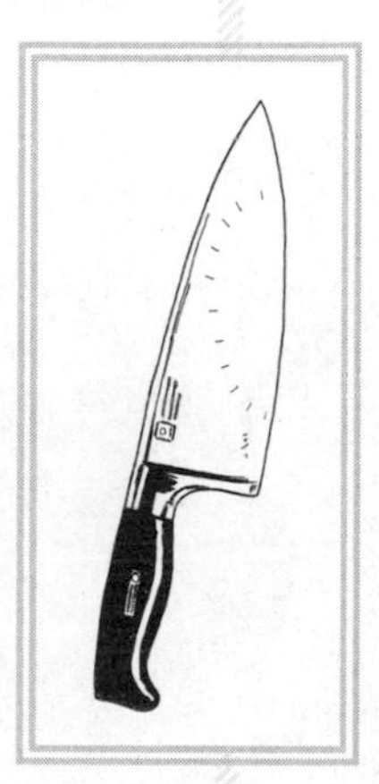

OVERVIEW: The one essential tool for every professional and home-trained cook, the chef's knife is also the best choice of weapon from your standard knife set to use against the living dead. Of the many types of kitchen blade available, the chef's knife meets all of our requirements for zombie combat. Chef's blades generally come in eight- to ten-inch lengths, more than adequate for the task at hand. Some modern-designed chef's knives have scalloped indentations that run along the length of the blade to prevent food from sticking during slicing tasks. This unique feature may also provide an advantage during zombie combat by enabling slightly easier withdrawal of the weapon from your adversary's skull.

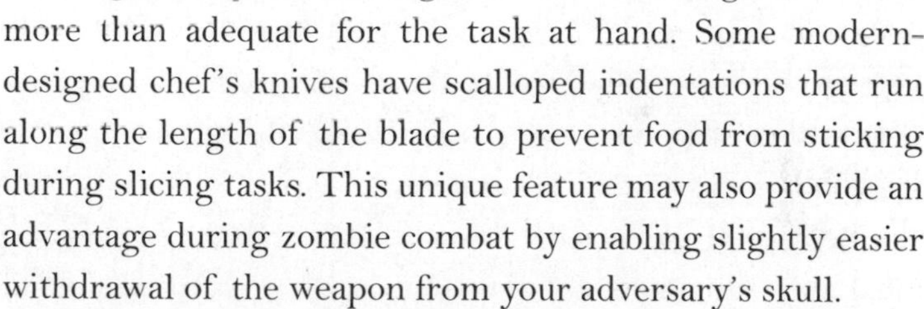

Just as with combat knives, quality and price points vary widely with kitchen cutlery. As this is a discussion on improvised weapons, it is recommended that you do not spend an exorbitant amount of money on a chef's knife specifically to use against the living dead. Should you have the time and financial means, purchase a quality, combat-specific blade. Regarding particular manufacturers, German-made chef's knives hold a slight edge over their Japanese counterparts when it comes to zombie weapon suitability. Reputable German kitchen knives tend to be thicker and crafted from heavier stock. Japanese blades, though often sharper, tend to have thinner blades, making them more fragile in repeated combat engagements.

WEAPON EVALUATION: FRYING PAN

EFFECTIVENESS: **MODERATE**
LIFE SPAN: **200+ ZOMBIE ENGAGEMENTS**
SKILL LEVEL: **MODERATE**
AVAILABILITY: **COMMON**
COST: **INEXPENSIVE**

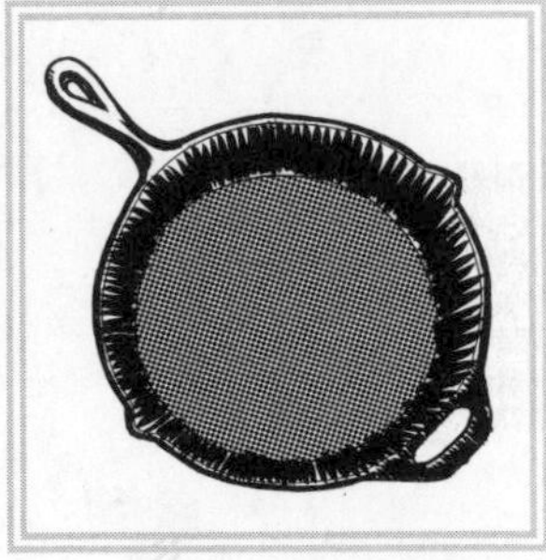

OVERVIEW: Although using this piece of cookware for combat purposes undoubtedly evokes images of slapstick comedy, a frying pan can function quite successfully as a weapon during a zombie attack. Of all the possible items in your cookware collection, this is your best option against an attacking corpse. The low sides and wide, flat bottom offer portability and a large striking surface. Given the wide variety of pans on the market, there are specific characteristics that you should keep in mind when choosing this unusual item to serve as an undead weapon.

Because the pan will act as a makeshift bludgeon, the most important trait for this tool is its need to withstand numerous blows to the undead skull without failure. It also must be heavy enough to shatter bone. As such, it is recommended that you avoid any pans that are not entirely manufactured from solid metal. Plastic-handled pans will not last more than a few blows against a zombie's thick skull. It is also suggested that you avoid lighter metals such as aluminum, which will dent and warp before doing your attacker any damage. Your finest choice among materials is, without a doubt, cast iron. Forged from a single, solid piece of metal, the cast iron frying pan has a history of being passed down through generations for use in kitchens, campgrounds, and the great outdoors. Should you become proficient enough with this improvised weapon, it can be passed down to future generations to serve a very different purpose.

WEAPON EVALUATION: CLEAVER

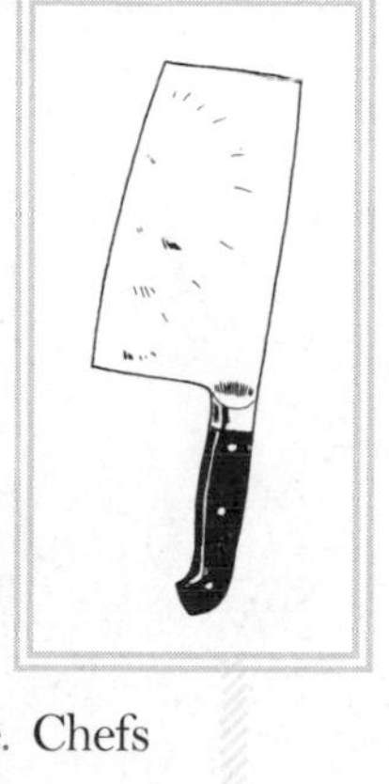

EFFECTIVENESS: **MODERATE**
LIFE SPAN: **50+ ZOMBIE ENGAGEMENTS**
SKILL LEVEL: **VERY HIGH**
AVAILABILITY: **COMMON**
COST: **MODERATE**

OVERVIEW: The kitchen cleaver is another piece of cutlery that you may have at your disposal, especially if you live in an Asian household. Designed to chop through animal flesh and bone, the cleaver is most commonly used in the preparation of Chinese cuisine. Chefs from this part of the world often use this blade alone for every cutting task to prepare all their dishes. Their dexterity with this large, seemingly cumbersome implement can be as precise and delicate as a paring knife and as powerful as a chef's knife.

As a zombie defensive tool, the cleaver has the potential to be a devastating close-combat weapon while also exhibiting some inherent shortcomings. Use of the cleaver is similar to that of an axe or hatchet. Because the cleaver's blade does not come to a fine point, it is exclusively a hacking and slashing weapon. Decapitation should be your principal attack strategy with a cleaver, because striking the skull may damage the blade beyond repair after protracted combat engagements. The length of the typical cleaver is also quite short, forcing you to move in close to your assailant in order to initiate your strike, similar to the bludgeoning claw hammer. Force and momentum are the keys to delivering an incapacitating strike with this utensil. It is imperative that you keep this tool razor-sharp for maximum effectiveness.

WEAPON EVALUATION: ICE PICK

EFFECTIVENESS: **HIGH**
LIFE SPAN: **100+ ZOMBIE ENGAGEMENTS**
SKILL LEVEL: **VERY HIGH**
AVAILABILITY: **MODERATE**
COST: **VERY INEXPENSIVE**

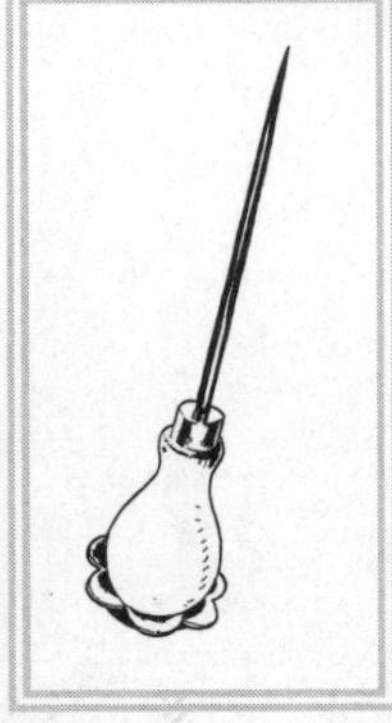

OVERVIEW: No longer as pervasive a household tool, the ice pick still retains a notorious reputation as an improvised weapon among certain criminal organizations. Its original purpose was to chip smaller pieces of ice from large blocks. The ice pick has now achieved status as a quick and efficient improvised close-combat weapon, and rightly so. Its sharp, pointed spike can penetrate clothing and flesh more easily than many combat knives, and the thin, cylindrical blade profile ensures trouble-free withdrawal from the target with minimal splatter.

As an improvised weapon against the living dead, the ice pick is just as efficient. The pick has penetrating power that rivals most bladed weapons, which provides you several target options on the undead skull. The ice pick's weaknesses are similar to those of any close-combat weapon. Its use necessitates being in close proximity to your opponent and thus requires a substantial level of speed and aptitude to wield effectively. Typical ice picks are also not exceptionally well made, hence their low price point. If you use this tool as your primary close-combat weapon, it is recommended that you carry a backup in case the pick fails you at an inopportune time.

The Stadium

Most families own a sizable quantity of sporting equipment for a variety of recreational activities. Because of the availability of items and the familiarity of use, you may gravitate toward selecting one of these tools during a zombie outbreak. Although any weapon is better than none, sports gear is your least favorable option. This is due to a single important reason: durability.

Most sports equipment that could possibly operate as a zombie weapon falls into the bludgeon class. This category includes instruments such as golf clubs, hockey sticks, polo mallets, and tennis rackets. Although this equipment was built to withstand the shock of striking a leather or rubber ball, experience has shown that in zombie combat, the failure rate of these tools is unacceptably high. These implements were not designed to inflict a great deal of damage. Quite the opposite, modern sporting equipment uses materials that are lighter, faster, and less likely to cause life-threatening injury from inadvertent contact—not an admirable trait when it comes to fending off a hungry ghoul.

As far as sporting goods that can serve as improvised weapons are concerned, only one item is worth evaluating in detail.

WEAPON EVALUATION: BASEBALL BAT

EFFECTIVENESS: **MODERATE**
LIFE SPAN: **20+ ZOMBIE ENGAGEMENTS**
SKILL LEVEL: **LOW**
AVAILABILITY: **VERY COMMON**
COST: **MODERATE**

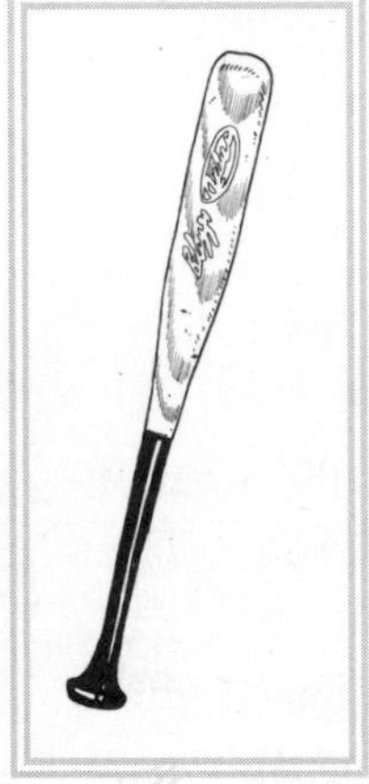

OVERVIEW: Possibly the most popular of all improvised weapons, the baseball bat is frequently selected by combatants as a weapon for both living and undead altercations. Though this implement may suffice against human opponents, research has shown that it is not the most durable weapon for undead combat. Traditional wooden bats have an average life span of only fifteen to twenty zombie engagements. Cricket bats, also made of wood, seem to exhibit a similar longevity. Bats constructed from aluminum stock have a slightly longer life span but also fall victim to dents and warping when repeatedly struck against the undead skull. Batting instruments made from higher-end materials such as composite fiber can cost hundreds of dollars and are susceptible to cracking and shattering in cold weather—not a good choice if you live in a frigid winter climate.

Although the baseball bat does not exhibit the best of life spans, it cannot be immediately dismissed as a poor choice for an improvised zombie weapon. What this tool lacks in resiliency, it makes up for in ubiquity and the required proficiency to wield it. Nearly all humans, regardless of age, gender, and experience with the sport of baseball, can swing a bat at an oncoming ghoul. Very little training is required to handle this weapon effectively, provided you know which areas to target. Most households, particularly those with children, will already have one of these implements handy, obviating the need to rush off and purchase a weapon should an outbreak unexpectedly occur. If you select this tool as your permanent melee weapon, be certain to inspect it for damage after each undead sortie.

Although sporting equipment does not make effective offensive weapons, some items can be used in a defensive manner. Pads and protective guards worn to minimize injury can be useful to shield against a biting and scratching corpse. We will discuss defensive gear in further detail later in this text.

Other Improvised Weapons

In trained hands, virtually anything can come to your defense against the walking dead; the leg of a chair, a piece of rebar, or a simple length of pipe can eliminate dozens of undead adversaries. If you find yourself embroiled in a combat situation, anything is better than facing the undead with only your bare hands. Once you are out of harm's way and have the time to choose a weapon to use on a permanent basis, keep in mind the following attributes:

- **Resilience:** Remember, metal is better than wood, and wood is better than plastic. Before you settle on a weapon, make sure that it will be able to last for at least ten combat engagements. Strike it against several hard surfaces to test its hardiness. Your first few battles will help determine whether the weapon you have chosen can survive the long haul. Be sure to closely examine it after each zombie encounter (see the section later in this chapter for additional maintenance tips).

- **Flexibility:** Can the weapon perform other tasks useful to your survival, or is it solely a combat item? Having a unitasking weapon that can easily crush a zombie's skull is fine, but a multitasking weapon that can also wrench open passageways, snip barbed wire, or split firewood is even better.

- **Mastery:** Regardless of the two previous attributes described, a weapon is only as good as the skill of its owner. A farming scythe may look impressive draped across your shoulder, but is useless if you cannot consistently use it to strike a single, terminating blow. Do not let pride cloud your judgment, and select a weapon best suited to your strengths and abilities.

WEAPON CUSTOMIZATION

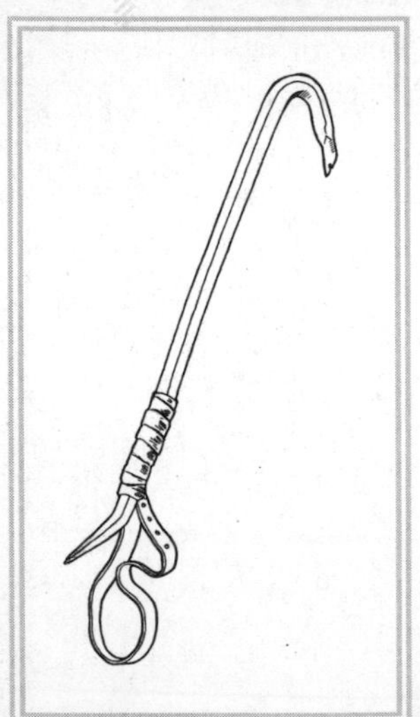

Everyday tools can play a major role in your conflict against an attacking zombie. As we have seen, improvised weapons often are inexpensive, plentiful, and function just as well as some dedicated combat armaments. There is no doubt that a collection of found objects can form the cornerstone of your arsenal against the living dead. The greatest weakness of an improvised tool is its inherent nature as a piece of equipment not originally designed for combat. As such, the implement may require some modification in order for it to perform optimally in its new task: disposing of a walking corpse. Here are several ways you can customize your weapon to improve its tactical functionality:

- **Craft hand grips:** If your weapon is not comfortable in the hand, it will rapidly become tiresome to wield during extended combat engagements. This issue may not be immediately apparent, but after disposing of ten, fifteen, or twenty consecutive undead attackers in as many minutes, you will quickly comprehend how an uncomfortable grip can affect your performance. Slight hand discomfort can transform into painful, technique-hindering blisters. A few lengths of duct tape–wrapped fabric around areas where you typically grasp your weapon can make a world of difference. Grips also create a tactile surface, making it easier to retain your weapon should it become coated with fluid, infectious or otherwise.

- **File down edges:** If the improvised tool you have chosen already has natural edges and contours, refine them further by grinding them down to a sharper bevel. By doing so, you make items such as shovels, scrapers, and screwdrivers even more lethal against the undead. Military personnel commonly use this technique on their entrenching tools, where a sharpened blade transforms the implement from a run-of-the-mill ditch-digging shovel into a de facto battle-axe.

- **Create retention straps:** A dangerous misfortune that can occur during undead combat is the loss of your weapon. This may happen if a ghoul manages to grab hold of your weapon and wrench it away from you during its attack. (This situation is rare and unintentional, as a zombie grabs at a weapon not to disarm, but to close the distance with its target.) Only after extensive combat engagements will you realize how exhausting it can be to simply keep a firm hold of your weapon. Your forearms will ache, your fingers will throb, and the muscles in your hands may begin to cramp, making it difficult to retain your weapon with each thrust or swing. This is the reason why many traditional arms are crafted with a retaining strap that can be looped around your wrist, enabling better security of the weapon. Replicate these straps by fastening a length of rope, leather, or fabric to your improvised tool so that even when you begin to tire, your weapon will still be close should it inadvertently slip from your grasp.

WEAPON MAINTENANCE

Be it a scimitar, battle-axe, or garden trowel, every weapon is a tool—a tool that can fail you if it is not properly maintained. Honing your weapons is as important as refining your fitness and combat skills. Do not be lulled by the misconception that simply because hand weapons do not have complex moving parts, unlike firearms or other ballistic weapons, they require no systematic upkeep. Just as you would clean your pistol after extensive firing and exercise your physique to keep it in optimum shape, establishing a customary maintenance routine for your armaments will maximize their fighting capabilities. After every zombie encounter, you should perform the following procedures once you have reached an area free of undead hostiles:

- **Clean:** Using a soft, clean rag or paper towel, wipe down the entire weapon completely. Repeat this step several times, rinsing the cloth in between wipes. After the initial mopping in which you remove most of the extraneous fluids, spend the time to ensure that no blood, bone fragments, or cranial tissue have worked their way into the recesses of your weapon. If you have the time and resources, pass the entire weapon under warm running water. After a methodical scrubbing, dry your weapon thoroughly with a clean cloth. Do not ignore this last step, as water can corrode metal, weakening it and making it more susceptible to failure.

- **Inspect:** From tip to tail, closely examine every inch of your weapon. Note every dent, nick, or bend, and determine whether the reliability of the weapon has been irreparably compromised. Even the tiniest stress fracture can weaken the structural integrity of a weapon such that it may shatter upon impact during your next battle. This is another reason why using wood-based weapons such as staves or baseball bats is not recommended, because they are much more likely to falter in intense zombie combat situations.

  Some cracks can be so minuscule that they can barely be seen by the naked eye, even with close inspection. A good way to determine whether your weapon has an unseen fissure is to rap it lightly against another hard object. Listen for your weapon to reverberate with a solid ring. If the tool makes an odd or buzzing sound, there is a chance that a fracture exists, which may result in weapon failure during your next engagement. If you hear the latter, strike it harder against a solid object, attempting to shatter it yourself. Better to destroy your weapon during a moment of security than to make this unfortunate discovery in the midst of an attack.

- **Preserve:** Keep your weapons in a constant state of combat readiness. If you are using a long-range weapon, make sure the head affixes to the handle solidly and without wobble. If you are using a bludgeon, make sure the handle wraps are in good condition and replace them if necessary. If you are using an edged weapon, sharpen it. Do not become lackadaisical and convince yourself that you will tend to it after the next battle. The unexpected nature of a zombie attack means that you will often be thrown in to battle when you least expect it. The less time you spend caring for your weapons, the more time you will need to finish off your undead adversaries with a slippery, filthy, or dull weapon.

EXTERNALLY-FUELED WEAPONS

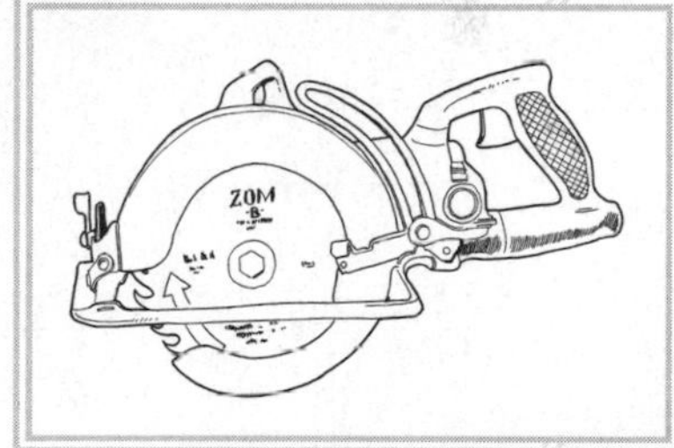

Note that regardless of the combat range covered and types of armaments discussed, we have not included evaluations of weapons that are powered by external energy sources. This was a conscious decision. Although electric, gas, or battery-powered tools such as circular saws and electric hammers may indeed be obtainable and devastating against the walking dead, they are not recommended as your primary combat weapons. Two of these reasons are obvious: The heft of these devices and the racket they generate when powered on make them cumbersome in transport and obtrusive in combat. There are two more reasons that are not as apparent, but just as significant:

- **Splatter:** As mentioned in our evaluation of the sledgehammer, certain high-trauma weapons suffer from what is known as the splatter effect. Many powered weapons most certainly exhibit this trait, as they often create wide, indiscriminate spray patterns during combat, a result of their cycling, shark-toothed blades. These whirling edges can send contagious bits of flesh scattering several feet in all directions, making you and those around you more vulnerable to infection. Weapons of this nature are also notoriously difficult to clean. Once a power tool has been used in zombie combat, it is nearly impossible to thoroughly scour all the blood and tissue that accumulates within its gears. For every two minutes spent in combat, expect to spend an additional thirty minutes post-engagement cleaning the weapon.

- **Energy:** A key to surviving in an undead world is to minimize your overall footprint. Instead of traveling by car, journey by bicycle. Instead of an electrical light, burn candles. The same philosophy holds true for your choice in weaponry. Just as ammunition may be hoarded and in short supply during large-scale outbreaks, fuel of any sort will also become a scarce resource. What will you do when the power drill you are waving menacingly in battle grinds to an unexpected halt? It is much better to not have to plan for that contingency, and instead train with weapons powered by the most efficient energy source available: the human body.

This is not to say that powered weapons cannot play some role in your undead combat arsenal. If you have access to tools in this category, be strategic in their activation. Just as with firearms, they should play a secondary role in your combat engagements, and only in specific circumstances. The best instance in which to use these unique tools is when you find yourself drastically outnumbered by the undead. When your energy level fades but several dozen ghoulish threats remain, start up the pneumatic drill. A fueled device can decimate a mob of ghouls in rapid succession, allowing you to finish the engagement with little physical exertion. Be judicious in their use and frugal with the energy they require, and these weapons can serve you best at times when you need them most.

WEAPON SELECTION— A FINAL WORD

Later in this manual we will describe combat techniques that complement many of the weapons detailed in this section. It is important to study these techniques and determine whether the armaments you have chosen as your first line of defense against the walking dead are truly appropriate for you. This may seem like an obvious statement, but it is not.

Individuals often find themselves enamored of a particular type, class, or size of weapon, even if it is poorly suited for their unique physical build, strength, or style of combat. Just as you need to honestly assess your physique to determine what type of zombie combatant you are, you should apply the same level of scrutiny to your choice of weapon. Simply because you've purchased a beautifully crafted, combat-ready battle-axe does not mean that particular weapon is your ideal match.

Remember, successful combatants throughout history have known that you need to fit the weapon to the fighter, not the fighter to the weapon.

DEFENSIVE EQUIPMENT

As we have seen in our overview of combat weapons, there are a multitude of options for offensive tools you can utilize in your skirmishes with the walking dead. There are also many defensive items that you can bring to bear that can stack the odds in your favor during a zombie encounter. Adding a few of these items to your arsenal will not only improve your chances of survival, but also make you a much more formidable opponent in undead battle.

Clothing

Your garments should be comfortable, close but not tight-fitting, and durable. Remember that during an attack, you will have ghouls clawing and pulling at your body. Clothing that is too loose will make it easier for the corpse to grab hold and hang on tight. At the same time, skintight clothing is not recommended, unless it is worn as a base layer with another outer layer for security. This recommendation is contrary to the popular opinion that tight clothing affords better protection from the grasp of an attacking zombie. This contrarian view is based on field reports of combat encounters in which a human defender wore extremely tight clothing, thinking it would provide better protection from a ghoul's clutches. In reality, skintight clothing presents another, more serious hazard.

Recall the description of the undead grip in our earlier discussion on anatomy. The fingernails on a zombie can often be jagged and sharp, making its hands a common source of infection to humans. An individual wearing skintight garments who is grabbed by a ghoul suffers a greater chance of having the fabric rip and tear, exposing the vulnerable flesh underneath. A person wearing tight clothing also runs the risk of having a zombie grab a handful of flesh underneath—an extremely painful occurrence and common with larger, endocombatant types. It is far better to wear clothing that fits close to the body but also has flexibility in the material so that a ghoul does not end up with a fistful of skin and fabric.

Ensure that the clothing material is of adequate thickness, as it may also provide protection from unanticipated assaults. Combat records show that victims have survived a zombie's attack simply because their clothing was sufficiently bulky to withstand bite penetration. Heavy leather coats make an excellent protective outer shell. Layering your outfit also helps prevent a zombie's infected fingertips from penetrating several levels of fabric, into your flesh.

Goggles

When fighting in close combat with a zombie, there is always a remote risk of having contaminated fluid spray against you, the chances of which increase dramatically depending on your proximity to the ghoul. A vulnerable area for this type of contact is the eyes. Research has shown that just a single drop of contagious liquid landing on the surface of the cornea will eventually lead to infection, death, and reanimation. Shielding your eyes during close combat with the undead is one of the simplest things you can do to protect yourself from infection.

Any eyewear, be it sunglasses, reading lenses, or bifocals, affords some level of protection during undead combat. Ideal optical defensive wear forms a seal around the entire perimeter of the orbital sockets. Examples of such eyewear include swim goggles, laboratory safety lenses, and skydiving goggles. If you participate in any activities that require protective eye shields, such as skiing, ATV racing, or scuba diving, use the lenses you have as a first option, as you will already have broken them in and become accustomed to their fit. Be aware that some goggles limit your field of peripheral vision, possibly affecting your ability to detect an oncoming attack.

Gloves

Protecting your hands in undead combat can be an even greater concern than shielding your eyes. This is particularly true when engaged in close-quarters combat, in which you will be seizing ghouls that may bear gory, infected wounds. A single cut on your hand that comes into contact with a zombie's open sores will end the battle in the ghoul's favor. Although, like goggles, any hand protection is better than bare flesh, some types are preferable to others. Choose gloves made of nonporous materials, such as latex, nitrile rubber, or other synthetic material. Cloth or wool gloves are not the best alternative, as fluid can soak through and make contact with your skin. Tactical hand protection can also assist in your offensive attack by enabling you to grip your weapon easier, even if it is slick with congealed blood.

Face Mask

This piece of equipment may be unnecessary, especially for trained individuals who have learned to keep their mouth closed during close combat, but for those who desire additional protection, a face mask will prevent a mist of infected gore from landing between your lips. Face masks are porous for the obvious reason of allowing oxygen to pass through the material, but choose one that ensures a tight seal around the mouth cavity. A painter's mask is your simplest, most inexpensive option. Face shields worn for sporting activities such as paintball also work well, as they were designed to safeguard against high-velocity fluid splatter.

Knee Pads

Defensive equipment protects your physique not only during battle, but also during the more mundane activities between combat engagements. During a zombie infestation, you may find yourself on your knees more often than you would expect. Whether you're crawling through brush to avoid detection from humans and undead adversaries, taking a knee to steady your aim, or scurrying under barricades, protection may come in handy to safeguard the delicate bony structures surrounding the patella. Damaged knees may affect your ability to evade or outdistance an attacking horde before you can reach the next safe house or rescue station.

Night Vision Device (NVD)

Once available only to the military and professional security organizations, night vision technology has advanced such that its price point makes it accessible to the civilian population. Traveling at night is never recommended during a zombie siege. It is, however, sometimes unavoidable. Although both hunter and hunted are impacted by the lack of daylight, humans are at a greater disadvantage. Despite the darkness, the living dead seem to be uncannily effective at tracking down prey in the dead of night. An NVD can help level the playing field should you find yourself on an open road, miles from safety, with the sun setting on the horizon.

Nose Plugs

Plugging your nostrils may seem like a negligible consideration but could very well mean the difference between defending yourself effectively and becoming a vomiting, teary-eyed victim. Recall our previous discussion in which we described the power a ghoul possesses simply in its noxious presence. Those who are sensitive to strong odors need to be particularly mindful. Nose plugs will prevent your olfactory system from being overwhelmed by the unrelenting stench of a walking corpse. This piece of equipment may be most useful when you find yourself engaging zombies in confined spaces or in multiple numbers. When using this piece of equipment, your breathing must obviously be done through your open mouth, which also can present a combat risk. It is recommended that you use a face mask in conjunction with nose plugs if you do require their use. Holding your breath is not advised.

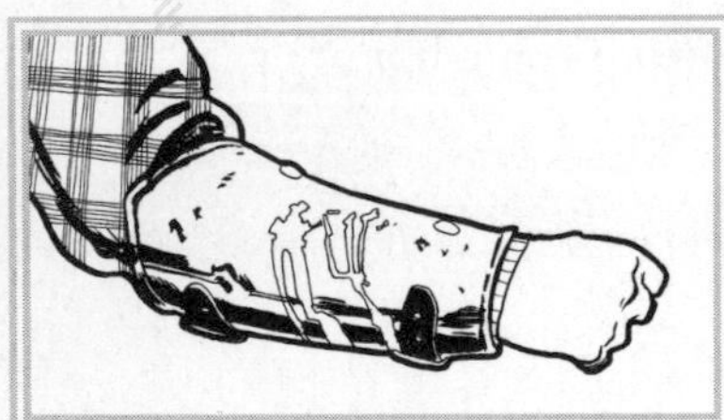

Forearm Guards

Also known as *vambraces* or *bracers*, this piece of protective equipment harkens back to a medieval age when archers protected their forearms from the snapping release of a drawn bowstring and knights guarded their arms from a slashing sword attack. Often made from leather or steel, bracers cover the area from wrist to elbow and can effectively shield against a repeated target of the living dead—the arms. Bracers are especially useful if you frequently engage in close-quarters combat or maneuver through narrow spaces during zombie-clearing operations, as this equipment makes freeing yourself from a ghoul's clutches on your arms that much easier.

Shin Guards

Another defensive item that has its origins in medieval history, shin guards, or greaves, protect the lower leg from knee to ankle. The modern equivalents of this ancient protective gear are the leg guards worn by athletes in sports such as hockey or lacrosse. Depending on the environment in which you normally operate, greaves may or may not prove to be a useful addition to your defensive outfit. Individuals in a jungle environment or those who regularly traverse heavily weeded areas, where ghouls may remain camouflaged in the brush, would benefit most from this type of protection. Full greaves, which protect both the front and back of the entire lower leg, are more effective than those that only guard the shin area, because the calf and Achilles' heel regions are vulnerable to attack by crawling ghouls.

Shoes

Choose your footwear carefully. It is one of the only pieces of defensive apparel that doubles as a zombie-neutralizing weapon. Avoid flimsy shoes such as sandals and flip-flops; these footwear choices may not last as long as a solid pair of hiking or combat boots and certainly do not provide the heft required to put a finishing stomp on a ghoul's skull. Safety-toe boots with steel reinforcements are an excellent choice, but remember that the comfort factor should not be overlooked. You may have to travel many miles on foot to safety during an undead outbreak, so your choice of footwear needs to be as comfortable as it is functional.

COMBAT REPORT: JAMES LITVIK

Clothing Designer, Indianapolis, Indiana

I step into James Litvik's workshop, located in an office park outside Indianapolis. The room is buzzing with the rhythmic sound of sewing machines and employees jostling back and forth with tall reams of fabric. I find Mr. Litvik standing in the back, inspecting some of his new tops that have just come off the machines. He explains that the disarray is a result of trying to complete a special rush order for the navy. "Customized wet suits for the special warfare teams," he says. Litvik's line of defensive garments has recently been awarded one of three government contracts to supply all branches of the armed services with "bite-resistant apparel." This line of work is strikingly different from the designs Litvik created to start his career, which were featured on the fashion runways of New York, Paris, and London. We retreat from the frenetic noise of the workshop to his office, which is just as cluttered with mannequins and fabric rolls, but more conducive to an interview.

JL: My father didn't hate me.

ZCM: Sorry?

JL: I said, my father didn't hate me. I wanted to get that out before we started. I've spoken some with journalists before, and my story's been twisted into your typical "queer son redeems self with military dad" cliché. I hope that's not what you're planning to do.

ZCM: I understand. How did your father feel about you?

JL: Pop was career army just like Grandpop, as "Hooah" as a man could get. He was also an amazingly open-minded person. Like most parents, he probably knew who I was even before I did. He was also a pragmatist. He knew it wouldn't be easy for me growing up where we lived. I remember him trying to teach me how to box when I was way too young to be interested in anything but blocks. It was his way of trying to protect me. And he never, ever made me feel like less of a son. When I think about it, being a military brat helped develop my style; being exposed early to different cultures and dress when we lived briefly in Europe and Asia, those experiences influenced me greatly later on when I was developing my couture line.

Still, an army dad loves to have an army son, and my brother, Jake, filled that bill. JROTC, West Point, Ranger Battalion, the whole business. While I was studying patternmaking and interning in Milan, he was "playing in the sandbox." Even though we saw each other rarely in between his extended deployments, he kept in close touch so we always knew he was all right, even if he couldn't tell us where he was. I had heard through Pop that Jake was being sent to deal with some events that were going on in the Middle East, and foreign reports started to filter in online about some new disease there causing mass outbreaks of civil unrest.

If you remember, back here in the States we were weren't hearing much from our own government. Thinking back now, I realize how oblivious we all were. All we kept hearing were things like, "Everything's fine. Go about your lives. Keep traveling. Keep shopping." I guess they figured that Uncle Mastercard would make everything better, so that's what everyone did. I launched my clothing line, made the rounds in Paris and New York, and dressed a few B-listers for some red carpet events. Things were going well, despite more news of casualties coming in from overseas. No one seemed affected by it here, just a passing paragraph on page three of the newspapers, far below the pictures of those celebrities wearing my fall collection.

Then the shit really hit the fan, and there was no keeping the lid on what was happening any longer. We didn't hear from Jake that often anymore. The communications between deployed soldiers and families became even more restrictive to the point where he was only sending two-word messages—"I'm okay," so we knew that he was. Until he wasn't.

To this day I don't know whether it was intentional or just coincidence, but I was visiting Indiana when the CACOs[9] arrived at our door. Either way, it's a good thing I was there. With Mom gone, I'm not sure Pop would have made it through that night if he'd gotten the news by himself. When we went to see Jake's body, I prepared myself for the worst. At that point, there were daily reports all over the news mentioning the horrific wounds our soldiers had been suffering. Some images had also been leaked online: bodies torn to pieces, sometimes barely anything left for a family to bury. I tried to steel both myself and Pop for seeing my brother's body ravaged by the living dead.

What I saw shocked me worse than any trauma could. At first glance, Jake looked untouched, except for the trickle of blood that ran from his nose. We were told by the casualty assistance officers that this was from the PRW, the "preemptive reanimation wound" given to infected soldiers after they've passed to prevent undesired reanimation. Other than that, he didn't look injured at all, until we looked closer. When we turned his forearm over, we saw a two-inch-long scratch, like that from an animal's claw, along the inside of his wrist. The coroner told us that this scrape was probably where the infection entered his bloodstream. I could hardly believe it. The wound looked no worse than a cat scratch. I didn't understand how he could be so vulnerable to such a

9 CACO: Casualty Assistance Calls Officer.

minor injury. Why didn't his equipment or uniform protect him more effectively?

From the look on Pop's face, I could tell he was thinking the same thing. He wasn't the most emotional person; this is a man who, at our mom's wake, made sure he ordered three full beer kegs for the guests. "People gotta drink, don't they?" he said. But when I saw him standing there by Jake's body, his hands gripping the coroner's steel table so hard that the veins in his forearms bulged, I knew that it wasn't just sorrow he felt for the loss of his son, but anger at the senseless way it happened. He said one last thing before quietly leaving the room—"He shouldn't have died this way."

We couldn't get Jake's personal combat uniform. It was incinerated as part of standard containment procedures for all zombie casualties, but Pop and I started asking around, trying to find out exactly what type of equipment the infantry grunts were being issued. I would've thought that our government would have taken into consideration the uniqueness of this enemy and outfitted the men accordingly. Unfortunately, our worst suspicions were proven correct. Everyone was being issued the same old standard BDU, made from cloth that couldn't withstand a rose thorn, much less rows of jagged, ripping teeth.

Sure, you saw plenty of high-tech military equipment being profiled by the media—the drones, heatsig cams, stalker bots. Everyone thought that we could tech-brawl our way out of this situation just like the other conflicts. You would have thought they learned something about technological reliance over boots on the ground after the last few flare-ups, but I guess the pull of the gadgetry was too strong. That was our first mistake. The second was not providing for the trigger-pullers doing the actual fighting. The defense secretary loved to show off the high-tech thingamajigs to the press, but the last innovation that made it down to the grunt level was a new camouflage pattern, and they even managed to botch that up.

I just want to make this clear; our family is a patriotic one. Pop was never the kind to whine about what the government does or doesn't provide our fighting troops. Our family's played a big part in this country's history of adapting to jungle fighting, desert warfare, urban combat, and insurgencies. With three generations of military in our family, the Litviks know better than most about the liabilities of "fighting the last war." In fighting the living dead, this axiom seemed to be coming true once again for the men and women going into harm's way. The difference this time was, if something didn't change soon, there wouldn't be a next war to adapt to. It wasn't about pointing fingers or whether what was happening was right or wrong. It was about finding a way to keep our men alive. And if the DoD wasn't going to do it better, maybe I could.

I decided to stay in Indiana while Pop used his military contacts to get field videos and postmortems of wounded soldiers, which we reviewed meticulously. Once we saw what was happening in combat and where the injuries on the body were occurring, the answer was so obvious. Seventy-five percent of the attack injuries were happening along the length of the arms, with most of the remaining twenty-five percent along the upper torso and neck area. The best analogy I can think of is being in a knife fight. If you're trying to fend off someone with a blade, you're going to be using your arms and hands. The same happens with a biting and clawing attack. The same thing happened to Jake. Once we realized this, I started doing what I trained to do—design clothing—except this time with a greater purpose other than satisfying vanity.

I knew the first priority in my designs needed to be durability. Any defensive attire had to be capable of withstanding dozens of bites or scratches without breaking the skin beneath. Second, it needed to be light and flexible enough so that any soldier wouldn't mind putting it on underneath his regulation uniform and all the other gear he'd be piling on top of it. Finally, it needed to be cheap. Sure, I could have used Kevlar or carbon fiber, but that would have driven the price of each piece up at least tenfold, and I wanted anything I created to be affordable to even the lowest pay grade.

We played with so many different fabrics—leather, vinyl, burlap. I even managed to test a small batch of engineered spider's silk. None of them were light enough to be comfortable while simultaneously being durable enough to withstand extensive bite trauma. I finally realized that we needed to think outside standard fabrics for our solution, and came upon this.

Litvik hands me what looks to be a roll of nylon wire.

ZCM: Is this fishing line?

JL: Braided multifilament line to be exact, much stronger and less give than your standard nylon monofilament, and up to ten times sturdier by weight than steel. Sewn in a trifold, quadruple basket-weave pattern, we found a solution that seemed to be flexible, durable, and cheap enough for even an E-1 recruit's paycheck. After getting our first container shipment of the line, I stayed up for two nights straight making twenty prototypes, sewing the weave by hand into the forearms, shoulder, and neck areas of athletic dry-wick tops. When I tried one on, it looked good, felt comfortable, and seemed to withstand trauma from knives and other sharp implements. There was, however, the small matter of making sure the prototypes worked in the intended environment.

ZCM: How did you test them?

JL: The same way we still test every prototype, in the Replication Room.

Litvik leads me up a staircase, past rooms of mannequins and sewing equipment to a padlocked door away from the rest of the workshop. He opens it, revealing a largely empty space, except for rows of garments hanging on portable racks on one side of the room and several steel tables lining the opposite wall. A steady hum from air-conditioning units drones in the background. On the tables, set on a long platform and individually encased in Lucite boxes, is a row of severed zombie heads, all of which are clearly still reanimated. Their eyes track us as we walk deeper into the room.

JL: I thought about using various types of testing methods, all of which had greater bite force than a typical human being—attack dogs, animal traps, mechanical presses. In the end, I knew that I couldn't really be sure, and no one would trust my work, unless I proved it against the real thing. Back in those days it wasn't so easy to get live specimens. Pop's military contacts that work on the darker side came through for me again. That one on the end there, I named him Quentin [*Litvik points to one of the heads, a male with an exceptionally large cranium*], he's been with me since the first prototypes. This is where I tested all the ones made those nights, just like we do now.

He slides one of the garments off the rack and slips his arm into the sleeve. Walking up to one of the heads, he lifts the plastic shield covering the head. It immediately begins gnashing its teeth. Litvik looks into its eyes and shoves his forearm into its mouth, which immediately begins gnawing on his arm. This goes on for several seconds, and he finally pulls away. Litvik removes his arm from the garment and rolls up his sleeve, turning his forearm over and showing me the skin, which is completely unmarked and intact.

JL: Once all the prototypes were run through this controlled simulation, my next goal was trying to get them into actual soldiers' hands for field testing. I knew this was going to be tough. Speaking with Jake over the years, I knew that the government frowned upon its soldiers using any types of non-official-issued equipment. I understood this reasoning. The military is all about consistency, uniformity; it couldn't have every other soldier wearing a nonregulation uniform or carrying some weird survival knife. I thought about contacting PMCs,[10] but those guys often handle personal protection rather than offensive operations, and I needed the samples to be run through the most difficult of paces.

As it turned out, it was Jake who helped me. I spoke to one of his old Ranger buddies who knew a contact involved in black ops. I couldn't believe my luck. These were the guys best suited to test my work, as they were in the thick of what was happening. Not only would they be involved in the most dangerous forward operations, but they're also the guys who don't look to Uncle Sam for their individual gear setups. They don't care where it comes from—regular military, an extreme sports equipment company, or a sweatshop in Colombia—they use whatever works. I was actually surprised that they didn't have custom BDUs already made. Some of the guys were using modified motocross equipment, but when they saw the video of my prototype tests, they requested all twenty of them for four teams deploying on covert sweep-and-clear missions. I shipped them off, and didn't hear anything for two months.

I wasn't sure what to make of the silence. I knew these were the guys who couldn't tell me where they were or what they were doing, but I figured I would hear if something went either outstandingly well or horrifically bad. I went back to

10 PMC: Private Military Contractor.

developing my spring line, thinking that maybe it was just all just a pipe dream, that someone like me couldn't possibly think I could help the likes of those guys. That's when I received the package from overseas. Inside the delivery was a walnut box, where I found this . . .

He points me to a plaque on the wall, which reads "For meritorious service by a civilian who, through his direct contribution to the military effort, saved the lives of twenty men several times over in intense combat operations." Alongside the plaque is a medal in the shape of a shield; the ribbon is patterned with alternating pink, white, and blue stripes. Below the award is a photo of a grinning soldier wearing one of Litvik's prototypes. He is holding up his forearm. What appears to be a human tooth is embedded in the protective fabric.

JL: The guys who got my prototypes made that one up for me on their own. Look at the stitching on the ribbon; someone on that team has some real talent. The call from JSOC[11] requesting three hundred more units came soon after that. The rest, as they say, is history.

ZCM: Your father must have been very proud.

JL: I'm sure he would have been, if he'd lived long enough to see it. He passed a few weeks before I received the package. Cancer . . . among other things. I guess I should be happy with how things turned out, though . . .

ZCM: Is there something else?

JL: Don't get me wrong, I'm pleased with what I've done. But I can't stop thinking that I should have gotten involved sooner. We all should have. Sacrifices should have been made. Instead, we all went blindly about our lives, while something I could have done earlier might have kept my brother alive.

---

11 JSOC: Joint Special Operations Command.

The day we went to see Jake's body, after my dad left the coroner's office, I stared at Jake on the examination table for a long time. My mind flashed back to all those times he'd protected me when we were kids. I was picked on quite a bit, despite Pop's boxing lessons. Jake was always there to watch over me. He made sure that any bully who picked on me once never was able to do it again. For all those times he watched my back, I swore that I would make it up to him someday. That if I made it big, he would never have to worry about living on a soldier's paycheck ever again. I never had the chance to make good on my promise. Nothing I do now or have done since can change that.

Hopefully we'll ramp up production for the rest of the regular infantry once we close on the full government contract. Funny thing is, now I have to actually come up with a name that can be listed on the GSA schedule. As much as I'd like to think that I could use my fashion label brand, I don't think that would go over well with the procurement office. Once I gave it some thought, I realized there was only one name that made sense.

ZCM: What's the name?

JL: Brother's Keeper.

CHILD PROTECTION

Our children. In a normal world, they represent what is best of our humanity: beacons of hope guiding our path toward a better future. In a world beset by the living dead, their beams burn a hundredfold brighter. Even the most despaired individuals, distraught over their own existence in a nightmarish reality, will often soldier on if they bear the sole responsibility as defender of their young.

The difficulties facing those who must ensure the safety of children from the clutches of the walking dead, however, should not be ignored. Whether you are protecting your own child, a relative, or a complete stranger in your care, this section will be invaluable to all who must defend those too small and weak to defend themselves. A key component of effectively insulating your child from a zombie's attack is the type of device you use to transport him or her.

The market abounds with hundreds of child transport variations—European buggies, integrated backpacks, off-road joggers. Selection of a transport type often becomes more about public perception and personal status than actual functionality. When it comes to surviving in a world filled with the living dead, many of these devices fall sadly short. Despite the endless variations that exist in carry method, size, and cost, most transport systems fall within one of three categories, each of which we will examine independently—strollers, mobility carriers, and slings.

Strollers

ADVANTAGES: **LONG-DISTANCE TRAVEL, MINIMAL ENERGY EXPENDITURE**
DISADVANTAGES: **HEAVY, INFLEXIBLE, SEPARATION POTENTIAL**

Strollers represent the most ubiquitous of all child-carrying devices; whether car seat conversions or all-in-one transport systems, strollers are an essential component of every family's child-rearing equipment. As a defensive system during an undead attack, however, they leave much to be desired. The stroller exhibits three primary liabilities as it relates to defending against the living dead:

Child separation: This is by far the stroller's greatest disadvantage. The nature of this unit is such that the child is physically separated from the guardian.

A child sits or reclines, often strapped into a harness, in a wheeled carriage that is pushed by his or her defender. Modern-designed strollers that elevate the child higher off the ground make this device even more hazardous during an undead attack. This same elevation that enables a caretaker to bend slightly and tend to the child enables a ghoul to quickly snatch the child out of the carriage and devour him or her before the guardian's very eyes.

It was once believed that this separation of child from guardian provided a greater degree of security during a zombie assault, as the child could be maneuvered out of harm's way while the protector executed appropriate defensive measures. Although this may be the case, the hazards of separating from a child, coupled with the probability of encountering more than one ghoul simultaneously, makes this strategy somewhat risky. Research has shown that given a choice, a zombie will focus its attack on the more vulnerable targets within a given group of prey, often the child. Whether this demonstrates a level of strategic analysis or combative insight by the ghoul is still unknown.

Maneuverability: The stroller's ability to operate in a variety of environments is also rather limited. On flat terrain, pavement, and concrete, the stroller performs as it was created: outstandingly. On any other surface material, such as sand, gravel, or soil, the effectiveness of this transportation device is hindered. Jogging strollers offer some terrain flexibility with their inflatable, off-road-type wheels, but this advantage is counterbalanced by another, potentially worse, liability—the possibility of a flat tire, rendering the unit all but useless.

Construction: At its core, the stroller is a heavily manufactured item—an assemblage of screws, joints, and semifragile components. When used in typical fashion, perhaps for a stroll through the park or a quick trip around the shopping center, a stroller can last for years. Its life span, however, drops precipitously during an undead siege, when you may be required to traverse miles of rough terrain to an operating aid station. Should you encounter an area where using a stroller is impractical, such as a hiking path, a mountainous region, or even a simple staircase, you must shoulder the weight of the unit. If you already bear the burden of transporting food, water, shelter, weapons, and your child, an additional twenty or thirty pounds is an unwelcome addition.

Given these liabilities, logic would dictate that you disregard the stroller as a viable transport option during an undead attack. On the contrary, it is of utmost importance that you keep one of these devices at your disposal, for one sole reason that trumps all of its disadvantages: convenience.

The greatest asset of the stroller transport class is its ability to easily cover long distances without requiring the guardian to continuously sustain the full weight of the child. This asset becomes more pronounced the greater the size of the child. The level of protection the child receives is directly correlated to the ability of the defender to ensure a safe environment. Thus, the vitality of the defender is of utmost importance.

Because the guardian does not have to carry the child when using a stroller, energy expenditure is minimal. The energy saved by using this device can be used for other essential tasks, such as foraging, perimeter security, and defense. This becomes an even higher priority if more than one child is being transported, or if long distances need to be traversed. Refugees of a zombie outbreak have been known to travel in excess of a hundred miles on foot to reach an active rescue station, all the while being pursued by the living dead.

Because of the perilous nature of using a stroller during an undead infestation, there are several points to consider when employing one:

1. **Choose carefully:** In the case of strollers, price does not necessarily denote benefit against the undead. As mentioned earlier, uber-designed strollers that benefit humans often benefit the living dead just as well. Pricier models also tend to outweigh their less expensive counterparts by seven to ten additional pounds—a consideration you cannot afford to discount when pursued by a flesh-eating mob.

2. **Tend your wheels:** Screws can be tightened. Straps can be resewn. But if the wheels literally come off your stroller, the unit has lost its utility. Make sure you care for the tires just as you would any other heavily used vehicle. Rotate them if possible, and ideally carry spares. Ensure that you possess the necessary tools to adjust any nut, bolt, or rivet on your device.

3. **Manage your straps:** Many stroller retention straps used to keep a child in place rival the harnesses found in a Formula One race car. These mechanisms may have usefulness in the normal world, but complicate the situation if the need arises to extract your child from the device while under the stress of a hovering ghoul. At the very least, rehearse unbuckling and dismounting your child quickly, as there may come a time when you must do so with the living dead bearing down upon you.

4. **Observe your surroundings:** If the situation seems relatively safe, and you anticipate a long road ahead, save your energy and use this transport device. If the environment is unknown or hazardous, or you foresee an imminent combat engagement with the living dead, use an alternative, less cumbersome means of transport.

Mobility Carriers

ADVANTAGES: **PORTABLE, MANEUVERABLE, MULTITASKING**
DISADVANTAGES: **LIMB EXPOSURE, WEIGHT-BEARING, COMPLEX MOUNTING**

Transport systems in the mobility carrier class include all back- and chest-positioned carry systems that strap the child into a harness, positioning his or her torso flat against that of the guardian. Carriers of this type hold distinct advantages over the aforementioned stroller class. They are lighter in weight, are portable, and enable hands-free use while simultaneously keeping the child close to the protector. There is a distinct difference, however, between carriers that mount the child in the front of the defender and those that mount him or her on the back.

Let's first examine the back-mounted carriers. These are harness types that position the child across the guardian's back and shoulders, much like a mountaineering backpack. There are benefits to positioning a child in this fashion, as it limits his or her exposure to a ghoul attacking from the front, keeping the guardian between the two. However, back-positioned carriers also exhibit some noteworthy shortfalls when confronting the living dead.

With the child on his or her back, the guardian has no visibility to any undead threats from the rear. In potentially lethal and unfamiliar situations, the child needs to be in full view of the guardian at all times.

Never discount the possibility of a ghoul that has lost the ability to moan (possibly because of a severe throat wound) attacking silently from the rear. Mounting a child on your back also inhibits your ability to use an actual backpack to carry other essential supplies.

Using a back carrier sometimes requires the help of two individuals to quickly secure and mount the child. If you are traveling alone, anticipate taking more time to situate your child in the back mount; time that you may not have at your disposal.

Chest-mount mobility carriers are a favorable option when facing the undead. Unlike the back mount, you have full visibility to your child, your back is available for another storage pack, and securing your child is much quicker from the front. Most important, your hands are available for other tasks, including defense, while you can visually monitor the child's safety. Individuals have even been observed engaging in long- and medium-range combat with the living dead while wearing one of these apparatuses. This is clearly not recommended unless you are suitably experienced in ghoul neutralization. Close-quarters fighting while wearing a child harness should be avoided at all costs, regardless of skill level.

Chest-mount carriers are also not without their drawbacks. First is the simple fact that the guardian shoulders the full weight of the child at all times during transport. With larger children, this can significantly impact a protector's energy levels, so much so that additional rest periods may be required, during which time both child and adult are vulnerable. Those who decide to only use a mobility carrier need to ensure that they are in superior physical condition to accommodate the child's weight for long periods of time.

The other significant drawback with these devices is the fact that, once secured in the harness, a child's limbs and head remain largely exposed. In normal situations, this provides a degree of freedom and comfort to the child. In a world clambering with hungry corpses, these exposed limbs not only are vulnerable to attack, but may impede the guardian's vision and mobility. This situation could prove deadly should a flailing child's arm cross a line of sight at an inopportune time. The best method for using a chest-mounted carrier is to supplement the unit with an additional cover that secures the child's limbs and minimizes his or her exposure to both nature's elements and the living dead.

Slings

ADVANTAGES: **LIGHT, INEXPENSIVE, HIGHLY PORTABLE**
DISADVANTAGES: **PROTECTOR BEARS WEIGHT, INAPPROPRIATE FOR OLDER CHILDREN**

Slings can also be considered a mobility carrier device, as they require the guardian to shoulder the weight of the child and also enable hands-free use for the defender. Styles of slings that either mount the child on the back or expose the limbs of the child suffer from the same disadvantages as the mobility carriers previously discussed.

However, a particular type of sling, one that envelops the infant completely like a peanut shell and secures him or her across the guardian's torso, is one of the best ways to transport and protect an infant during a zombie outbreak, for several reasons:

Security: Because exposure of your child to the external environment is minimized, there is less likelihood that an exposed limb will find its way into the mouth of a hungry corpse. The baby is also positioned lower on the guardian's torso in a sling than in other mobility carriers, keeping his or her body out of close range of a ghoul's snapping jaws.

Flexibility: Not only is this type of carrier inexpensive compared to the other options discussed, it packs well into a small space and requires a minimal footprint. It also enables hands-free use by the guardian, so that he or she can execute other tasks.

Comfort: One of the benefits of this carrier type is that it secures the child close to the guardian's body in a soothing position. During a plague of walking corpses, there is no better time to provide maximum comfort and reassurance to your child.

Like other mobility carriers, the greatest disadvantage of the sling is that it necessitates bearing all the weight of the child during transport. This device may also be less appropriate for larger or older children. However, it is the ideal mechanism for newborns—the most vulnerable humans during a zombie attack.

Which Carrier Is Best?

Given the pros and cons of the various carriers described, which one is the ideal choice during a zombie attack? If only the answer were that simple. Just as there is no one single weapon that is suitable for every undead combat situation, there is no perfect transport system that will solve all of your child protection needs. It is therefore recommended that, if possible, you prepare one of each device described. Should you lose or damage one system, you have an alternative at your disposal. This also enables you to switch between devices depending on your outbreak situation, which will no doubt be in constant flux. Depending on the scale and duration of the infestation, you may find yourself starting with a sling, moving on to a mobility carrier as the child ages, and switching to a stroller when it is appropriate or when you can no longer continually bear the child's weight.

If you can manage only one transport device, you should then ask yourself the following questions to help inform your final decision:

- Is the child you're guarding a newborn, infant, or toddler?
- Do you have the strength to carry the child at all times?
- Are you alone, or will you have the assistance of a second party?
- Are you shepherding more than one child?
- Do you live in a metropolitan area, a suburb, or the countryside?

Safeguarding the welfare of children is challenging during the best of times. In a world in which the dead are feeding on the living, it may seem like an impossible task. You can, however, better prepare yourself for the situation by not only having the proper equipment, but also understanding how that equipment will perform in such dire and unusual circumstances.

COMBAT REPORT: DR. JUDITH BALLANTINE

Child Psychiatrist, Walla Walla, Washington

Dr. Ballantine agrees to meet with me before one of the dozens of seminars she conducts across the world's secured regions, educating parents on dealing with the psychological trauma that zombie outbreaks have caused their children. Her sharp gaze and serious demeanor hint at her standing as one of the pioneers of child psychiatry as it relates to the living dead. In addition to the seminars she provides free of charge, she is a distinguished visiting professor at the newly founded Covington Child Study Center, whose specific charter is the study and treatment of children suffering from mental trauma precipitated by an interaction with the undead. Dr. Ballantine is the author of three books to help children deal with existing in a world inhabited by walking corpses. Her latest title, Mommy's Different Now, *addresses how guardians should educate toddlers on coping with the loss of a parent to infection. She is also a qualified senior instructor of* Shigai-jitsu, *a martial art created to combat the living dead, having received her instructor's sash directly under tutelage from Grandmaster Eric Simonson. Before we even begin, the doctor makes it clear that her priority today is her work.*

JB: We may have to cut this short when the participants start arriving, so please, ask your most pressing questions first.

ZCM: Certainly. What should parents know about protecting their children against a ghoul attack?
JB: I don't use that term.

ZCM: Sorry, which term?
JB: *Ghoul.* It has supernatural connotations. Derivations of

the occult. That's not what these specimens are. I'm begrudgingly resigned to using the word *zombie* because it's such a ubiquitous expression at this point. Sorry, I can be somewhat sensitive to the terminology. On to your question . . .

Unfortunately, the greatest threat to children during an undead outbreak is often the parents themselves. Before teaching their children about the danger of the living dead, parents must first introduce the concept of death itself. This is the first hurdle, and it's a significant one. Addressing death is one of the least desirable discussions adults want to have with children, and based on my experience, second only to conversations about sexual education. Under normal circumstances, parents may be able to avoid this subject for some time, perhaps until their child is well into the toddler years. Some never broach the subject at all, allowing the outside world to deal with it for them. In a world filled with attacking corpses, avoiding this discussion is tantamount to child neglect and increases your child's vulnerability at least fivefold.

Before the dead began to rise, a child's first encounter with death was often from a nonhuman loss—typically a household pet. Some children experience the loss of an elderly grandparent or neighbor. You would occasionally read these stories in which a parent expires unexpectedly at home, and the child stays with the body for days, sleeping next to it, trying to wake it up. In a dead-infested world, a child who remains in the house when a parent succumbs to infection typically does not survive. In the postzombie era, eight in ten children have suffered the demise and reanimation of someone they knew closely—a classmate, a sibling, or, worst of all, a guardian. You see the sense of urgency we had? It was literally a life-or-death situation to make people understand that having these conversations with your child should be the highest priority.

The added difficulty of the situation is that after introducing the fundamental concept of death to a child, you then have to explain a phenomenon that flies directly in the face of that concept—the living dead. This is clearly not a simple conflict to explain. Children already have a difficult time understanding the permanent nature of death. Layer on top of that the possibility that the person they see die may *rise* from the dead, and you understand how complicated and confusing the explanation can become.

This is why many areas of developmental child psychiatry needed to be clearly delineated between the pre- and postzombie periods. An entirely new branch of treatment emerged to deal with this unique situation. We needed to rethink how we dealt with explaining concepts such as death, dying, and monsters to our young. As long as a child is old enough to understand the concept of life and death, he or she is old enough to understand the threat of the living dead.

This is why I recommend keeping it very simple. Explain the concepts as completely as possible, so that in the tragic case of the loss of a family member, the child understands that the person is permanently gone. Once this occurs, the deceased should be dealt with appropriately so as not to reanimate, or be immediately removed from the child's field of vision. Without a doubt, the most difficult situation to manage is if a loved one passes and subsequently reanimates in front of the child. In these cases, the child needs to understand that it is no longer the same individual and poses a mortal threat. This becomes additionally complex when adults give a metaphysical explanation of death to their children. Saying something like "Daddy's in heaven" can prompt the child's question "Why did he choose heaven over us?" Seeing that person reanimate may be construed by the child as "Daddy changed his mind!" ending with the child running to embrace the reanimated individual. I've tried to address it as best as I could in my books, but I'm the first to admit that this is not an easy process. It's why I still conduct seminars like this one today.

ZCM: How was your information received by the public?

JB: We had our work cut out for us. Getting people to pay attention wasn't easy. During large-scale infestations like the ones we were dealing with, this type of information is the last thing people want to think about. Medical crisis resource management teams were overwhelmed enough in dealing with the physical distresses of undead assault; the psychological response was often ignored or implemented too late. In areas where we were able to blitz the population with information, leaflets, and seminars, we saw dramatic decreases in child mortality rates, resulting both from the undead and from the living.

ZCM: What do you mean, "from the living"?

JB: One of the tragic ancillary effects of an undead outbreak is a steep increase in family annihilations—in which one family member decides, for the sake of the household, that it is better to end the family's existence by his hands than those of the living dead. I say "his hands" because traditionally annihilations are committed by a male family member. However, there are times when it is both parents committing the act together. Very sad, especially when you consider that children actually have a very high survival rate during outbreaks, even more so when taught by their parents how to protect themselves.

ZCM: Is that a fact?

JB: It may be hard to believe, but it's true. This is one thing that the public still doesn't completely understand. Children are highly resilient beings, much more so than we give them credit for. Although it's difficult for them to grasp the initial concepts, they are open to the idea of bogeymen that they need to avoid and escape from.

The other problem we faced was parents who waited too long to have these discussions with their children. Most believed that they would be able to protect their families, that they wouldn't be infected, and as a result, they didn't plan for the situation in which one or both of them were contaminated. This plays directly into the insidious nature of the infection. In our research, we meticulously analyzed the virus' pathology in an attempt to decipher a pattern in the reanimation sequence. If we could find any consistencies in the time from death to reanimation, we could educate adults who wanted to wait until the last possible moment to say their good-byes. We wanted to give the public the specific amount of time after infection before "P&T"—passing and turning—so they could plan accordingly.

We looked at dozens of external factors—healthy or sick, overweight or thin, young or old. After analyzing data from countless infections, we could find no consistency between the degree of injury, speed of demise, and time of reanimation, and so we were never able to develop an accurate predictive model. A healthy woman in her mid-twenties suffering from an infected scratch may P&T in ten minutes, whereas an obese, diabetic man in his forties with an entire knob of flesh taken out of his arm may linger for three days. The inconsistency frustrated us to no end, mostly because we knew that it would result in adults who waited too long to establish an arrangement for their children and inevitably reanimate with kids still in their care. We knew the best advice we could give is to tell parents to have a three-step strategy if they become infected: plan in advance, say your good-byes, send them on.

The flipside of this tragic coin is parents who are turned by their own reanimated children. There are thousands of recorded cases of this type of transmission occurring. What we could not determine is whether the infection was accidental, the result of a parent not realizing the child had turned, or an intentional transmission. There was not much we could do to influence this population. Adults know the consequences. Unfortunately, when it comes to their own children, some parents choose to ignore the signs, or don't care.

ZCM: Does the age of the child factor into what you tell them?

JB: With infants, this is not an issue at all. You simply need to ensure that babies are well fed, well protected, and comforted as much as possible so that their cries do not reveal your position and make them vulnerable to attack. With colicky babies, there's not much that can be done; the best you can do is ensure that you are not traveling on open terrain, as a baby's wail has been shown to draw in living dead from up to a mile away. Although this can be a significant liability, having an infant among your group can also be an asset, as they seem to have the ability to detect approaching zombies from a distance much greater than adults. If a baby starts to stir and whine for no apparent reason, it is most likely that a reanimate is near.

As they grow to become toddlers, they still have a limited understanding of the permanency of death, but this is the point at which guardians need to introduce the idea that a reanimated human is a threat and should be avoided at all costs. As children get older, certainly beyond preschool age, they should have a full understanding of the danger the living dead pose to their well-being.

ZCM: Why did you decide to study one of the sanctioned undead self-defense systems?

JB: I'm first and foremost a physician. But I'm not so much of a clinical academic that I don't realize the value of knowing what it's like in the field. Although my primary focus is the psychological care of those exposed to the living dead, physical defenses could not be ignored. To remain uneducated about such a key element to surviving in an outbreak would be bordering on malpractice in my eyes. In order to impart the greatest level of treatment to my patients, I needed not only to learn how to defend myself, but also to be able to teach it to others.

There is also no question that if you are safeguarding children, you must know how to eliminate a reanimate without a firearm. How do you think a six-month-old is going to react when a twelve-gauge round from a Remington 870 goes off next to his ear? How many other undead will be drawn to your location from a wailing child, upset by the deafening sound of gunfire and the choking smell of smokeless powder? It is inarguable: if you're defending the welfare of children against the undead, it's imperative to know how to defend yourself with a weapon that doesn't fire ammunition.

ZCM: Should children be taught to fight the undead?

JB: As much as I would like to encourage it, I can't. Human children, even preteens, face a difficult task confronting even another reanimated child, much less an adult specimen. Children simply do not have the strength to deal a terminal blow to the undead skull. They are, however, very effective at evading an attacking corpse, which explains their high survivability rate.

The best defense that can be taught to children under age thirteen is how to escape and steer clear of a zombie's grasp. Anyone with children knows how fast crawling infants can speed away from you. Given the specimen's poor coordination, children often can escape by simply dropping to their hands and knees and quickly crawling away, before the reanimate can stoop down and launch an attack.

People begin quietly filing into the room. Some of the adults are alone. Others are leading or carrying children.

JB: I'm sorry. We're going to have to end it here.

Dr. Ballantine leaves the interview table. As I see her approach the attendees, the steely demeanor that I experienced during our meeting seems to soften as she draws closer to the group. She bends down to greet a young girl, who whispers something about keeping monsters away. The doctor's face breaks into a warm, comforting grin, and while embracing the child, she says "Yes, I will."

V.

COMBAT STRATEGIES AND TECHNIQUES

War is a brain-splattering,
windpipe-splitting art.

—LORD BYRON

Now that you have primed your mind, your body, and your weapons, it is appropriate to discuss the methods to bring these components together to most effectively engage the walking dead in combat. For those who have never encountered an attacking cadaver, the techniques described in this section may seem vicious, brutal, perhaps even excessive and gratuitous. Let us be perfectly clear: Combat with a walking corpse is unlike any struggle that you have ever faced in your life. There exists no equivalent comparison in human combat. There are no knockouts, no submissions, no standing eight-counts. Confrontation with a zombie ends with only one of two possible outcomes—a neutralized ghoul or a devoured human.

Before we explore detailed strategies suitable for the various ranges of undead combat, it is important to discuss the unique dynamics that factor into your success or failure in a physical engagement with the living dead. Normal human combat follows a nonlinear progression of difficulty that depends on many external factors, including strength, size, and skill level of your opponent. Battling a walking corpse is a different matter. Though no encounter with a zombie should be deemed "easy," the general degree of difficulty seems to be heavily influenced by the distance between combatants.

Dr. James Bane, an eminent clinical researcher in the field of undead combat, conducted a comprehensive study of human-versus-zombie conflict to specifically analyze the importance distance plays in survivability. Because of the predictable nature of a zombie's combat tactics, Bane surmised that it was possible to accurately forecast the probability of any successful engagement regardless of the enemy, provided it was undead. A graph depicting one of his most significant findings is shown here:

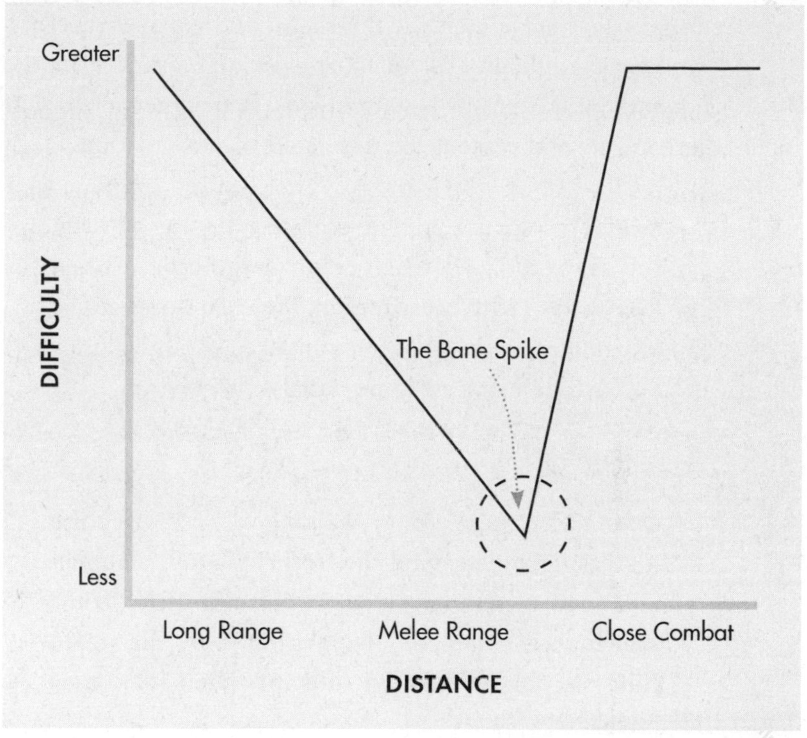

Bane discovered that long-range combat with the undead is most difficult because of the expertise and weaponry required. As the distance between combatants closes, this difficulty steadily decreases in direct proportion to the relative distance between opponents; the closer a zombie is, the easier it will be to dispatch. Eventually, the target enters what is considered the "sweet spot"—the optimal combination of distance, difficulty, and force required to successfully end the confrontation. Although this region will differ for each individual, this spot predominantly exists in the melee range of zombie combat, approximately three feet between combatants.

However, once a particular threshold has been crossed and the engagement evolves from a melee altercation into a close-combat encounter, the degree of difficulty skyrockets. The rise in difficulty is much steeper than earlier in the encounter and is nearly instantaneous. Bane determined that there are several reasons for this rapid transformation:

- **Fear:** The closer a zombie comes to its human prey, the more terrified that person may become when face-to-face with the attacker. This fear seems to be augmented if the ghoul has suffered grisly wounds and decay during its reanimated existence.

- **Odor:** The scent of a walking corpse becomes increasingly distasteful the closer it is to the human olfactory receptors. Once in close contact, some humans are completely incapacitated by the smell, thus becoming easy victims of their ravenous attacker.

- **Panic:** Once a person is engaged in close-quarters combat with the living dead, panic may overwhelm the human defender. When a human being panics, hormones flood the body, causing a cascade of consequences, one of which is the decreased ability to execute movements that require a precise, steady hand. This loss of precision may affect one's ability not only to draw a close-combat weapon, but also to execute a neutralizing strike at a specific target on the zombie skull.

Bane's formula for this sharp swing in the curve is known as the *inverse combat distance coefficient*, and the severe flux point created by the rapid change in combat difficulty is known as the *Bane Spike*. Once the zombie is engaged at this range, two things may occur—either the human defender resets the distance between combatants to his or her advantage, or the engagement ends, with either human or ghoul victorious. Further studies have determined that most human deaths occur after the point where the Bane Spike has been surpassed.

So what does this mean for you, the readers, who are clearly looking to improve your odds in zombie combat? One vital point to extrapolate from Bane's analysis is that, unlike the innumerable variations you may encounter in a human combat scenario, you do not need to master a vast array of maneuvers to defeat the living dead. The greatest liability of the zombie's offensive attack is that it is predictable to a fault. This predictability enables you to use a limited but effective collection of fighting techniques successfully, regardless of your opponent's physical attributes.

A ghoul does not have the tactical acumen to employ feints, lures, or deception. You will be able to use the same technique time and again without your opponent "catching on" or "getting wise" to your strategy. Use this ignorance to your advantage. Better to master two or three methods and execute them impeccably 100 percent of the time than to learn fifty techniques and master none.

It is also recommended that you take Bane's findings with a grain of salt. The doctor's analysis is based on a vast and diverse sampling of civilians who have engaged in undead combat. Statistical averages should not take precedence over your personal traits and talents, regardless of what these figures convey. If, for example, you find that it is easiest for you to dispatch ghouls at long distance with a sidewalk scraper, there is no need to wait until your opponent enters the Bane sweet spot. Remember to take an accurate inventory of your abilities and develop a personalized combat strategy. Study the techniques in the following pages. Learn at least one for each practical combat range. Practice them. Make them your own.

COMBAT REPORT: STEVE SHANAHAN

Police Officer, Retired, Chicago, Illinois

Steve Shanahan comes from three generations of Chicago police officers. Now retired, he runs his own consultancy specializing in "dead issues," or security situations involving the living dead. Throughout his career with the Chicago Police Department, he has handled more than one hundred undead situations, including home invasion, perimeter breaches, and hostile containment.

SS: I've had to take down EDPs[12], tweakers, hard-core gang-bangers. Nothing comes close to going mano a mano with a DG.[13] Sure, it's easier now that we know so much more about how to handle them—strikes, maneuvers, defensive tactics—but when Chicago PD was initially fielding these calls, no one knew jack. At that point we were getting very little intelligence from the CDC or DHHS, so we had to figure everything out on our own. They damn well couldn't send SWAT down to every incident call. In those initial outbreaks, they were also being categorized as domestic or civil disturbances—people thought it was someone hopped up on coke

12 EDP: emotionally disturbed person.
13 DG: dead guy; slang commonly used by law enforcement to denote the walking dead.

or speed. I don't blame them for miscalls; it's easy to pinpoint a zombie after it's been walking around for a month or so, but when it's first turned, it was really hard to tell, especially if the infection point was not caused by a high-trauma wound. They almost look like everybody else, until they start biting. Hell, some of them look better than a lot of skels I've brought in. And when you're in a hot situation with people running around like headless chickens, it's real easy to get pulled into some dead guy's mouth.

The type of housing structure you were called to made a big difference. Single-family homes were easier to handle. At least you can start by knocking out the windows and clearing a lot of the rooms from the outside. The first thing I would do with a house job is to smash any ground-floor windows open with my baton. Not only can you clear the floors faster, it starts airing the place out in case everyone's been fermenting in there for a while.

If it was a slow and deliberate search, I wouldn't even bother entering for the first fifteen minutes. That's the thing about DG jobs—you don't need to worry about being quiet. In fact, it was just the opposite. You actually wanted to let them know you were coming and clear out as many "walkers" as you could before you actually entered. Hell, if I could've tied a cowbell around my neck, I would have. Typically I'd set myself outside, tap my foot, and whistle a tune, just waiting for them to come to me. This wouldn't work all the time, though. There would always be "brooders"—zombies that, for whatever reason, just sat where they were rather than responding to sound. Most of the calls weren't the slow and deliberate type. Most of them were dynamic entries—someone calling because they were being attacked or were trapped by a DG. You couldn't be slicing the pie and quick-peeking these types of situations. In a dynamic-entry situation, it was all about speed, power, and overwhelming violence of action.

Apartment complexes are a whole different story; they were the worst. We called them "chambers of horrors." You respond to a DG job in one apartment, knowing full well that there are probably dozens of other residences where zombies have taken control, and there's just no one left to make an emergency call. And these places reeked. Some residences would stockpile bodies, both dead and undead, in one or two rooms or apartments. As soon as you arrived on scene, you could smell that it was going to be a hell call. I was smearing menthol rub under my nose so much I should've bought stock in the company; stocks—remember those? Now there's a blast from the past.

I'll never forget one of the early calls I responded to in New Cabrini. There were already five units and two fire trucks on scene by the time I arrived. I was helping clear some of the upper floors when I opened up a bedroom to see a DG feeding on his wife. I pushed him off and cracked my steel-toed Danner over his temple. I was on the radio calling it in when what felt like a metal vise clamped down on my tricep. Sure enough, the wife had already turned. I spun around, but before I could clear my weapon from the holster, she was on me. She wasn't a big lady, probably a buck-thirty, but fighting her was like trying to fend off a rabid chimpanzee. Now I've rolled with some pretty strong characters—wrestlers, judo guys—and never in my life have I felt anything like this woman. I'm damn lucky I wasn't wearing our summer-issue uniforms; otherwise my forearms would have been torn to ribbons. I finally managed to get my weapon clear and get off two rounds—one that went wide right, and the other that took off her left ear. She grabbed my forearm and wrenched it so hard that it caused a hairline fracture in both the ulna and radius bones. That's what caused me to drop my service weapon.

We wrestled around the room for the better part of five minutes; on the bed, against the bureau, back onto the bed. She had this crimson sludge running down the side of her head from where her ear used to be, and I just kept praying that none of it would drip into my eyes. I was exhausted. No matter what I did, I just couldn't keep her off me. I didn't have the strength left.

We ended up writhing on the floor, in the narrow space between the mattress and the wall. I grabbed her by the throat to keep her snapping jaws away from me, but I knew it was just a matter of time before my arm gave out. I turned my head and saw her ragged bedslippers under the box spring. "So this is how it ends," I thought to myself, "staring at pink fuzzy slippers?" And then I heard the voice of my academy instructor in my head, cursing my stupidity for not pairing up on the room clears.

My arm started to give way, and I closed my eyes as I saw her mouth descending onto my carotid. Just then I heard a loud whack, and the woman's jaw slammed shut, cracking several of her teeth. I looked up and saw the prong of a Halligan tool sticking out of the top of her skull, the other end held by one of Chicago's bravest. He yanks her up by the head and tosses her aside. He then shoves the clean end of the Halligan toward me and helps me to my feet.

Who says cops and firemen don't get along?

LONG-RANGE COMBAT

SAFETY LEVEL OF ENGAGEMENT: **HIGH**
COMBAT SKILL REQUIRED AT THIS DISTANCE: **MEDIUM-HIGH**
RISK OF INFECTION: **2–5%**

Long-range combat is defined in this manual as combat with an undead attacker at a distance of 6 to 8 feet (1.8 to 2.4 meters) between opponents. Combat at this distance affords you the greatest level of personal safety to fight the living dead. Studies have shown, however, that it is also the most difficult range to engage and eliminate your attacker quickly. It takes substantial skill to wield a long-pole weapon and consistently deliver destructive blows, so armament selection, training, and practice are essential if you are frequently engaging the living dead at long range.

Long-Distance Combat Strategies

Regardless of the scenario, there are a few general strategies you can apply to all long-distance combat situations.

Maintain Your Balance

Because of the size and weight of the weapon you are handling at this distance, it is easier to be thrown off balance when fighting at this range more than any other. You must always focus on maintaining your balance when striking with your long-range weapon. Many people become captivated by the size and potential destructive power of a weapon such as a halberd or poleaxe. This makes them prone to engaging in an undead version of Home Run Derby, swinging the weapon with all their might. Witnesses have seen people stagger, lose weapons, even stumble into a mob of ghouls as a result of an overextended swing. Do not give in to this temptation. Always maintain even footing, and be in control of your weapon throughout your swing regardless of your target. Better to take two or three balanced strikes to eliminate a zombie than try to do so in a single, awkward rotation.

Avoid the Eyes

With a long-range stabbing weapon such as a spear, you may be tempted to try to attack the brain by driving the weapon through one of the eye sockets. In theory, this is a very effective strike point—it will cause minimal damage to your weapon and does not require excessive strength. In actuality, however, thrusting a weapon into a moving target the size of a quarter requires a great deal of precision and coordination. Untrained individuals have been seen attempting this technique, only to miss numerous times and have the attacking ghoul grab hold and pull the weapon from their hands. Unless you have practiced this technique incessantly and can execute it without fail, it is recommended that you use a different strategy.

Be Wary of Crown Attacks

Another possible enticement for an individual using a heavier bladed weapon is to "cleave the crown," or attack the top of the head in an attempt to split the ghoul's skull in half. Although it is undoubtedly a striking sight to behold and can be accomplished with a battle-axe or claymore, it is not recommended. Even if you have the strength and skill to do so, there are several reasons why you should not:

1. **Your weapon may get stuck:** With enough power behind your strike, splitting the skull like a piece of dry cordwood is definitely possible. However, the momentum of the blow may drive the weapon down into the body, embedding it in the neck and torso area and making it difficult to dislodge. The precious seconds required to extract and ready your weapon for another attack may cost you your life, particularly if another undead assailant is waiting in the wings.

2. **Your blade will rapidly dull:** Your weapons are the lifeline to your survival. Bladed arms need to be sharpened consistently, and persistent contact with bone will shorten their life span under normal wear. Why accelerate the process? Quality long-range weapons can be especially difficult to replace once damaged during a zombie outbreak.

3. **It is overkill:** You are not auditioning for a barbarian film. An effective neutralizing blow is one that does just enough damage to the zombie brain to prevent it from attacking further. Any additional damage beyond what is minimally required needlessly expends energy, energy that can be put to better use to dispatch another zombie.

Combat Techniques

Because of their significant length and heavier weight, fighting with long-range destructive weapons requires more strength and skill than fighting at other distances. If you find yourself equipped with such a weapon, you can use certain techniques to make your battles with the undead quicker and easier. Recall the vulnerable attack points of the undead physique covered in the section on anatomy. Given the physical properties of your weapon, nearly all of those points can be effectively targeted when fighting at long-range distance. Here are several tested techniques that you can use to target those vulnerabilities.

THE BLINDSIDE

TARGET AREA: **TEMPORAL REGION**
MOST EFFECTIVE WITH: **HEAVY POLEARMS AND BATTLE-AXES**
TECHNIQUE: **WHILE STANDING IN FRONT OF YOUR OPPONENT**

1. Hold your weapon near the middle and end of the shaft with both hands.

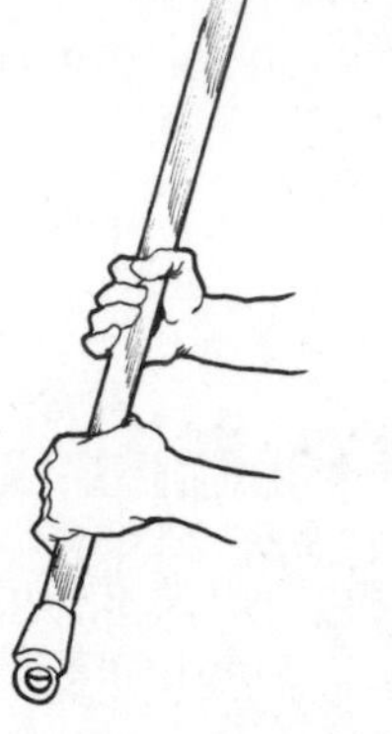

2. Raise your weapon and pivot at the waist.

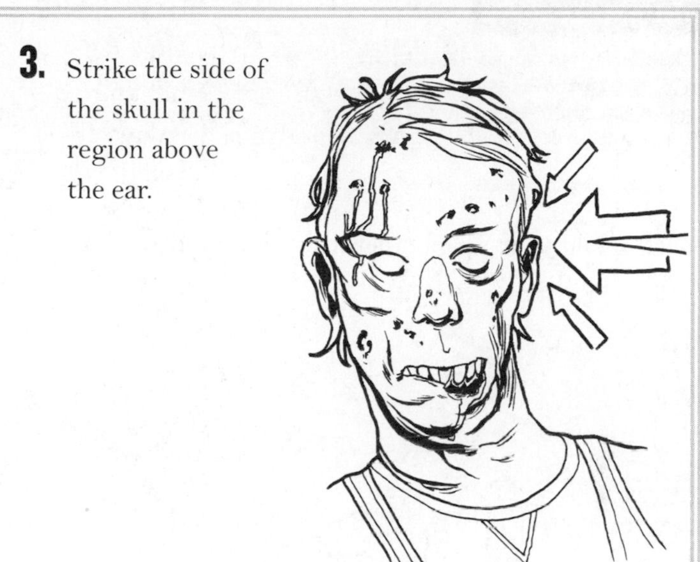

3. Strike the side of the skull in the region above the ear.

4. Follow through on your swing.

THE SKULLCAPPER

TARGET AREA: **NASAL/ORBITAL REGION**
MOST EFFECTIVE WITH: **FLAT-BLADED POLEARMS (SPADES, SHOVELS, AND SCRAPERS)**
TECHNIQUE: **WHILE STANDING IN FRONT OF YOUR OPPONENT**

1. Hold your weapon near the middle and end of the shaft.

2. Aim for the bridge of the nose.

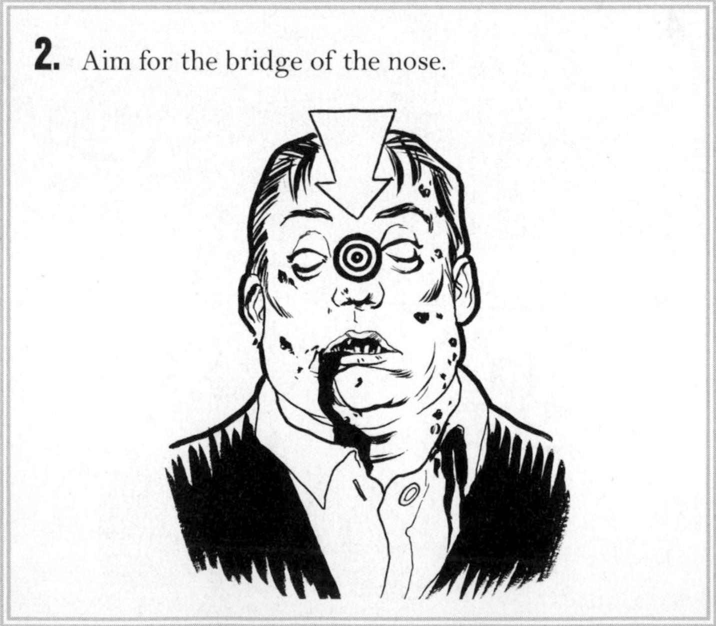

3. Thrust forward aggressively, driving the blade through the skull.

4. Retract your weapon to ensure that it does not get stuck within the skull cavity. A powerful enough thrust can shear the top of a ghoul's head clean off.

THE MUSASHI

TARGET AREA: **NECK/DECAPITATION**
MOST EFFECTIVE WITH: **BLADED POLEARMS, BATTLE-AXES, AND GREAT SWORDS**
TECHNIQUE: **SIMILAR TO THE BLINDSIDE ATTACK, WITH THE EXCEPTION OF YOUR FINAL TARGET**

1. Raise your weapon and pivot at the waist.

2. Strike the side of the neck, following through on your swing.

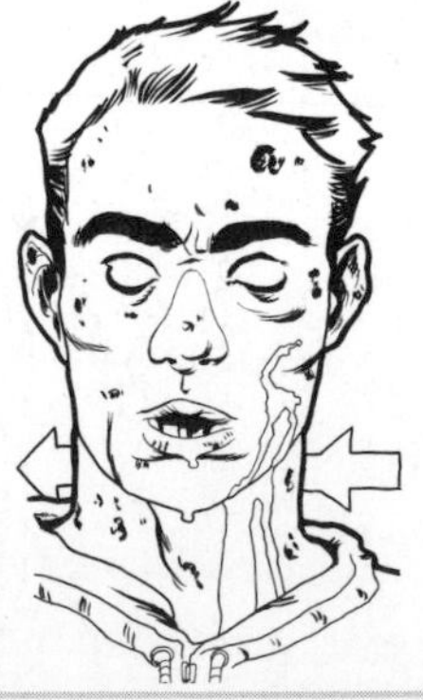

3. Repeat until the head is separated from the torso.

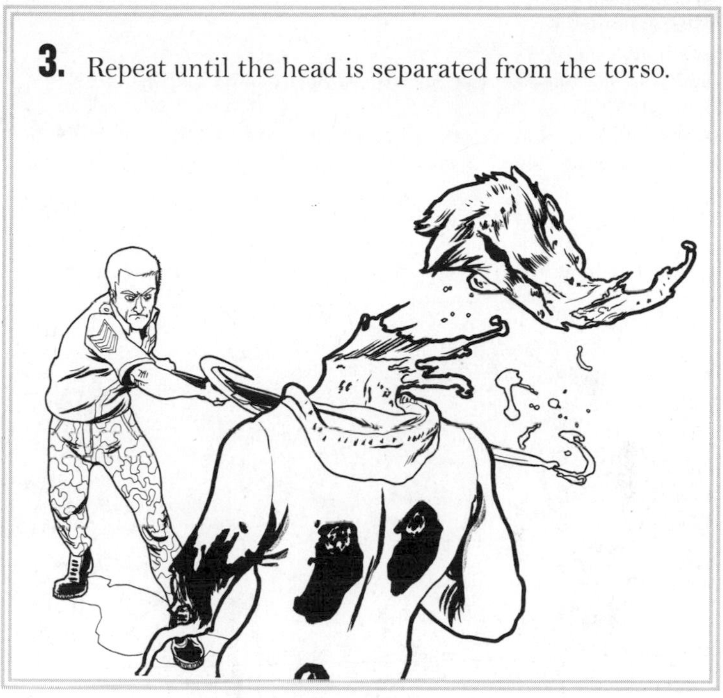

4. Finish with a neutralizing blow to the severed head.

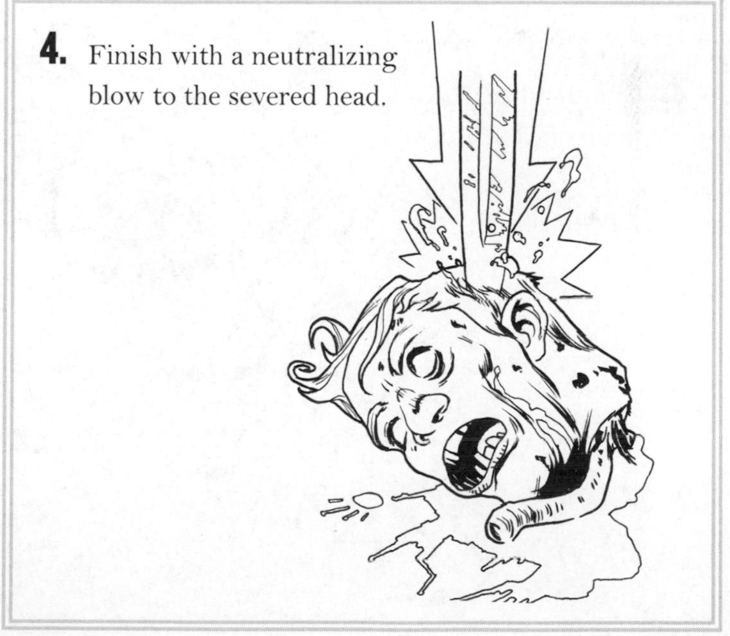

THE KABOB

TARGET AREA: **MIDDLE CRANIAL FOSSA (MCF)/UNDERSIDE OF BRAIN**
MOST EFFECTIVE WITH: **STABBING/POINTED POLEARMS (SPEARS, PIKES, AND LANCES)**
TECHNIQUE: **ONE OF THE MORE DIFFICULT TECHNIQUES TO EXECUTE, BUT PERFECTLY SUITED TO A LONG-RANGE STABBING WEAPON**

1. Hold your weapon near the middle and end of the shaft.

2. Aim the sharpened point of your weapon at the base of the ghoul's throat.

3. Raise the point until it is under the chin, just inside the mandible.

4. Drive the weapon through the jaw and upward into the braincase.

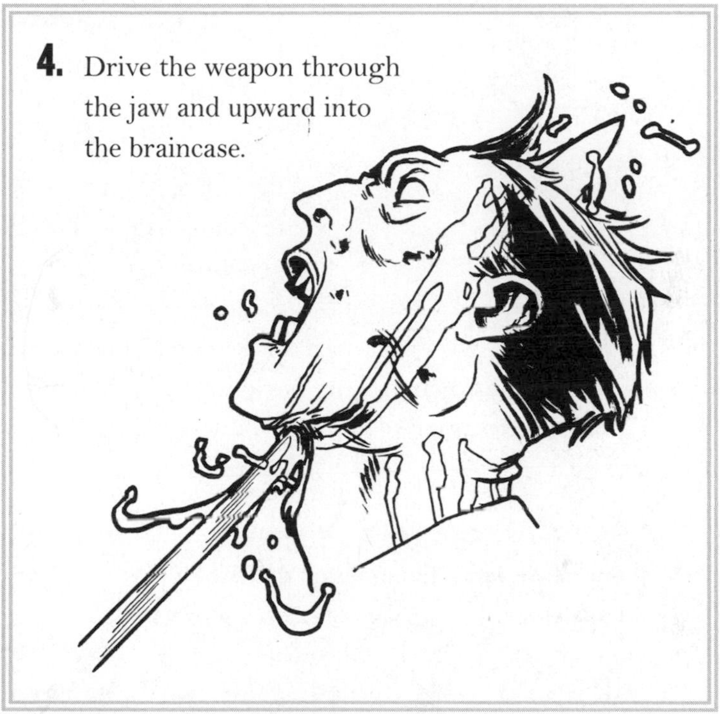

Weapon Throwing

There may come a time when, as a result of media influence, poor advice, or simple overconfidence, you may be tempted to hurl your weapon at a ghoul in the distance in order to neutralize it. This is generally not recommended. Even in situations in which you witness a partner or family member in imminent danger, throwing your weapon is not a suggested option. There are several reasons why this technique is highly discouraged:

1. **Weapon design:** Armaments that are thrown are often explicitly engineered to do so. Weapons that are crafted to be hurled have better design, weight, and balance qualities that facilitate their aerodynamic properties. Although any weapon can be thrown, there is a high likelihood that an inexperienced thrower who tosses an ordinary edged weapon at an undead opponent will watch in dismay as the wrong end bounces harmlessly off the target's body, if it hits the mark at all. Even if the throw manages to reach the target, remember that the blow is effective only if it penetrates the assailant's white brain matter.

2. **Skill level:** Should you happen to acquire a throwing weapon, the skill required to consistently "stick" such a weapon requires years of dedicated training. If you fling your armament in order stop an impending attack on a loved one, you run the risk of hitting the person you seek to protect rather than your intended undead target. Remember that you are aiming for a small, moving target—the undead skull. Striking such a target with sufficient force to neutralize an attacking zombie would be a challenge even to a seasoned, professional knife thrower.

3. **Retrieval:** Throwing your weapon means losing your weapon, even if it is a temporary loss. Unless the armament you pitch is a backup to your primary weapon, being unarmed, even for a few moments, is a precarious risk during a zombie assault. If you follow our earlier recommendations of having a weapon handy for every combat range, you should have another means of protection available. In any case, having to spend time retrieving a thrown weapon means less time accomplishing other tasks, such as eliminating other undead threats in the vicinity.

Should none of these reasons convince you that throwing your weapon is a poor combat decision, try tossing your weapon at a stationary target at a variety of distances. Unless you achieve 100 percent accuracy in hit and penetration rate, you should probably avoid this tactic altogether. Use an appropriate long-range or ballistic weapon for distance neutralization, and keep your hand weapons where they belong—in your hand.

A Few Words on Decapitation

We have seen it depicted repeatedly on both the big and small screens—the conquering hero, facing off against a throng of opponents, draws his mighty saber. With a single, effortless swing of his blade, he lops the heads from his adversaries with ease. Were it only so easy.

Because decapitation has been so dramatically embellished in entertainment media, most of the population is unaware of how difficult it is to actually separate a head from its attached torso. Let's examine the actual physical dynamics necessary in a decapitation attack. The average zombie neck is approximately fifteen inches in circumference. Not only must you slice through several different sets of muscle groups, you also must sever the spine and the cartilaginous rings of the trachea. Unlike what is depicted onscreen, only the most proficient and trained warriors are able to decapitate adversaries with a single swipe of the blade. For the average civilian, it may require up to six swings to completely chop through a zombie's neck. Although long-range weapons are heavier and more likely to make decapitation easier, it is still an intensely strenuous act.

The death of Japanese author Yukio Mishima is quite possibly the best nonzombie example of how difficult the act of decapitation actually is. In 1970, as an act of defiance against the emperor, Mishima committed seppuku, ritual suicide, in the Tokyo headquarters of the Japanese Self-Defense Forces Eastern Command. In the tradition of this act, Mishima was to be decapitated at the end of the ritual. This important task was assigned to his friend, Masakatsu Morita. Morita was untrained in the use of a sword. After three attempts to decapitate his friend using the author's own priceless samurai sword, Morita ultimately failed. Hiroyasu

Koga, another friend who was present and a trained *kenshi*,[14] grabbed the sword and decapitated Mishima. Koga watched as Morita also committed seppuku, and then decapitated him as well. Why Mishima chose his untrained friend rather than the experienced Koga to execute the finishing act in the first place is unknown.

What can we learn from this historical incident? Reality can be a harsh teacher; although most of us would like to believe we could perform like the trained Koga, most of the population will fall into the Morita camp. This is nothing to be ashamed of. In due time and with the experience gained from even a single zombie encounter, your skill levels will steadily increase to where you may eventually perform like a skilled swordfighter. What is important is that you recognize that regardless of what you have seen onscreen, the actual act of decapitation is far more difficult than you can imagine.

14 *kenshi:* swordsman, practitioner of *kenjitsu*.

MEDIUM-RANGE/ MELEE COMBAT

SAFETY LEVEL OF ENGAGEMENT: **MEDIUM**
COMBAT SKILL REQUIRED AT THIS DISTANCE: **MEDIUM**
RISK OF INFECTION: **10–15%**

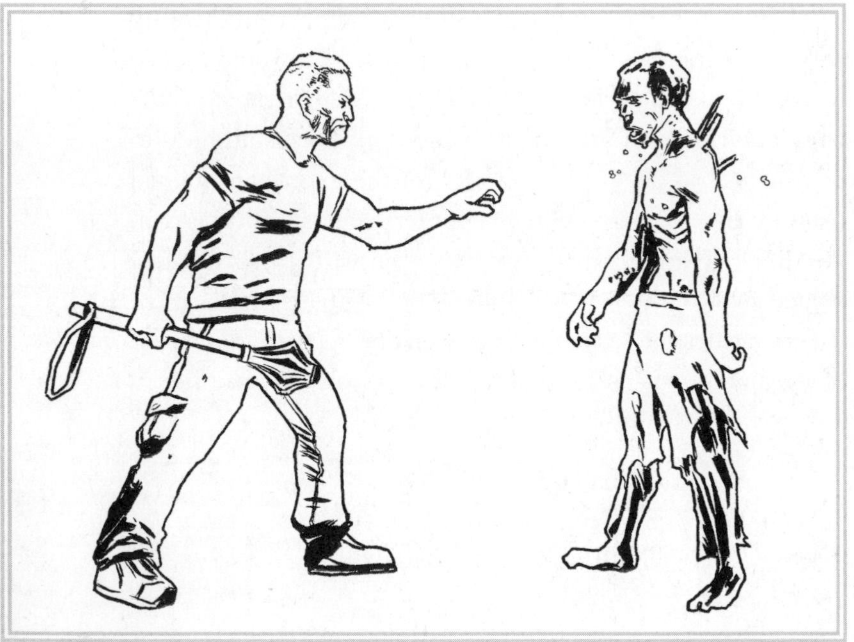

Medium-range or melee combat is defined as engagement with the undead at a distance of 2 to 3 feet (0.6 to 0.9 meters) between opponents. The striking areas on the skull addressed previously in long-range combat are the same regions you should target at melee range. In fact, you may have a greater opportunity to attack these points given the improved control you will possess with a shorter, easier-to-handle weapon. For this reason, as well as weapon availability, terrain, and skill level, melee range is the most common distance at which undead combat takes place. Of all the possible undead combat ranges, melee combat requires the least amount of technical skill. It does, however, present its own unique set of challenges, the greatest being that you will be fighting at a distance where you are vulnerable to a ghoul's reach.

Melee Combat Strategies

Just as in long-range combat, you should be aware of a few general strategies during any engagement that falls within the melee range.

The Fatal Funnel

The method by which you confront your undead opponent at melee range could significantly impact your level of vulnerability. The most common mistake untrained combatants make when engaging an attacker at this distance is walking into "the fatal funnel." Those with law enforcement experience may be familiar with this term, as it traditionally describes the vulnerable area an officer faces when entering the doorway to a room or hallway containing potential threats. In relation to zombie combat, we're describing the scenario of confronting an undead attacker at melee range from the most dangerous position—directly head on.

Unfortunately, many individuals mistakenly engage an attacking ghoul this way, as it is how we universally confront human adversaries. Never forget that your opponent is now anything but human. You must contend with not only a zombie's gnashing mouth, but also its scratching, infected hands, which at this point will be outstretched and seeking to pull you toward its open jaws. The triangular area comprising the ghoul's mouth and two hands is what's known as the fatal funnel. Your strategy in this situation should be to take advantage of the zombie's restricted speed and coordination and work the perimeter of your opponent for your attack.

Dismembering the Undead

When employing an edged weapon in melee combat, you may experience the urge to begin hacking away randomly at your attacker, turning it into a pile of chopped zombie detritus. This tactic seems to be taken advantage of most often by individuals who suffer from PUCT or have recently experienced intense emotional distress from a zombie attack, such as the loss of a friend or loved one. Resist this inclination, as it is not encouraged for several reasons:

1. **The undead feel no pain:** Although you may believe that you are delivering some form of "human justice" by slicing your opponent into ribbons, hacking off the arm of a zombie does no more to injure or inflict pain than tapping it on the shoulder. Your opponent will remain unfazed and continue its attack. Save your energy for a single, finishing strike.

2. **You amplify the risk of infection:** You may contend that severing a zombie's hands eliminates its ability to grab you. This is true. By cutting off its hands, however, you have only eliminated its means of grabbing you, not its desire to do so. Instead of two groping hands where the infection is somewhat contained, you will have two infected, gelatinous stumps reaching for you, leaking contagious fluid.

Remember that the second-highest cause of infection results from contact with existing wounds on a walking corpse. Any laceration you inflict that does not result in threat neutralization causes an open sore packed with infectious tissue, making the ghoul a more hazardous opponent.

3. It is overkill: Just as smiting the top of a zombie head with overwhelming force may be overkill, so is excessive hacking at melee range. Using an edged weapon in undead combat requires that you keep your blade sharpened and ready at all times. By using your weapon to dismember rather than eliminate a target, you not only waste precious time, strength, and energy, you create more work for yourself once the engagement has ended by needing to rehone your blade's edges. Your objective in any zombie combat situation is to end it as quickly as possible, not to prolong your encounter out of rage or personal satisfaction. Any strike that does not contribute to stopping an attacking ghoul is an unnecessary one.

Combat Techniques

Many of the strategies detailed in long-distance combat such as the Musashi and the Blindside can also be used in melee-range encounters. Some specific techniques particular to this distance can also prove very useful for fighting the undead while at the same time avoiding the fatal funnel.

STRACIRS TECHNIQUE

TARGET AREA: **TEMPORAL, NASAL/ORBITAL, OR OCCIPITAL REGIONS**
MOST EFFECTIVE WITH: **BLUDGEONS (MACES, HAMMERS, CLUBS)**

Technique: One of the simplest techniques to employ at melee range to neutralize your attacker while steering clear of the fatal funnel is the StraCirs (pronounced "STRAY-cers") technique. This technique is composed of three movements that will keep you clear of the zombie's primary threat zones while creating options for your own attack. As you enter melee range, a zombie will most likely have its arms extended, hands grasping for you, attempting to grab your body—at which time, you will begin the first movement:

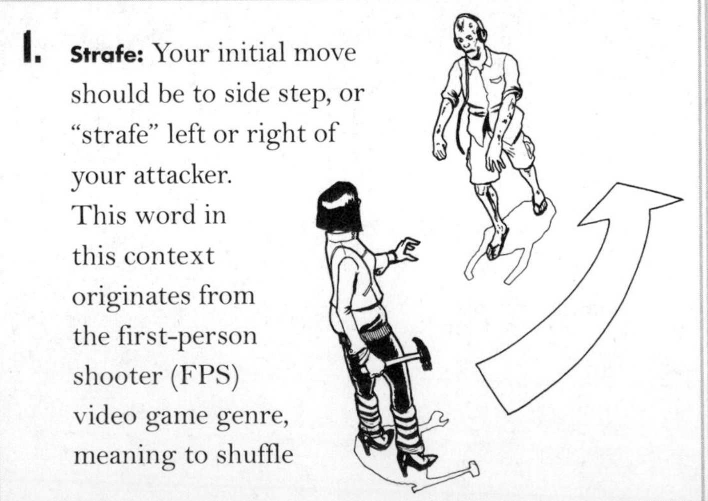

1. **Strafe:** Your initial move should be to side step, or "strafe" left or right of your attacker. This word in this context originates from the first-person shooter (FPS) video game genre, meaning to shuffle

side-to-side while keeping your torso constantly facing the same direction. The intention is to move out of reach of the zombie's grasp while not losing sight of your opponent. Do not turn away from your attacker during this movement. At melee range, zombies have been known to lurch suddenly in an attempt to grab their victim.

2. **Circle:** Once you have strafed to either side, begin moving in a circular pattern around your opponent, ending at the left or right side of your attacker; you could continue circling until you end up directly behind it, but this obviously requires more time. By moving in a circular pattern, you are taking advantage of the zombie's lack of coordination. A normal human attacker would most likely pivot at the same speed and in the same direction should you attempt to outflank him. Using the ghoul's lack of speed against it, you are able to remain out of reach while exposing several prime anatomical targets for your assault.

3. Strike: Once you have circled your opponent and find yourself in an advantageous position, you have several target options. Depending on where you complete the movement, the occipital region, the temporal region, and the nasal/orbital region are all available targets. Remember, the zombie does not possess the intellect to block an oncoming blow, so choose whichever target suits your weapon best. Strike quickly and decisively.

As you become proficient in this technique, you will be able to combine the first two movements into one smooth transition, known also in gaming terms as the *circlestrafe.*

As we covered in the discussion of weapons, you will employ one of two kinds of armaments at melee range—either a blunt instrument or an edged weapon. Bladed arms, such as a sword or machete, tend to be less effective at direct strikes to the zombie cranium. Blades have a tendency to either glance off the skull or embed themselves deeply in the head of a zombie after your blow. Striking the hard cranial bones can quickly dull your fine cutting edge. With an edged weapon, a more efficient strategy is to decapitate your opponent.

As the act of fully decapitating an opponent is much more difficult than most people realize, we have developed a technique similar to the StraCirs maneuver, but specifically designed for edged weapons.

THE LUMBERJACK

TARGET AREA: **NECK AND THROAT REGION**
MOST EFFECTIVE WITH: **BLADED IMPLEMENTS (SWORDS, MACHETES, AXES)**

Technique: Watch any woodsman's technique as he is in the process of felling a tree, and you will note that he does not hack away at an identical spot on the trunk over and over. Rather, he approaches his target from several angles, "notching" the log before splitting it all the way through, thus minimizing the likelihood of his tool becoming wedged and speeding up the entire process dramatically. You can use a similar approach with an edged weapon against the neck of the undead:

1. **Circlestrafe:** Just as in the previous blunt-trauma-weapon maneuver, your first step should be to shift out of the ghoul's fatal funnel.

2. Strike: Chop the neck with your blade, making sure you use an ample amount of force to inflict a deep, severe laceration.

3. Repeat: If your initial blow does not sever the head from its torso, do not panic. Circle approximately twenty-five degrees and strike your target a second time.

4. Finish: Repeat the preceding sequence of maneuvers until your undead opponent's head is separated from its body.

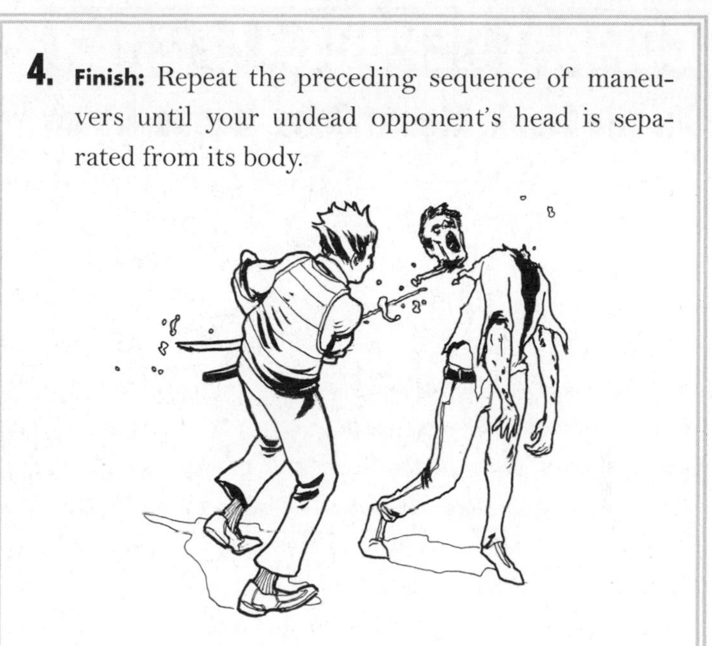

Using this technique, most individuals are able to finish the engagement within two to three strikes. Should you find yourself unable to completely separate the head from the undead body, you have at least seriously compromised the ghoul's ability to retaliate. Most important, you have kept yourself out of danger during your offensive attack. Remember, the severed head of a zombie requires a final, terminating blow to the brain.

COMBAT REPORT: LEE ZHEN

Shaolin Monk, Mount Song, Henan, China

I'm escorted up a craggy mountain trail by a brigade of warrior monks armed with Chinese long-pole weapons. Along the route, we hear the moans of several roaming zombies that have sensed our oncoming presence. Before I can even see the ghouls in the distance, the scouts in our party dash ahead and eliminate them before they are within a hundred yards of our position. Finally, we come upon a clearing that looks to be a large, well-tended vegetable garden. Monks and villagers work side by side to help cultivate the young, delicate shoots. It is here I am greeted by Lee Zhen, the Shaolin monk chosen to speak with me because of his command of English, which is remarkably good. Lee explains that he learned the language mostly by watching rebroadcasts of the American television show Hunter *on CCTV. "Growing up, I wanted to be Fred Dryer," Lee tells me as we sit down for tea while watching the work in the fields continue.*

LZ: Most people in the outside world, even within the mainland, had a misunderstanding of the Shaolin lifestyle. Many believed it to be an austere existence, one filled with fetching water, tending wheat fields, and hours of meditation, similar to what they saw on film and television. They thought it was, how you say, that phrase young people say meaning traditional, established?

ZCM: Old school?

LZ: Yes, that's it. They did not realize that, just like the rest of China, the monastery had adapted with the changing times. We had cell phones, an e-commerce website, even a reality television show. Though many did not completely agree that this open adoption of modernism fit well with the historical spirit of Shaolin, no one argued that it brought additional funds to the temple, helping us prosper. It was not technology, however, that brought the living dead to our attention, but the will of the Henan people.

As you can imagine, the spread of information by public broadcast was somewhat restrictive in those days. Early outbreaks were attributed to dissidents, radical factions, Falun Dafa, and the like. It was at this time when we began receiving individuals at our gates, fearful of what they had been hearing from family and friends in other cities. It was a trickle at first: the lone farmer, a street vendor or two. This trickle slowly began to expand into a river. At this point, there were still limited actual sightings of any walking dead. But there was a feeling in the air; the people sensed it. Something terrible was soon to be upon them.

Finally, the dam burst. People by the dozens arrived daily, some already with their heads shaved, women and children included, wearing bedsheets tied into makeshift robes to show their devotion and commitment, anything to allow them to enter. We took them all in. At this point there was no covering up the situation—reports of infection were reported in Beijing and Shanghai and quickly spreading to the smaller outlying cities. Those with money—and there were many—fled the country to take refuge in the neighboring islands—Taiwan, Malaysia, the Philippines. But those who came to us for help, these were the ones without the funds, without any means of escape.

ZCM: Why not reach out to the government, or approach the local officials?

LZ: You're not very familiar with how things work here. There's an old proverb that says *"Qiang da chu tou niao"*—"The bird that sticks out its head gets shot." In this particular case, there was fear that the phrase would be taken literally. Besides, the government was too focused on major urban areas. They had no time or desire to help those left in the countryside. Soon, the temple's sleeping quarters, training rooms, and courtyard were filled with crude tents, structures, and bedding from the hundreds who came to us for help. Many of them were *ganranzhe*,[15] weakened and frail. There was a concern among many of the monks that we would not be able to feed or care for everyone, especially those who were already sick. When confronted with this situation, the abbot simply replied, "Many of these people were forgotten by our country once already. Let us not have it happen to them again."

Early on, before any of us realized what he was doing, the abbot was laying the foundation for his plan to manage the dire situation he knew would be coming our way. When villagers first began arriving at the temple, he quietly delivered messages to former students who were now employed in surrounding cities as bodyguards, security officers, and policemen. He also sent envoys with messages to the heads of kung fu schools within a two-hundred-mile radius of the temple. I am unsure of the specific content of the communication, but within days, many of the top students of various schools arrived. The abbot assembled all of the guests and the most skilled and senior of our monks together to articulate his plan.

ZCM: His plan?

LZ: For half a fortnight, the abbot met long into the evening with various groups within the temple. At the time I was busy doing as I was told—feeding and tending to all the incoming refugees—so I was oblivious as to what exactly was happening. I did see many groups of monks coming and going from the temple at all hours of the night, many

15 *ganranzhe:* Literally translated to mean "infected people"; many villagers throughout the Henan Province contracted the HIV virus as a result of tainted equipment used in blood transfusions.

carrying tools and supplies. This went on for several weeks as we continued to receive countrymen by the wagonload.

One day when I awoke, nearly all of the villagers were gone, as were the guest students and roughly a quarter of the monks. It was after morning prayers that we were all finally told of what was to happen over the next several days. Roughly forty kilometers north of the temple lies a vast, open field where we often would assemble, meditate, and train. To the north of the field is the Yellow River. Mountains lie to the west, and fifty kilometers to the east, the city of Zhengzhou. The field is an idyllic place, an ideal location for the abbot's intentions. We set out on foot and horseback just after breakfast, and arrived just before nightfall.

There was an odd smell in the air as we approached our destination. When I set eyes upon the field, I could hardly believe what I saw. A large bamboo platform had been erected, upon which sat two of the large meditation bells from our temple. Alongside the bells were racks upon racks of weapons from our armory. Each of the top instructors from the temple and neighboring schools was responsible for dividing us all into groups based on a single weapon class. We had teams wielding spades, axes, spears, broadswords, and a multitude of other weapons. It was then I noticed that most of the villagers were also present and separated into their own group, including many of the sickly ones. Given their lack of formal training, they were given their own choice of weapon, many selecting a simple cudgel or broadsword. Some preferred to wield a farming tool they brought with them. Everyone then sat down to dinner. When the meal was finished and the tables cleared, one of the bells was rung three times, and we all began to chant.

Our chanting continued unceasingly throughout the night, pausing only to punctuate the repetition with the deep gong of a meditation bell. The sounds echoed off the mountain ranges to the west and south. Then, just before daybreak, we began to hear them. The sounds were faint and low at first, barely audible above the sound of the wind gusting through the trees. Slowly, they began to grow louder in volume, as the air began to fill with a pungent odor. They were approaching from the east, just as the abbot had planned. The moans began to crescendo as they drew closer, blending with our chants into a single, horrific chorus. As hundreds of walking corpses began to wander onto the field, we rose from our *zazen* positions and prepared for battle.

The abbot summoned onto the field the first wave of monks equipped with polearms: spears, spades, and axes. Of all the hours we spent on the battlefield that day, this initial moment was the most dangerous. We heard many rumors about how to deal with this unknown enemy, none of which we knew whether or not to believe. Strike the head, strike the heart, remove the head from the body—all of these techniques needed to be tested during these critical first minutes. Several of the monks ran through their opponents with the seven-foot long *qiang*, only to have the creatures pull themselves down the length of the shafts to continue their attack.

We soon realized that head strikes and decapitation were the most effective. Those armed with *yuèyáchǎn*[16] and broad axes were well prepared to sever heads from torsos. I witnessed Li Baobao, the monk most skilled among us all with polearms, decapitate seven bodies with a single whirl of his *guandao*,[17] as if he were channeling General Guan Yu himself! The monks needed to watch where they stepped, as the heads of the creatures continued to snap at them from the ground. The abbot then set loose other waves armed with

16 *yuèyáchǎn:* monk's spade.
17 *guandao:* Chinese polearm, similar to a broad axe.

shorter broadswords and bludgeons to follow alongside their long-range brethren. A rhythm began to develop between the ranks, where a polearmed monk would decapitate an attacker and then kick its head back to the short-range ranks to deal a final blow. It was quite a spectacle—rows of fighting monks, whirling, flailing, and striking. Our flowing, brightly colored robes presented a fiery contrast against the dulled landscape of thousands of walking dead.

The most impressive, however, were the *ganranzhe*. What they lacked in technique, they more than made up for in tenacity, especially the women. The abbot was cautious about sending them into the fray, but once engaged in battle, it is with no exaggeration that I say they fought with the fury of a thousand dragons. I believe it was because of the frustration they felt; not about having to leave their homes or their livelihood, or even about the living dead, but the faith they held that their country would help them in their time of need. That belief was tested twice in their lifetimes, and twice they were let down. They battled with a reckless abandon, with no concern for their safety or survival, and suffered greatly for it. Many I saw simply dove straight into a mass of creatures, flailing away until they were bitten, and then continuing to fight until completely overcome. Maybe that was their intention all along. Perhaps losing your life is less of a concern when you ultimately feel in control of your fate. Whatever the case, it was an epic battle, the most spectacular since Wengjiagang. Truly a valiant loss.

ZCM: Loss?
LZ: I use that word in the traditional sense that the dead were not vanquished that day. Nor was that ever the intention.

ZCM: What was the intention?
LZ: The abbot was a man of peace, but he was not naïve. There

were seven million people in Zhengzhou alone. Even if only one half of one percent of the population was infected and made its way toward the sound of our chants, they would vastly outnumber our own ranks that day. His greater purpose was to use this situation as an opportunity to test both our weapons and our will. It had been almost five hundred years since monks of Shaolin had to confront an enemy in mortal combat. And this enemy was different from any we had ever faced in our history. These were not pirates or bandits. He knew that facing these adversaries, of whom we knew so little and who looked not like hardened fighters, but very much like the same, poor countrymen that fought alongside us, could affect the monks' ability to do what was necessary.

As the battle took place, scribes stood next to the abbot, furiously recording notes as fast as he could relay his thoughts. As the abbot watched, he noted the performance of each of his disciples—which monks overcame a normal sense of fear and resistance to destroying unarmed attackers, which ones needed continued assessment, and which needed to be placed in more of a support role in the future. Even in those cases, he was very conscious of making the reassigned monk not feel like a coward. The abbot would say to him, "Your level of compassion is great indeed," and he truly believed it.

Our weapons needed assessing against this new adversary as well. As closely as he was evaluating each monk's abilities, the abbot also monitored which of our historical armaments performed most effectively, and which might need further technique refinement given our opponent's vulnerabilities. The spear, broadsword, and axe all seemed to fare well during battle. Other weapons, such as the chain whip, fan, and rope dart, did not.

We fought for hours, until just before sunset, as ghouls continued to swarm from the east. Teams of monks were responsible for continuously clearing bodies toward the outskirts of the field as the battle raged. The dead were piled in such great numbers that they formed a perimeter several meters in height around the battlefield. As it turns out, this too was intentional. As everyone began to tire and our weapons dulled too quickly to resharpen, the abbot declared a full retreat from the field. Once the last of our combatants was clear, he ordered a group of archers to release a volley of arrows tipped in flame. Upon landing, they sparked an inferno that engulfed the entire battlefield. It was then I recognized the odor we had encountered when approaching the field that morning—kerosene. The edges of the field were soaked in the flammable liquid, and large kettles were also overturned to augment the flames. Not only did the blaze devastate much of the remaining horde, themselves trapped by the wall of corpses, but the fumes helped guard our nostrils from the stench of the ghouls during combat. The abbot truly thought of everything. We stood alongside the battlefield, now a massive funeral pyre, to say a prayer for the dead. As night was falling, the flames helped light our path as we made our way back up the rugged mountain pass, returning to Mount Song and sealing the trails behind us.

It was almost daybreak by the time we returned to the temple, and awaiting us was a breakfast prepared by the villagers who had stayed behind. It was during our meal that I learned that other groups of monks were sent forth along the opposite side of the mountain to gather supplies and the experienced farmers and their children were coordinated to prepare the neighboring fields for the growing season.

Zhen stares contemplatively toward the vegetable field. He points to a child who, startled by an insect, is being calmly soothed by his mother.

LZ: Life here is not easy. The earth on this mountain is hard and rocky, difficult to farm. We have survived, though, just as we have for thousands of years. This will be a time to return to ways that were forgotten by us in our recent past. We now exist in a world much like our ancestral monks before us—uncomplicated, simple, austere . . .

Lee pauses and smiles.

LZ: Old school.

CLOSE-QUARTERS COMBAT

SAFETY LEVEL OF ENGAGEMENT: **LOW**
COMBAT SKILL REQUIRED AT THIS DISTANCE: **HIGH**
RISK OF INFECTION: **30–50%**

Zombie close-quarters combat (ZCQC) is defined as engagement with the walking dead within a two-foot (0.6-meter) range between opponents. Combat at this distance frequently occurs indoors, and many times unexpectedly. Two common scenarios when ZCQC takes place are during undead home invasions and in urban search and rescue operations in an apartment or housing complex. Because of the proximity with the undead and the confined space where combat usually takes place, it is a harrowing and treacherous range in which to battle a corpse. At this range, the zombie most likely will have its hands on your body and will be seconds away from a lethal bite. In order for you to survive at this distance, your skills need to be razor-sharp and your execution flawless.

Close-Quarters Combat Strategies

Although engaging in close-quarters battle with an undead opponent is not encouraged, you can use several strategies to lessen the risk of infection and to make these types of encounters easier to manage.

Sloth Kills

Whatever you do, do it fast. Research has shown that the risk of infection triples for every additional second you remain engaged in close-quarters combat with a ghoul. This is due to not only the increased chance of being bitten or scratched by your attacker, but also having undead fluids spray onto your exposed areas. This risk also depends on your protective garments, the zombie's state of decomposition, and the injury status of both you and your attacker. The more exposed wounds and lesions either opponent has, the riskier the engagement. As mentioned previously, experts in zombie close-quarters combat can finish an altercation within three seconds. It should be your goal to do the same.

Loose Lips, Safety Slips

The major risk of infection during ZCQC warrants addressing another recommendation when fighting at this range—keep your mouth closed. Because a zombie's blood does not course through its decaying veins, there is less risk of being splattered by infectious fluid if you sever a major artery. However, there is always a chance that aberrant drops of fluid will land on your body. Ingestion of undead flesh or fluids has been shown to cause death within sixteen hours. It has been difficult for researchers to measure the exact quantities of undead contagion that have to be ingested to cause a fatality. (Is your fate sealed should a single drop land on your tongue?) Regardless, it is better to err on the side of caution in these situations.

Targeting the Eyes

In long-range combat, we recommended avoiding the eyes because of the likelihood of a misdirected strike given the small area you are targeting. Although close combat affords you better accessibility to these attractive targets, it is still recommended that you proceed carefully. Shoving a blade into a zombie's orbital socket may seem effortless in theory, but when you have a writhing, decomposing corpse in front of you, its rotting hands flailing away at your vision, the maneuver can be quite difficult. Should you be unfortunate enough to miss your target, your arm may be positioned in a highly vulnerable location—close to the zombie's mouth. Only after extensive close-combat experience should you even consider the eye sockets as primary targets.

Combat Techniques

The most important zombie close-quarters combat technique to keep in mind is, if at all possible, to avoid it. Never engage a zombie at close range by choice. If you are able to convert a close-quarters encounter into a melee-range engagement, you run much less risk of death and infection. This first technique can be used to plant space between yourself and your undead attacker:

THE LAUNCHPAD

TARGET AREA: **CHEST/TORSO AREA**

Technique: Recall the section on conditioning, where we detailed Blaster push-ups and Kickout exercises. This technique is a direct application of both movements in a combat setting. The launchpad tactic is a straightforward maneuver to execute in lieu of engaging in a wrestling match with a zombie.

Upon initial contact, before the ghoul has an opportunity to latch itself to your body, take the palms of both hands and slam them against the zombie's chest, forcing it backward. Alternatively, you can use your leg to jam your foot into the attacker's pelvis and force it away, noting that this movement requires slightly more balance and coordination. Ensure that you shove forcefully, driving from your heels with the weight of your entire body behind you.

Executed correctly, this action should cause the zombie to stumble back several steps, after which you can draw your melee weapon and execute a neutralizing technique as described in the section on medium-range combat. This technique is most effective when encountering an undead attacker outdoors or in a wide open setting where there is more room to maneuver. It is less successful in cramped conditions such as an apartment hallway, bathroom, or office cubicle.

As we described in the section on anatomy, the grip of a zombie is one of its most dangerous attributes. Some have even claimed that it is impossible to escape once you are caught in the clutches of the walking dead. This is a complete falsehood. Not only have many people been able to break free from the tight hold of a zombie, it is relatively simple to do so. It does, however, require a specific technique and dedicated practice to perfect the movement.

BREAKING THE GRIP

TARGET AREA: **UNDEAD HANDS/FINGERS**

Technique: In most standing ZCQC encounters, the zombie will grab you in one of two places: the upper or lower arms. Given this high likelihood, there are two defensive techniques to keep in mind:

Avoid pulling or pushing: The reason why many people fail to release themselves from a ghoul's clenches is often that (1) panic overwhelms them, and (2) they attempt to force themselves free by either pushing or pulling their arms. Not only is this ineffective in dislodging the zombie's grip, it actually puts you in greater jeopardy. If you pull your arm away from the attacking zombie, you risk pulling its open mouth closer to you. Additionally, pulling away may result in having infected fingernails ripping deeper into your flesh. Pushing your seized arm is equally futile, as you may push your body closer to your attacker, becoming even more entangled.

Roll your wrists: The most effective way to break a zombie's hold on your arm is a technique common in several different martial arts. The objective is to apply the greatest amount of pressure on the weakest part of the ghoul's grip. If the zombie grabs the outside of your forearm, forcefully roll your wrist around the zombie's hand, exerting pressure against where its rotting thumb and forefinger come together. Apply

aggressive downward pressure, and you should be able to free yourself from its grasp. If the zombie grabs the inside of your arm, execute the same maneuver, this time rolling your wrist toward the inside. This maneuver places a great deal of force against a zombie's grasp while requiring a nominal amount of strength on your part.

Practice the wrist-rolling grabs with a partner and you will see how easy it can be to free yourself from any adversary's grip, be they living or living dead. With regular drilling and practice, you should be able to consistently escape a zombie's hold within seconds.

The first rule of conventional weapon-disarming tactics is to control the weapon itself. Once you negate the weapon's advantage, your opponent becomes much less of a threat. This is no different when engaging in close-combat with the undead. In these cases, the primary weapon you must manage is the zombie's bite. If you are able to effectively keep a ghoul's mouth from snapping at you, you provide yourself valuable time to draw your weapon and deliver your own lethal blow.

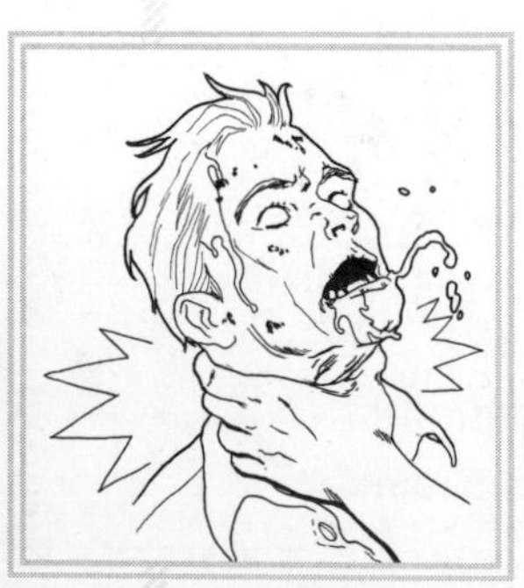

THE FULL THROTTLE

TARGET AREA: **NECK/THROAT REGION**

Technique: Grab the zombie with your nondominant hand by the top of the neck, directly below the chin. Using your thumb and forefinger, forcefully squeeze the soft tissue alongside the throat (the Adam's apple on a male zombie). This will enable you to keep the zombie's mouth at a distance from your body, while also forcing it slightly shut from the pressure you exert on the mandible. Grabbing near the top of the throat also prevents the ghoul from craning its neck down and taking a chunk out of your wrist or forearm. This maneuver can also set the stage for the two techniques described next.

MIDDLE CRANIAL FOSSA (MCF) ATTACK

TARGET AREA: **UNDERSIDE OF CHIN, SOFT PALATE, BRAIN**
MOST EFFECTIVE WITH: **EDGED WEAPONS (COMBAT KNIVES, CHEF'S KNIVES, SCREWDRIVERS)**

Technique: The MCF attack is identical to the Kabob technique described in long-range combat techniques, the obvious difference being the distance at which it is executed. This technique is by far the most effective method for ending a close engagement quickly. The middle cranial fossa area of bone is the thinnest on the entire skull and can be easily targeted during ZCQC. It does, however, require that you move quickly and without hesitation:

1. Draw your weapon from its sheath (ideally mounted on your chest in the cross-draw position).

2. Position the weapon so the point rests directly under the ghoul's chin.

3. Drive the weapon straight up through the jaw into the brain. You will feel resistance once you puncture the soft and hard palates, and finally reach the brain. Keep driving the weapon upward.

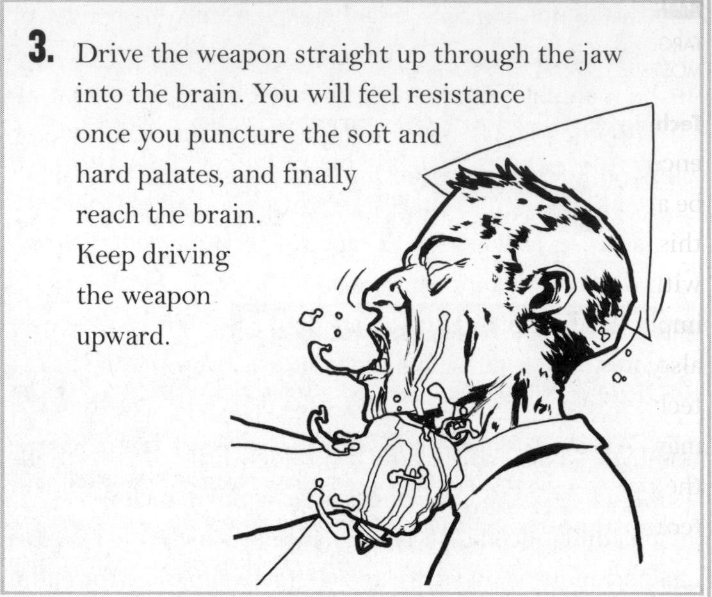

4. Forcefully retract your weapon to avoid catching it in the skull cavity.

5. Push the zombie away so its carcass does not fall on your body.

THE Q-TIP

TARGET AREA: **EAR CANAL**
MOST EFFECTIVE WITH: **SPIKED WEAPONS (ICE PICKS, TRENCH SPIKES, AWLS)**

Technique: An alternative target during a close-quarters encounter is the ear canal. This technique, however, should be attempted only when using a weapon suited to penetrating this specific orifice. The weapon should be long and thin with a stabbing point, such as an ice pick or trench spike. An improvised weapon such as a screwdriver or scratch awl is also effective. A combat knife is **not recommended** for this technique. The flat, wide blade of a traditional edged weapon may have greater difficulty driving through the canal into the brain. The attack sequence is similar to that of the MCF technique, except for the target area on the zombie cranium:

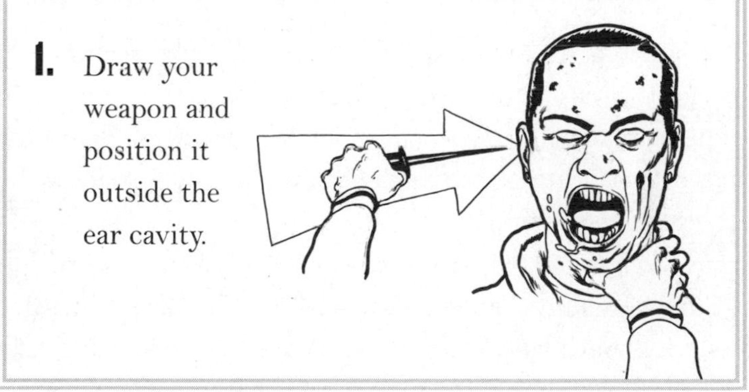

1. Draw your weapon and position it outside the ear cavity.

2. Forcefully thrust the weapon into the ear canal upward toward the brain, driving the weapon to its hilt.

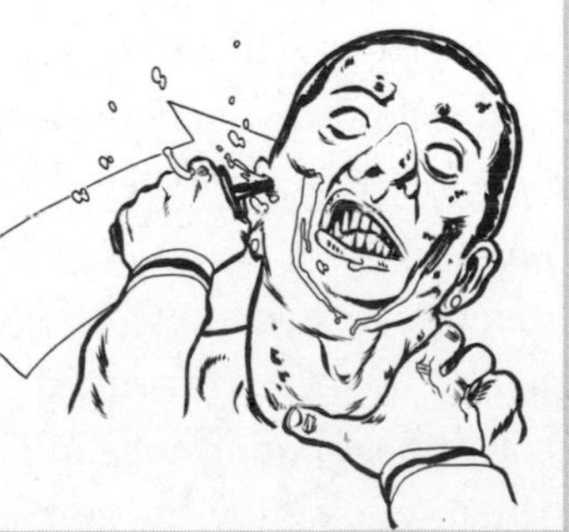

3. Twist the weapon, which aids in weapon extraction.

4. Extract your weapon vigorously and push the body away.

The various techniques just described may seem fairly straightforward and no more complicated than the techniques previously described at longer distances. Why, you may ask, is fighting the undead at close quarters so difficult? The reasons are simple.

During a ZCQC encounter, several intense events will be occurring simultaneously. Your face will be inches from an undead ghoul, its arms thrashing in front of you menacingly, its hands looking to seize any available fleshy portion of your body. Its neck will be outstretched while its teeth gnash at you. Its moan will be howling in your ears. With your body's cells soaking in epinephrine and your hand clutching the opponent's neck to keep its mouth at bay, you will have to then draw your weapon and plunge it into your target while attempting to control the volatile actions of a ravenous ghoul. For these reasons, drilling close-quarters techniques is of utmost importance in order to train your body to react instinctively and with calm assertiveness.

UNARMED COMBAT

SAFETY LEVEL OF ENGAGEMENT: **CRITICAL**
COMBAT SKILL REQUIRED AT THIS DISTANCE: **EXTREMELY HIGH**
RISK OF INFECTION: **90%**

In a world filled with walking nightmares, this is the most hellish of all encounters. Whether duc to poor planning, unfortunate circumstance, or just plain bad luck, you may at some point find yourself completely unarmed and inches from a rotting corpse. There is no more dangerous fighting scenario than engaging in unarmed zombie combat (perhaps with the exception of such combat with multiple assailants). Not to begin with a pessimistic view, but statistics show that the odds are not in the human combatant's favor. Nine out of ten fighters engaging in unarmed combat with a ghoul end up infected and, as a result, mortally wounded. Regardless of your background, fighting skill, or prior combat experience, in an unarmed engagement against a zombie, the living dead always have the upper hand.

It is exceedingly difficult but not impossible to escape an unarmed encounter uninfected and with your life intact. The sharper your skills and the faster you act, the greater your chance of survival. Several strategies previously mentioned are equally effective in an unarmed engagement—moving fast, maximizing the distance, and keeping your mouth closed. There are also a few additional strategies to keep in mind when fending off a ghoul with nothing but your bare hands.

Unarmed Combat Strategies

Remain Calm

This may seem like an obvious recommendation, but it demands emphasis in unarmed combat. Even experienced combatants may literally lose their head when their primary weapon is suddenly unavailable to them. Often fighters will focus on reacquiring a weapon before the undead threat is fully controlled. Even with your adrenaline in the red and a zombie clawing at your face, remain calm, take a deep breath, and remember your training.

Avoid Hair Pulling

Because of the proximity to your attacker, you may be tempted to grab a handful of the ghoul's locks in order to control it or keep its biting jaws away from you. This may be even more tempting if you face a walking corpse with long, bountiful tresses, as it may seem like a natural hold. This is not recommended for two simple reasons. First, the successful reaction derived from a hair-pulling tactic is primarily due to the pain elicited by such an action. Because the living dead feel no pain, the value of this technique is limited. Second and even more crucial is the fact that a rotting corpse, walking or not, has begun to decay. Therefore, the epidermal components surrounding the hair and scalp are in a fragile, unstable state. Many who have attempted this maneuver have ended up with a fistful of dying follicles and decomposing scalp.

Combat Breathing

A method used by professionals to help stimulate a sense of serenity during an otherwise anxiety-ridden situation is known as combat breathing, also referred to as tactical breathing. Knowing how to properly control your breath during times of extreme stress can make your combat engagements that much more successful. Although the technique we will describe can be used in any undead encounter, it may be of particular use during a gravely dangerous situation, such as an unarmed engagement with a zombie.

Despite its aggressive name, combat breathing actually has its origins in the most peaceful of endeavors—yoga, meditation, and contemplative reflection. These practices all require you to transport your body and mind into a tranquil, reflective state by consciously controlling the ventilation of air through your lungs. Military and law enforcement personnel have adopted this technique to induce a state of calm in the body during a hostile encounter. The technique can be used to equal effectiveness when facing the living dead.

It is a natural physical reaction to react intensely when seized by a walking corpse. If you are unable to control this reaction and instead allow it to escalate, death is almost certain. Your pulse rate will soar. Your breathing will become shallow and rapid. You may begin to hyperventilate. Finally, when your eyes fill with a glaring white fog as you start to lose consciousness, you'll realize the battle is over. By using a combat-breathing technique, not only do you keep your mind from being paralyzed with fear, you also enable your body to physically execute the undead combat techniques you have rehearsed without losing control of your muscles.

The method itself is rather simple—inhale through the nose for a count of three to five seconds, hold the breath for an equal amount of time, and finally exhale through the mouth for the same count. By controlling your breathing, you are able to soothe the mind during moments of high stress, calm your muscles so that they can react appropriately, and decrease your heart rate to a less frenzied tempo.

There is one caveat unique to using this breathing method during undead combat. Remember that one of the physical assets a zombie possesses is its intense, overpowering odor. Therein lies the dilemma—how can you execute a technique that requires breathing in through the nose if you will simultaneously inhale the potentially incapacitating scent of a ghoul, especially in close range? This can be addressed in several ways. First, each individual has his or her own sensitivity level to a zombie's rancidity, so you may be able to take in oxygen through your nostrils without being overwhelmed. Second, a filtered face mask or menthol gel rubbed underneath the nostrils can help alleviate the symptoms associated with zombie stench. Third, you can use the same combat-breathing technique and inhale through the mouth, but be watchful—not only are you at risk for hyperventilation, an open mouth in close combat is susceptible to ingestion of errant zombie contagion.

Combat Techniques

Although we recommend that any tactic you employ in unarmed zombie combat is driven by your need to escape, there may be times where this is not possible, such as in an elevator, a narrow corridor, or a room with blocked exits. With absolutely no armaments available and no room to escape, you will have to eliminate the undead threat using your own body as your primary weapon. This can be done, provided you attain mastery in two specific combat techniques:

OUTSIDE SWEEP AND STOMP (OSS)

TARGET AREA: **OUTSIDE THIGH/CALF REGION**

Technique: Always exploit the living dead's liabilities to your advantage. The liabilities we are focusing on in this particular technique is the zombie's poor balance, coordination, and lack of ability to defend against a simple leg sweep:

1. Mitigate the zombie's bite attack by securing its neck, as detailed in the Full Throttle technique.

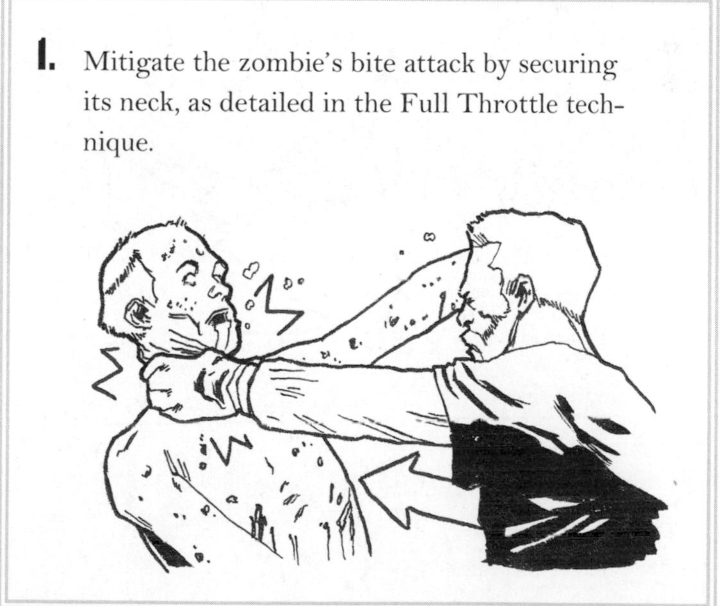

2. Hook one of your legs behind the ghoul's opposite leg. Remember that your throttling hand and your hooking leg are on the same side (right hand throttle, right leg hook).

3. Aggressively smash your leg against the zombie's leg while simultaneously pushing against its neck, forcing the zombie's weight backward. This should cause the ghoul to topple backward to the ground.

4. Once the ghoul is on the ground, move toward its head and stomp on its skull with the heel of your shoe. It is recommended that you wear appropriate footwear at all times in anticipation of this very purpose.

The following illustration shows the sequence in its entirety:

INSIDE SWEEP AND STOMP (ISS)

TARGET AREA: **INSIDE CALF/ANKLE REGION**

Technique: A variant of the sweep technique, this particular maneuver works best if you notice the zombie standing with its legs wide apart, as you will be attacking from the inside of the leg rather than from the outside:

1. Control the zombie's bite attack by securing its neck, as detailed in the Full Throttle technique.

2. Place your foot between the legs of the ghoul and hook your heel around the ghoul's calf.

3. Sweep your leg back while pushing against its neck, forcing the zombie to the ground.

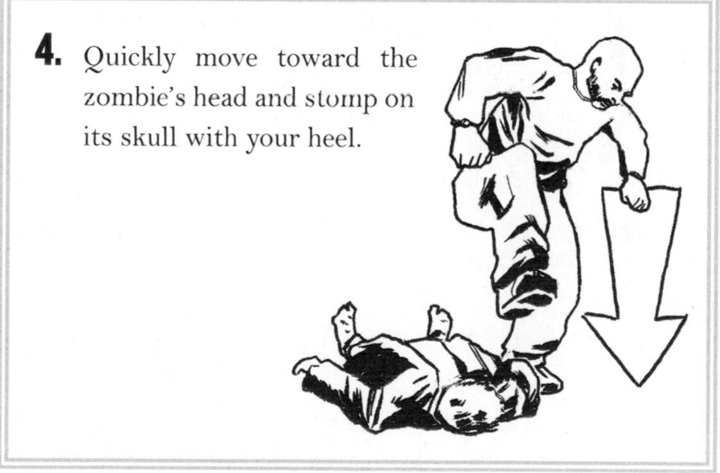

4. Quickly move toward the zombie's head and stomp on its skull with your heel.

Here again is an illustration showing the sequence in its entirety:

Those of you with previous martial arts experience may recognize both of these maneuvers as variations of two classic techniques—the *osoto-gari* (major outer reap) and the *ouchi-gari* (major inner reap). Martial artists may be tempted to try other techniques learned in various self-defense classes against an undead adversary. Unless you are willing to sacrifice your life to the benefit of your art, testing other random techniques is not encouraged. This is not to say that other movements would not work on a walking corpse, but are you prepared to take that chance?

These two variations on traditional techniques work well because (1) they are executed easily, (2) you are in constant control of the attacker's mouth, and (3) grappling with the zombie is kept at a minimum. If you are tempted to try other maneuvers such as shoulder throws, hip tosses, or back throws, you are likely to feel a set of undead teeth sinking into your shoulder, forearm, or neck. The biting and clawing attacks used by a zombie are banned in every professional human combat sport setting. They are also tactics that many martial artists are not used to defending against regularly, unless they have extensive experience in the most vicious of street brawls.

No disrespect is intended to any individual style or category of martial arts, but many classical methods do not translate well against the undead. Techniques that rely on pain to generate a calculated response from your adversary are particularly ineffective. Recall our discussion on melee combat regarding the futility of hacking a ghoul to pieces. Unlike a human being, a zombie will never surrender or "tap out," and it will let you snap every bone and hyperextend every joint in its body, all the while attempting to bite you as you do so. Traditional kicks and punches are not only ineffective against undead adversaries, they may actually do more harm than good should you lacerate the skin of your fists against the infected flesh of your opponent. For advanced training, you should study one of the specific zombie combat arts to gain knowledge in techniques that have been tested to work specifically against the walking dead.

COMBAT REPORT: ERIC SIMONSON

Grandmaster, Shigai-Jitsu
Red Rock, Arizona

I drive up to what looks to be a nondescript warehouse. From the outside, the structure could pass for a storage facility, retail wholesaler, or lumber supply depot. The only evidence of its true purpose is the snaking coils of concertina wire that encircle the complex and a black wooden placard etched in white lettering that reads "Shigai-Jitsu: All Are Welcome." Eric Simonson stands beneath this sign awaiting my arrival. He is dressed in a traditional black martial arts uniform known as a gi. *With a warm smile and surprisingly soft handshake, he leads me into his training center. I address him by his official title as "Grandmaster," which he immediately waves off, feigning embarrassment. "Grandmasters are old men with long, white beards, usually dead. Call me Eric."*

His humility is surprising, even for someone who was previously told of Simonson's lack of ego. His modesty belies his status as the head of one of seven internationally recognized and federally funded styles of undead self-defense. He is a wiry man with a triathlete's build and looks decades younger than his actual fifty-four years, the only hint of his age being the streaks of white in his long hair, which is pulled back in a ponytail.

Classes are in session as we walk through the training center. Nearly all the students look identical and drastically different from Simonson—shaven heads, cargo pants, boots, and athletic compression tops. The instructors are dressed the same, with the exception that most wear their hair slightly longer than the students. We arrive at Simonson's office in the back of the complex, which adjoins a large, open training space. Unlike the areas we passed, this training room contains no equipment or padded surfaces. Dark blemishes stain the concrete floor.

ES: I still remember where I was during those initial reports. Guess it's like that "Where were you when Pearl Harbor, JFK, 9/11 . . ." kind of thing. I actually wasn't in town at the time of the first EMS broadcasts.

ZCM: Where were you?

ES: Los Angeles, at this semiannual West Coast martial arts leadership conference. They liked to refer to it as a "Gathering of Warriors." *Pfffft.* Most of the guys I knew were going for three reasons: to get new business, get hammered, and get tail. It was always a good time, and it gave me an opportunity to catch up on some of the newer training methods. Once televised mixed martial arts became the highest-rated sporting event on broadcast television, man, we just couldn't keep up with the demand. At the same time, we had to differentiate ourselves and stay up-to-date with the latest training techniques coming out of Asia. I was in the exhibit hall looking at some guy connected to what looked like thirty-five rubber bands when a Muay Thai boxer I knew called me into the lobby.

They had the news up on the flat screens. I swear, half of us thought it was some sort of guerrilla marketing campaign or performance art piece—like those collective dance groups or that guy who takes pictures of people bare-ass naked in public. I remember they just kept rolling the same footage coming out of Miami over and over again: this huge mass of them, like some giant, rolling wave of gray and brown. I'd heard some news reports here and there, but nothing like this. I still didn't believe it until they started showing the footage coming in from around the world—Mumbai, Tehran, Hong Kong. When I saw the stuff from Hong Kong, Jesus. The short hairs on my neck were still standing up as I was speed-dialing my airline to get an earlier flight.

ZCM: You wanted to leave?

ES: Damn straight. I remembered what happened when the shit hit the fan in New York in 2001 and then later in Chicago. At the time I didn't know whether this was some Al-Aqsa attack or superpandemic or what. I just figured that Red Rock sounded a hell of a lot safer than L.A. Didn't matter, flights were already being delayed or canceled, and I was stuck with all the other guys at the conference.

ZCM: What was the reaction of the others?

ES: That was what was most interesting. The reactions I saw in those initial hours exemplified the attitudes I continued to see throughout the initial outbreaks, when we were all too stupid or arrogant to be scared. There was a bunch that were, like any normal human beings, basically freaking out. Some, like me, incorrectly believed that the government would handle the mess before it got too out of control. A majority of them, though, a lot of my friends included, saw this as a unique opportunity to prove themselves.

ZCM: Prove themselves?

ES: As combat practitioners. After forty years of doing this stuff, this much I know: I don't care what style, what origin, what country—if you spend a good percentage of your life hitting pads, kicking bags, and rolling around on mats, at the end of the day you want to know that what you're doing actually works when it counts. Much of what we all practice is theoretical, especially the weapon-based arts. Sure, you can say "I'll block this strike and then snap the arm at the elbow," but very few in the civilized world, instructors included, know the specific level of force required to crack a radial bone. Even fewer have actually done it. This is even truer in the blade arts, given that most legal systems frown on people slicing each other to ribbons.

I'm not sure how much you know about how mixed martial arts got ramped up in the States. For decades, it was that age-old "My kung fu is better than your kung fu" boasting. Then fighters of all styles started getting into cages in the early nineties. That's when the entire martial arts world got flipped on its ear. It caused a sea change throughout the fighting styles. Everyone realized that unwavering commitment to any one style, regardless of what it was, wouldn't work in a real fight. Bruce Lee, smart SOB that he was, said it best way back in the seventies: Be like water. Be flexible—keep what works, toss what doesn't, keep learning. Everyone had to get out of their comfort zone and train in a different set of techniques: wrestling, jujitsu, boxing, judo. And you know what? In the end, we were all better for it. Better martial artists, and better people. More humble, more open, more willing to learn.

After years of being flexible, we started to get cocky again. A lot of us thought we had it all figured out, and now some of us wanted to prove it. Against them.

We had come full circle, and were back to seeing whose kung fu was best. I remember this one guy at the convention, a huge, tattooed judoka, turned to me, wrung his hands in delight like a kid in a cupcake shop, and yelled "Rock and roll!" A bunch of the other guys laughed. They saw this as open season—a prime opportunity to use techniques that would normally get them tossed from competition or thrown in jail. You would have thought that these guys would know better; they were supposed to represent the vanguard, the leadership from their respective styles. I wish I could say that these feelings were isolated. I don't know what it was—validation, insecurity—but in those first months, I saw a lot of good men, good fighters, throw their lives away. For what?

ZCM: You didn't have the same urge?

ES: Never. Maybe it was because I was older, had a family. Maybe I worked out all that testosterone-fueled horse crap in my twenties. It also just didn't make sense to me, especially early on, when no one had a clue what the hell we were up against. It was just blind ignorance. No fighter in his right mind would get into a ring before studying his opponent, right? At that point, we knew less than nothing about what was going on around us. All we saw were these slow, lumbering mental defects. "Eric, it'll be like kicking fish out of a barrel," I remember one guy saying. We had no knowledge, and no respect for the opposition. We underestimated them. And in a fight, that's precisely when you lose.

The boxers took it on the chin the worst, no pun intended. Everyone had to swallow at least a small chunk of humble pie when all was said and done, but the boxers, they were the first to suffer. A boxer's weapons are his fists, and what good are they against an opponent that does not, *cannot* get knocked out? There was this one friend of mine, Manuel, awesome fighter out of Albuquerque. Golden Gloves three years in a row, most of his Ws by knockout. I had him out to the dojo a few times to run some clinics for the group.

He points to a picture on the wall of a stout, handsome Latino, his hands raised in a boxer's stance, standing alongside Simonson and other students.

ES: He was in town when we saw one of those things roaming the streets. I tried to tell him to get his ass out of there, but goddamn that Manuel, just too much pride in his Mexican blood. He just stepped right up and threw a right cross that you could hear ten blocks away. All it did was pivot that thing ninety degrees sideways. He threw a couple of jabs, another right. No effect. When he started throwing body blows, that's when it got its arms around Manny's shoulders. I barely got there in time to kick it away, and caught a thundering left hook to the jaw for my efforts.

By the time I woke up, Manuel was sitting on the curb next to the corpse, its head completely caved in. Manny's hands were a mess—broken fingers, the flesh on his knuckles peeled back almost to his wrists, and covered with that thing's slime. He didn't realize how bad off he was, but I was keeping up with the medical news reports. I took care of him at my place most of the night. Manny was tough. He held out for hours, and turned just before dawn.

Manuel wasn't the last of my friends to end up on the wrong side of an attack. We took some serious hits, and the dead didn't discriminate. Kickboxers, jujitsu players, karate-kas—whatever your style or the color of your belt, it didn't matter. That's when I realized that we needed another sea change. We had to throw out the old book again and take nothing for granted—no weapon, no style, no technique.

Boxing is a good example. All we heard was, "Go for the brain, the skull is the weak link." What we didn't realize then, what no one knew, was that whatever happens when you turn into one of those things, the brain isn't the same any longer. It doesn't respond to external trauma, like Manny's right cross, the same way a human would. When a fighter throws a knockout punch, the force of the blow slams the brain against the inside of the skull, causing shock to nerve clusters in the brain stem. Unfortunately, that don't work so good on the walking dead.

The same reality was true for pretty much every other combat style—everyone experienced a big-time wake-up call. Try to put a rear naked choke on a zombie, you two will stand there until your arms are screaming from lactic acid buildup, that is if you don't feel teeth sinking into your forearm first. Want to execute a *harai-goshi* on a ghoul? You'll probably have a chunk taken out of your trapezius before it hits the ground. Pankration, tae kwon do, krav maga—every style and technique needed to be placed under a different lens and evaluated under new physical constraints: those of the living dead. That's when I started trying to get the right people—senseis, professors, physiologists—together in the same room to talk through what worked and what didn't from each fighting style.

ZCM: How was that received by your peers?

ES: They were . . . unenthusiastic, to put it politely. No one wants to hear their baby is ugly, and there isn't a small amount of ego that goes into leading a fighting style. For a bunch of other instructors to sit around a table and hear that their techniques were worth bunk, well, you can imagine how well that was taken. As time went on, the egos started dissipating as more of us started falling victim. We would hear about this teacher and that teacher not being around anymore, and the students dwindled rapidly. Eventually I was able to get anyone who was left in my circle to come around.

Those were some tough nights. We tried to be as meticulous as possible, breaking down everything we knew about zombie anatomy, physiology, movement, anything that could help us develop a complete defensive style specifically around them. Plus, doing all of this while still trying to just keep our collective asses alive. Things got a lot easier when we all moved into the same western rescue station. We researched and trained furiously, pulling from this art and that. We even interviewed other civilians who were willing to describe some of their personal experiences and then tried to replicate them during training. After what felt like years of training and scribbling, we finally arrived at the foundation of the system you see today.

That's when we also started trying to let the authorities in on what we were trying to do, and organizing classes in the rescue camp. We even started training the Guardsmen when they were off duty. That's when some of the senior officials started to pay attention, and got us on a Pave Hawk to visit some of the other stations up the coast. We then made our way east to the other safety nexuses. The rest you already know—we were able to secure some funding through FECDA,[18] pressed some palms at the new White House, and then set up shop again back here.

ZCM: How realistic is the training to actual combat?

ES: As real as it can be for the novices while keeping everyone safe, and once you reach a certain level, as real as stepping outside your house and finding one in your front yard. My goal is to not only train anyone who walks through that door, but to get their spouse and kids in here as well. Especially the kids. For guys like you and me, we can only do so much with our creaky old bones. But children, if you get them started early enough, we can build the muscle memory into their systems and give them a psychological edge as well. For the next generation, it'll be like playing pat-a-cake to them. But I'm getting off track; you asked me how realistic the training

18 FECDA: Federal Civilian Defense Act, enacted to supply federal funding to private institutions that provide self-defense education to the civilian population.

is. Why don't we go into the Advanced Sim room and I'll show you.

We move into the space adjoining his office. The temperature is markedly colder in here than the other areas of the facility. Simonson guides me to a viewing area encased in Plexiglas and instructs me to stay inside.

ES: Sorry for the temperature, it's necessary in here to slow down the rot. This is an advanced room, only open to those whom I've personally tested and passed through our initial program, which doesn't take a long time. One thing we learned from the Israelis is getting people trained and combat-ready fast. We don't have the luxury of toiling for years before being ready to deal with actual threats.

He picks up a short rattan stick and presses an intercom button on the wall.

ES: Tim, send in a quartet, please.

Simonson loosens his ponytail, allowing his hair to cascade over his shoulders. An amber warning light flashes as a gate buzzes and slides open on the opposite wall. The room grows silent. Simonson begins rapping the stick methodically against the concrete. A faint moan begins to fill the large chamber. Simonson clips a plug on his nostrils and stretches his limbs as the wail grows louder, joined by several other moans. Suddenly, four ghouls burst forth from the opened gate. They are in varying states of decomposition—one is nearly skeletal, its sex undeterminable. The others—two males and a female—are in a fresher state. The four begin lumbering toward him.

ES: You can see these trainers are in full battle mode—hands and mouth fully exposed. For those new to this room we'll start by muzzling them or flex-tying their fingers.

Simonson moves slowly toward the group in a zigzag pattern. His movements seem to confuse the group, which begin to separate and spread across the hall. He takes two bounding steps toward the skeletal zombie and tucks himself into a ball, rolling forward past it and emerging slightly behind the ghoul. Without standing, he sweeps its legs, sending the creature crashing to the floor face first. Simonson is immediately on it and pulls a nylon handcuff from his gi *pocket. He binds the zombie's hands behind its back.*

ES: The first thing we teach is evaluating the threat. Of the four, this trainer seemed to be the easiest to handle, given its size, weight, and current state.

He picks the ghoul up and with a single shove sends it careening into another two zombies, causing all three to tumble to the concrete.

ES: The second thing we teach is assessing engagement. If you can, run. If you just need to carve a path for your escape, knock a few down. Don't waste your time and energy unnecessarily cracking skulls.

Simonson is on the other two fallen ghouls. He places his foot on the neck of one subject while securing the female corpse and then cuffs the remaining male. The only zombie left untethered is the largest—more than six feet tall. Given the state of decay, it appears to be recently infected and wears green digital-camouflage fatigues.

ES: The third thing we teach—use what's between *your* ears before attacking what's between theirs. The greatest advantage you have is up here *[he taps his head with the stick]* and their greatest disadvantage is here *[he taps the uncuffed ghoul's head]*. Don't make the mistake of playing their game. If you grapple with them, you're playing their game. Play yours.

He circles the ghoul as it lurches out and lunges for him. As he circles, he strikes its skull with pinpoint strikes to the temples, nose, and back of the head. Simonson grabs another stick from a weapon rack and begins striking the zombie's skull from all angles with both weapons at blinding speed. The strikes echo through the room with the staccato pattern of a marching band's drumline.

As he spins around the ghoul, it manages to catch a handful of the instructor's long mane in its fist, pulling his head sideways and knocking him off balance. The ghoul pulls him in close and opens its mouth. Simonson's sticks clatter to the floor. I'm out of the viewer's case running toward him when he extends his hand, telling me to stop, and then grabs the creature by the throat. His other hand quickly reaches inside his uniform to reveal a short, hooked blade. Simonson slices the strands of hair clenched in the ghoul's fist while simultaneously sweeping its legs from under it, sending it rolling to the floor. He flips and cuffs the final zombie and leaves it writhing on the concrete, unable to rise, along with the others.

ES: Well, that was a bit of excitement, and a fine example of the fourth thing we teach—never, ever underestimate your opponent, even if it's dead.

Simonson bows slightly to the group of bound, moaning ghouls and begins picking them up off the floor. He forces each one toward the doorway, and cuts their flexible cuffs just before pushing them through the electronic gate, which shuts after the last ghoul has passed through.

ZCM: So, you don't . . .

ES: Finish them? No. My students, I leave the decision up to them, but I don't. First of all, do you know how tough it is to corral these things in the wild? More important, I'm trying to live the true spirit of this style, even in training. Shigai-Jitsu is at its core a pure defensive art. The most important elements are not attacking, not crippling, and certainly not "killing." They are escape, evasion, and defense. That's what is most ironic about all that has happened. In a world that's been turned completely inside out, we have finally been able to develop a style that is the quintessence of martial arts—the art of defensive survival.

We walk back through the dojo and stop to watch a group in session. The class is composed completely of children who look no older than ten.

ES: The other positive thing that's come out of all this is a new respect from the younger generation—a generation raised on the misdirected reality of video games and action films. Kids from all over the world thought they could outfight those things, even if all the exercise they got was an hour of P.E. once a week. Their perspective was completely skewed. When you're able to run, shoot, and swing a weapon all from your gaming chair and your life force resets at the next power-up, what do you expect?

Now everyone understands. Surviving isn't as easy as it looks, and you're never as indestructible as you think.

UNCONVENTIONAL ENVIRONMENTS

Combat with the living dead does not occur in a vacuum. In an ideal situation, you will face your undead attacker on a level field on a clear day with an unobstructed line of sight to your target while remaining out of hostile range. Unfortunately, reality will interfere with this model situation more often than not. Weather, terrain, and unique surroundings can dramatically influence your ability to survive an undead combat engagement. Although dozens of environmental variations can be evaluated, we will provide analysis on the most prevalent factors.

Weather

History is filled with examples of the event-altering impact Mother Nature can have on the field of battle. This potential impact is no different when confronting the living dead. Although some weather patterns have a more dramatic effect than others, it is important to keep in mind that strategies and techniques that work during one particular forecast, such as a bright, cloudless summer day, may not perform as effectively in another, such as an overcast, rainy spring evening. Be certain to consider your own weather-related vulnerabilities—for example, those who have severe seasonal allergies need to be dutifully aware that this could affect their ability in combat come springtime and fall.

IUCS researchers have analyzed some common weather patterns in relation to their effect on a zombie confrontation.

Precipitation

Precipitation can both positively and negatively effect a combat engagement with a flesh-eating corpse. The level of impact will largely depend on the severity and type of precipitation. Not only are warfare variables such as speed, mobility, and weapon retention affected by this type of climate, but basic sensory variables such as hearing and the ability to see your undead opponent may be impacted as well. Let's examine the two most common forms of precipitation that you may encounter during an undead outbreak:

- **Rain:** Fending off an attacking ghoul during a torrential downpour can be quite unpleasant. Retaining a strong grip on your weapon may become difficult, and your agility and clarity of vision may also be impaired. At the same time, a zombie may have a more difficult time grabbing hold of a rain-slicked arm or torso. Be aware that your ability to detect approaching ghouls during a rainstorm will also be hindered. Your typical cues—odor, moans, the sound of shuffling feet—will be dampened and harder to perceive as the droplets fall.

- **Snow:** Thankfully, this type of precipitation has more of a negative impact on the zombie than the defending human. Although a snowstorm can inhibit your visual acuity, it has a more severe effect on a ghoul's maneuverability, given the slippery ice and snow crystals underfoot. This makes evasive action after a blizzard easier than during temperate weather. Should the temperature drop below freezing, the limbs of the walking dead will also begin to stiffen and solidify, making it even slower in its movements.

As during a rainstorm, you may have difficulty picking up sounds of an oncoming corpse both during and after a snowfall. However, you should also use this natural resource to your advantage. Take note of any prints created in the snow. With practice, you should be able to quickly discern the tracks of the living from the lumbering gait of the undead.

Heat

When assessing the effects of heat on zombie combat, both temperature and humidity of the surrounding air must be taken into account. Both of these elements can have a profound influence on the body's performance in combat. Although every person is uniquely affected by higher temperatures, it has been generally observed that the higher the temperature, the lower the performance level of the individual. This is particularly true for those engaged in highly strenuous activities, which include fighting off a flesh-hungry cadaver. Cramps, fainting, exhaustion, and heatstroke are some of the maladies that can result from being ill-prepared when facing a zombie in warmer climates.

The most important precaution to take when fighting the living dead in a sweltering environment is to ensure that the body is properly hydrated. It may be impossible for you to take a sip of water while embroiled in combat; make certain you do so immediately after delivering your final blow. Should you expect an approaching confrontation, prepare yourself in advance with a cup of water or juice, which you will inevitably lose by sweating during the heat of undead battle. Alcohol is not a recommended hydration fluid, as it will actually dehydrate your body in addition to impairing your performance.

Be sure to consider the impact of heat during evasive maneuvers. You may typically run at a certain steady pace in temperate climates. This rate of speed, however, may slow considerably as the mercury rises. Athletes have shown a differential of 10 to 20 percent off their typical pace in hotter climates. This difference is critical to account for when calculating the time required to reach a safe station or to elude a mass of ghouls. Also note that although excessively high temperatures seem to impact the speed of human movement, they do not at all affect the pace of the living dead.

Aquatic Combat

There may come a time when, for any number of reasons, you will confront a ghoul in a waterborne environment. You may need to cross a riverbed, traverse a flooded underpass, or swim toward a rescue vessel in the open sea. Fighting the living dead in any type of aquatic setting presents a unique set of challenges and negates some of the inherent advantages humans have over the undead on dry land. This negation of advantage is the reason it is important to understand the various types of marine combat and the limitations that each presents.

Slight Submersion

This level of aquatic engagement is defined by an immersion level at calf height or lower and presents the least amount of difficulty. At this submersion level, land is often a short distance away. Given the proximity to dry terrain, it is recommended that you avoid undead confrontation until you have safely exited the water. If you must begin an engagement while your feet are submerged, note that your leg speed and dexterity are vastly diminished, making any combat techniques you attempt more awkward to execute. This is especially true when facing off with a ghoul in a lake bed filled with slippery algae-covered rocks. Use extra caution to keep a safe distance, and take a wider stance so as not to accidentally lose your footing and slip, waiting to be pounced upon by your undead, water-logged assailant.

Partial Submersion

Engaging a ghoul when partially submerged up to your waist can be quite hazardous, as this effectively counteracts any speed advantage you have over your reanimated opponent. In addition, you must not only contend with the ghoul you can see, but also watch for ones you cannot. At this water level, a zombie can be completely submerged below the waterline and remain unnoticed until a set of moss-coated teeth sink into your ankle. If you absolutely must engage a ghoul at this submersion point, it is recommended that you do so with a partner. While you contend with the upright corpse, your cohort can stand at your back and sweep the water for any unseen attackers.

Full Submersion

Engaging an attacker while you both are entirely submerged in water is the most dangerous of all aquatic encounters. In a full-submersion scenario, your speed and maneuverability advantage is utterly negated, your eyesight is diminished, and any weapon that requires a swinging motion is completely useless. You are limited to using thrusting and piercing weapons, such as stakes, knives, and spears, in this type of aquatic combat. One advantage you do have is that regions on the undead skull that are normally difficult to target when on land, such as the eye sockets, can be somewhat easier to strike when fully submerged.

The attacking ghoul faces a disadvantage as well, as it will have a much tougher time grabbing hold of a submerged forearm. If at all possible and available, it is advised that you don swim goggles before entering a full-submersion encounter in order to improve your underwater vision. In a fully submerged situation, your best defense may be to simply swim away from your attacker, as the speed of your paddling will undoubtedly outpace a bloated, floating corpse.

Night Combat

What can be more frightening than being attacked by a walking corpse? Not being able to see the attack coming. Imagine opening your eyes to pitch blackness, knowing that a rotting cadaver is within striking distance, but being unable to spot it until its teeth rip into your flesh. This is what makes low-light undead combat so nerve-wrackingly intense.

In the dark, the dead have an edge over the living. Although they do not possess any exceptional or extrasensory perceptive abilities that make locating prey at night easier, zombies seem to have no less difficulty finding unlucky victims in the wee hours of the evening as they do in the daylight. Humans without adequate illumination or a night vision device, on the other hand, awkwardly stumble through the dark, staggering around locations that are well familiar to them in the daytime. Luckily, you can use several strategies to improve your odds in situations in which light is lacking, but the living dead plentiful.

Avoid the Darkness

The first logical tip to successfully fighting in the dark is to avoid it altogether. Plan your travels accordingly, and ensure that you are already settled in a secured zone or temporary shelter by the time the sun sets. If you find yourself out in the open as dusk approaches without enough time to reach a safe fortification, locate a short-term refuge where you can allow time for your eyesight to adjust (see the strategy that follows).

Let Your Body Adjust

The eyes require an average of twenty to thirty minutes to completely adjust to darkness, plenty of time for a ghoul to attack. As night falls, it is better to stop and permit your eyes to acquire their own natural night vision abilities, rather than press onward and risk running into an attacker you cannot see. Individuals have varying degrees of night vision, and there are several ways to improve it naturally. Be sure to ingest adequate amounts of vitamin A (carrots, mangoes, and cantaloupe are all excellent sources) and avoid nicotine, which can impair eyesight in general. The flickering ember of a cigarette also hampers your eyes' ability to adjust to the dark.

Open Your Senses

A diminishing of one particular sense means relying that much more on the others. In the absence of light, your sense of hearing and sense of smell should provide you with clues as to the presence of a zombie. Just as in daylight, an attacking ghoul will make itself clearly known by its mournful groans, which hopefully will provide you with its approximate position. Its odor should also help you determine its general location and distance. Thankfully, your cadaverous opponent does not have the forethought to use a covert approach in its attack.

Keep Low

Rather than standing starkly upright, taking a slightly stooped, crouching stance may help in low-light situations. Not only will you make yourself a smaller target to any assaulting ghouls, staying lower than your surroundings can help silhouette approaching individuals against any existing light sources, such as a star-filled, moonlit sky.

Stand Ready

Keep your body prepared for night combat by holding your arms up and in front of you, much like a boxer's stance, with your preferred weapon in hand. You can also use your long-range weapon effectively as a "feeler," much as an insect does with its antennae, to help pinpoint and locate a ghoul within a viable combat distance. Do not, however, extend your arms fully in front of you as if to feel for any oncoming obstructions. This is a common error made by those who believe that an extended hand may keep the attacking ghoul at bay before being seen. More often than not, your probing fingers will wind up in the jaws of a waiting zombie.

Watch Your Back

Should you find yourself in an unfamiliar location in the black of night, attempt to guard against as many attack angles as possible until your eyes have time to adjust. An unnerving aspect of low-light attacks is the potential for an unseen attack from any direction. Mitigate ambushes from the rear by moving with your back pressed against a solid structure. "Dig the corners" by situating yourself in a corner position, thereby thwarting unknown assaults from the back, left, and right positions.

EVASIVE MANEUVERS

> I met Chris along a stretch of Highway 51, right outside Porthill. Huge guy, had to be about six-three and two-fifty. Biceps the size of my thighs. I was just about to ask him if he played any football in high school when we met up with a nest just past Copeland. It seemed like too large of a pack to manage with just the two of us, but Chris just plowed into forty of them, hatchets swinging. I told him to ease up, that he'd brought down enough of them for us to get going, but he bellowed that he was having too much fun. By the time he was done and we were back on the

road, he was pretty beat. I suggested we take a break while I stand watch, but he waved me off and told me to go on ahead, that he'd be right behind me.

After a few miles, I decided to slow down and wait until he caught up. I stopped for a while, then finally decided to head back for him. I got that sinking feeling in my gut when I came upon three ghouls that looked like they'd recently fed from a fresh kill. I found him another two miles in, not far from where I left him. His hatchets lay across his lap, like he never even saw them coming. If I had to guess, he probably sat down to catch his breath, lay back, and fell asleep.

I waited another fifteen minutes, until he started to stumble to his feet. I put him down quickly, buried him in a shallow trench by the side of the highway, and was still able to make it to the Bonners Ferry rescue station just before nightfall.

—*Sam, Sandpoint, ID*

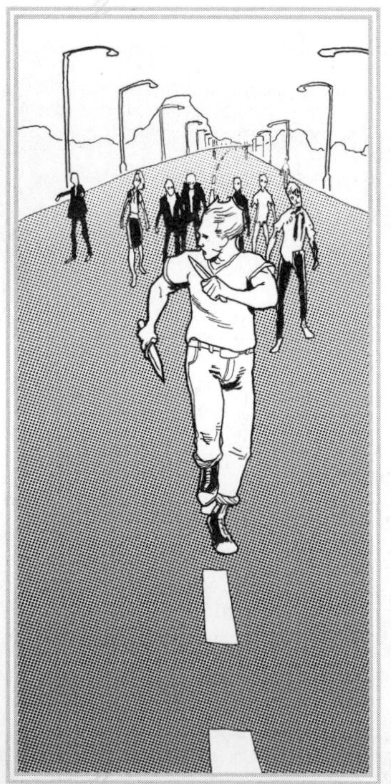

One trait is universal among all seasoned, successful warriors. It is not strength, aggressiveness, or body count. All expert combatants have the ability to accurately assess the moment at which withdrawal from the field of battle is necessary. Experienced fighters know that evasion is not synonymous with cowardice, dishonor, or "cutting and running." It is also a required element of fighting the undead, just as important as weapons training and physical fitness. Detractors who believe that running from the living dead "only means you'll die tired" have not experienced the fatigue of eliminating an entire throng of walking corpses, only to face several dozen more behind them.

Just as there are combat strategies appropriate for the various combat ranges, there are specific strategies you can use in evasive maneuvering to improve your degree of success.

Do the Math

Earlier in this manual we provided specific research data to compute a walking corpse's average pace. This data set will be critical to your calculations when determining how much time you have at your disposal once you have evaded an undead adversary. For example, imagine encountering a ghoul and deciding to evade rather than engage your opponent. You jog five miles at a pace of ten minutes per mile before deciding to stop and rest. How much time do you have before your adversary reaches you?

At a pace of 23 minutes per mile, a zombie requires 115 minutes to cover five miles. Subtracting the 50 minutes necessary for you to cover the same distance, you have approximately 65 minutes before that same ghoul reaches your position. Remember this simple calculation:

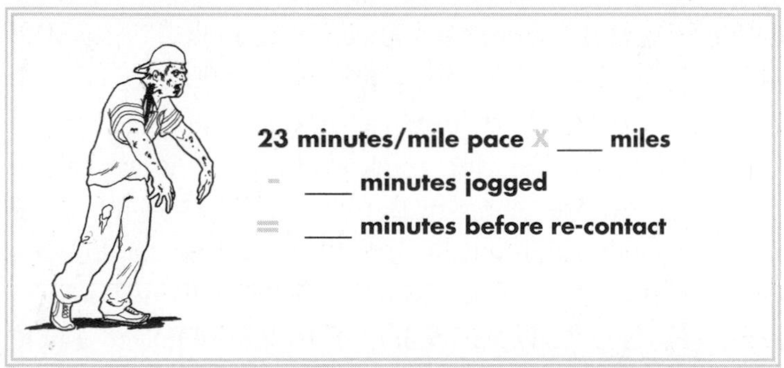

If you have difficulty calculating the figures quickly, carrying a portable calculator in your supply gear is advised in order to do these computations in the field. **Caution:** This formula only establishes the time remaining from your last zombie encounter. It does not account for other ghouls who may also be in your immediate vicinity, closer to your position than your previous adversary. Thus, your calculations will determine the maximum time available before you meet the same opponent again, with the understanding that *other zombies may stumble upon your location sooner.*

Use the Terrain

A positive aspect of evading a somewhat mindless adversary is the fact that you can use a variety of terrain imperfections to your advantage. Hills, barriers, and obstacles, both natural and artificial, will slow down your opponent's progress considerably. If at all possible, traverse paths that are impeded by ditches, potholes, or destroyed walkways. A zombie does not have the physical or mental judgement to leap across dangerous ledges and will blindly step off the end of a precipice in pursuit of a victim without a moment's hesitation.

Train for Distance

One important conditioning regimen you should implement in preparation for a zombie outbreak is to develop your endurance level for long-distance excursions. The need to initiate this type of training during peacetime is critical; once an outbreak occurs, you lose the opportunity to head to your local park or jogging track. Although running can be a difficult exercise for many, light jogging or speedwalking is within most people's capability. Speed is not the ultimate goal; distance is. At peak performance levels, you should be able to cover at least 13.1 miles, a distance equal to a half marathon, at a moment's notice. Based on our formula, it would take a standard undead specimen slightly more than five hours to cover the same distance. At a pace of twelve minutes per mile, this would provide you roughly two and a half hours' advance start—not a great deal of time if you need to rest, resupply, and continue onward until you meet your adversary again.

Tend Your Soles

What may sound like a trivial concern of caring for your feet is in fact critical to your ability to successfully evade the living dead. Those who have participated in long-distance marches or charity walks can attest to the potential for podiatric damage caused by extensive pounding of feet on pavement. Many individuals have succumbed to their undead pursuers not because they lacked the physical endurance to continue, but because of the acute pain resulting from miles of nonstop trekking. Corns, sores, and blisters caused by ill-fitting shoes can severely impact your maneuverability. It is not uncommon for the skin from the bottoms of both feet to slough off entirely after a refugee trudges dozens of miles to reach a secure area.

There are many remedies, both medically based and homegrown, for insulating the feet during long-distance expeditions. Vaseline, duct tape, moleskin, and tincture of benzoin are all solutions that work to varying degrees. Individual experimentation can help determine the most effective solution for your particular pace. None of these remedies, however, is a substitute for comfortable, properly fitting footwear and building up your feet's tolerance by disciplined training. Evading the undead can be an exhausting war of attrition, against an enemy that will not attrite.

COMBAT REPORT: MARTIN RANDESH

Ultramarathoner, Big Bear Park, Colorado

Martin Randesh greets me in typical athlete's fashion—covered in sweat. He's reluctantly agreed to speak with me for this interview, having just concluded his "short" afternoon group training run of fifteen miles. This brings him to a total of thirty-five miles already completed before lunch, twenty-five miles from the total he will run before he lies down to rest for the evening. Although a staggering count for even an advanced long-distance runner, this is the average number of miles that many in his training class cover on a daily basis. We sit in a fenced gazebo while the rest of his group slowly arrives behind him to begin their cool down and stretching exercises.

MR: I still have no clue why you want to talk to me. From what I've heard about the folks you're interviewing, I'm not one of those types.

ZCM: Which types?
MR: I'm not one of those macho zombie fighters you seem to be interested in.

ZCM: You have a compelling view on dealing with the threat.
MR: Yeah, running from them, there's a real page turner. Look, I'll talk about it if you want, but I'm not going to jazz it up for you. It is what it is.

ZCM: That's fine.
MR: I'll be honest and tell you what I tell my students—I think we're all better off now. If there's anything to be said for what's happened, it's that it got people off their asses. It was so easy for people to say "Just run. Run in the other direc-

tion. Hell, just walk, they'll never catch you." All you need is a second-grader's math skills to figure out that wasn't going to work for most people in this country. Before the outbreaks, do you know the number of minutes Joe American walked, not ran, during an entire week?

ZCM: How many?

MR: Twenty. Twenty goddamn minutes a week. Now, let's say that Joe is able to cover one and a half miles in those twenty minutes, which is being pretty damn generous, since most people can only cover a mile in that time. That means he's clocking about thirteen-minute miles, about ten minutes faster than your average zombie. So, if you've got dead on your tail and start walking for say ten miles, you've bought yourself a hundred minutes. That's an hour and forty minutes to eat, sleep, crap, hunt, gather, before that same ghoul is on your ass again and you have to go another ten miles to buy yourself another hundred minutes. You see what I'm getting at? Mr. Barcalounger who used to walk a mile and a half a *week* now has to trot sixty miles a day to get six measly hours without being harassed by dripping corpses. And that's not taking into account other zombies he may run into along the way. Needless to say, the people I know who survived the dead weren't the ones sprawled on the couch watching *America Can Samba.*

Even myself, before the outbreaks, I was just a regular nine-to-five stiff getting in a three-mile run a couple of times a week if I was lucky. Then there was the state of emergency, the evacuations, the sealing off of the cities by the National Guard. Suddenly I found myself on a stretch of Interstate 25 with a bunch of other refugees. There was a lot of talk about transportation in those early days: "I've got an SUV, I've got a Harley, I'm riding my tricked-out fixie." Yeah, all those types were in our group, hoofin' it just like everyone else. The fossil-fuelers aren't even worth talking about—if you were dumb enough to think you'd have enough gas to make it anywhere safe, even with one of those hybrid jobs, you probably didn't make it past the first week.

So there we were, a handful of us trudging along this expanse of highway. We were told that a functioning rescue station was only five miles away. Five miles came and went, and the only change was the size of our group. We passed three, maybe four so-called "safe havens" that were completely abandoned. At one point, this group of cyclists zipped by us, screaming for us to get out of the way. They were totally decked out in their spandex outfits, too. I had no idea what they were doing. We caught up with them a few miles afterward, walking their bikes after they hit a pool of shattered glass from a seven-car pileup. I guess those tights don't leave much room for a patch kit.

We were on the interstate for about fifteen miles when the whining started. People were tired, people were hungry. This one jerk-off yuppie even suggested taking all the food and dividing it equally. And wouldn't you know it, he didn't bring any of his own. Typical. I had to listen to everyone yammer on for another thirty miles until we arrived at what we thought was going to be the final stop, the outpost we were all sure was still going to be operational in Cheyenne. It was operational all right, just not by anyone living. That's when everyone started running. And running. For almost three hundred miles, we ran. People started dropping off quick. We would try to stop and rest when we could, with someone standing watch. It worked for the most part, until some idiot fell asleep on his shift. That cut our group down by another two thirds. I tell you, I really didn't think I was going to make it, but it just goes to show that when you dig down deep, everyone's capable of amazing things.

ZCM: Was your family with you?

MR: Nah . . . I tried to reach my ex, but she's the one who wanted sole custody and milked me dry in the settlement. She didn't need me before the outbreaks, so I assumed she didn't need me after. I also realized that if they were with me on that stretch of blacktop, none of us would have probably made it; I had to take care of myself first, you know, before worrying about everyone else. That sounds cold, doesn't it? Yeah, well, it's that attitude that's kept me breathing until now. Do you think a pre-outbreak Martin would have been able to knock out twenty miles before breakfast? Not on your life. That's what I'm saying—all of this, all that's happened, it was all part of a larger purpose.

ZCM: A larger purpose?

MR: Do you remember all the crazy biological shit that was going on before the dead started walking? Not many people think about this stuff, but I do. Mad cow. Avian flu. Rodent flu. Sky-high autism rates. Huge increases in miscarriages. You don't think that was Nature telling us she was pissed off? I'm telling you, all those "natural disasters" were hints to try to get us to get our act together, and we flipped it off. We were always top dog, and no one was going to tell us to stop screwing, and stop crapping where we screwed. We dodged a bunch of her bullets, but good old Mother Earth wasn't going to let us dodge this one. She couldn't whittle our numbers down fast enough to keep us from constantly dumping on her, so she'd have our own dead do it for her.

And whittle down we did. That group along I-25 was like a little microcosm of our society, and a perfect example of how things began to shake out for the rest of the world. There were your geeks who thought technology would solve our problems. There were the yuppie whiners who wanted to be waited on hand and foot. There were the lazy bastards who wanted to stop and rest every fifty feet. And then there were the people who toughened up, made the best of the worst situation, and survived. Janey and Alan over there along with me are the only three of the original refugees who made it all the way to the safety nexus in Colorado City.

He points to a middle-aged woman and a young man from his running group, each assisting the other to stretch their calves.

MR: This wasn't about who was the fittest and healthiest. This was about heart. The outbreaks not only eliminated the weak, but made the strong realize that they were capable of so much more than they were already doing in life. Janey was a housewife in an abusive relationship for twenty years; Alan was a high school dropout who weighed two hundred seventy-five pounds. Now look at us. We're thinking of forming a team for some of those necro-race challenges overseas. We'll see.

ZCM: Do you ever feel that you're in denial?
MR: Denial about what?

ZCM: About the reality of what's happened.
MR: . . . and where did you get your psychiatry degree?

ZCM: I just mean . . .
MR: Whose reality are you talking about? The reality that, after everything that's happened, I should go back to slogging through a regular workweek and paying alimony to my bloodsucking ex who took my kids away from me? That was my reality for a long time, and you know what? It sucked. I'm happier now that I've ever been in my life, and if it took the dead to rise and start eating the living for it to happen, I sure as hell ain't complaining. We're done here.

Without another word, Randesh begins running up the path toward the blazing afternoon sun. His group, seeing that he's back on the move, dart off and follow. Within minutes, they are dots against the hillside, slowly drawing out of sight.

MULTIPLE ATTACKERS

During a zombie outbreak, it is almost certain that you will face multiple undead assailants at the same time. Do not interpret this to mean that zombies exhibit any semblance of a hive or pack mentality. Every ghoul is its own singular entity—it does not follow leaders, give orders, or form alliances with other undead creatures. The reason why hordes of walking dead are often seen clustering themselves together is simple—that's typically where the food is. Zombies have been known to recognize the moan of another ghoul as a signal that food is nearby and turn to follow the direction of said moan, eventually ending up in a packed swarm of walking corpses.

Just as we've detailed strategies for handling a single zombie, you can use specific tactics when facing multiples of undead. Battling a group of walking dead with a hand weapon is a tiresome and dangerous venture to undertake. Depending on your strength and skill, it is recommended that you engage only with groups of ten or fewer ghouls. For numbers greater than this, evasive maneuvering is always a better option, as the tactics described herein may be difficult to execute against larger clusters of undead. Evasion is also the preferred choice if you notice more zombies in the distance closing in. By the time you have eliminated one group, you may then have to engage with another sizable force, only this time in a fatigued state.

If escape is not possible and the only way to survive is to eliminate every zombie in the surrounding vicinity, follow these strategies to make your engagement smooth, efficient, and as short as possible.

Patience Is a Virtue

Fighting one zombie at close range is stressful enough. Having to engage five, six, or ten at a time may drive you to the brink of madness. Seeing so many undead figures eagerly lunging for your flesh will most likely cause your stress levels to increase, possibly throwing you into a panic and tempting you to simply begin battering away at the group. Doing so is a sure way to end up joining their ranks. Maintain your composure. Stopping multiple zombies can be as simple as stopping one, the key difference being the time required to complete the act. Remember that the group will not use their greater numbers to strategically overwhelm you. Use your intelligence, outwit them just as you would a single opponent, and take your time to make each of your blows count.

Gain the High Ground

When the odds are stacked against you, you must exploit every advantage at your disposal, including terrain. If you can lead the fight to even a slight elevation where you stand above your attackers, it will be much easier to dispatch your opponents. Additionally, a zombie's lack of coordination means that the mob you originally faced will most likely stumble, fall, and disperse slightly, making them easier to pick off individually.

Outflank and Attack

A common strategic error individuals make when engaging multiple zombies is to dive straight into the center of the pack on your initial approach. Striking the zombie in the middle of a group provides an opportunity for the others to close the distance around you, flanking you on either side, while you are preoccupied with that one opponent. Without a means of egress, there is a high probability that you will then be pulled apart by the mob.

Use what you already know about the undead to your advantage. Recall that ghouls move at a slow, consistent pace, even during pursuit of prey. Use this weakness to flank the group, and attack the zombie closest to the tail end. Once you eliminate that opponent, circle the mob again until you see another opportunity to strike a vulnerable ghoul. Continue this flanking maneuver until all zombies have been eliminated. If this technique sounds similar to a maneuver you have heard before, it is. You are basically applying the StraCirs technique and adapting it for use against a mob of undead opponents.

Culling the Herd

In a combat situation in which you face a solitary undead opponent, executing any strike that does not immediately end the engagement is a waste of energy. If you have the strength to shatter a ghoul's kneecap, then you should have the strength to destroy its brain. When facing simultaneous attackers, however, it may be advantageous to administer bone-shattering blows to the vulnerable areas of a zombie's lower extremities—the knees, shins, and feet—so that the attackers cannot pursue you as a collective horde.

In these situations, thinning their undead ranks may make it easier to battle the entire cluster. Move from ghoul to ghoul, pinpointing the tertiary targets in the legs described earlier in the section on vulnerabilities. As you continue to hobble their numbers, the shambling mob that once posed a grave collective threat can be reduced until one upright zombie remains, with a parade of crippled ghouls following in its wake. You can then choose to dispatch the crippled zombies or make your escape.

Remember, it is not enough that you strike a perceivably "painful" blow to the legs, as such a concept does not exist to an undead combatant. Your blow must be severe enough to completely shatter the patella, destroy the tibia (shin bone), or snap the Achilles tendon; otherwise your opponent will continue its pursuit, along with its undead cohorts.

The Whack-a-Mole

In addition to using the environment to your advantage, you may encounter a structure that you can exploit to effectively dispatch a mass of undead attackers. This strategy requires that you find an object that can elevate you to a height such that the attacking brood has difficulty reaching you, but not so high that you are unable to mount a counteroffensive. Effective structures include natural objects such as boulders and hilltops, or artificial obstacles such as automobiles or shipping containers. Stand atop the structure and wait for the attacking horde to approach. As each ghoul raises its head high enough to be targeted, strike it down. By repeating this process until all ghouls are eliminated, you can dispatch a large gathering of zombies with relative safety. Consider both the weight of the structure you mount and the number of attackers confronting you before committing to this tactic, and choose your structures wisely. A large enough number of zombies may be able to shift or overturn a lightweight obstacle, foiling your strategy.

The Bum's Rush

This is an advanced technique that should be used only in certain situations by strong, experienced fighters, or as a last resort to escape. When you find yourself attacked by a pack of zombies, grab hold of one by the neck. Using that ghoul as a shield, barrel through the rest of the undead cluster. The zombie shielding you should flatten others in your path like pins in a bowling lane. Once cleared of the pack, you can release the shielding ghoul at arm's length, or dispatch accordingly. This technique is most effective when you are in a confined space, such as a house or an apartment complex, and have no other means of escape except through an undead mob.

As you can imagine, this is a highly risky maneuver, and should be used only in specific situations in which you have no other viable alternatives. When using the Bum's Rush, keep the following key points in mind:

1. **Pick an adequate shield:** Choose a shielding zombie that is thinner and lighter than the average adult ghoul, a size that enables you to handle it through the undead throng. Examine all specimens closely, and select one appropriately. Young and elderly zombies seem to work best. Lighter female zombies may also be an option, but be sure to glance at their fingernails to determine if you need to be wary of its scratching and clawing.

2. **Move with speed:** There's fast, and there is the speed you need to execute this technique. You need to move with extreme velocity, force, and aggression through the mob in order to prevent any one of the ghouls from grabbing hold of you, stopping your momentum, and taking an infectious bite. Once initiated, you must fully commit to completing this maneuver, as any hesitation midstride means certain death.

3. **Watch your feet:** As you batter ghouls out of your path, there is a chance your legs will be vulnerable to attack by any zombies crawling along the ground. Moving with speed and a light step will help prevent this hazard, as will wearing equipment that guards your lower legs.

COMBAT SIMULATIONS

You have conditioned your physique, chosen your weapons, and studied the tactics. The only task that remains is to refine your technique. During a large-scale zombie outbreak, this will not be difficult, as your skills will most likely be honed in actual battle. During peacetime, however, how do you ensure that your fighting abilities are as sharp as your machete? Through effective combat training simulations.

Depending on your situation, you may be training alone, with a single partner, or in a group. Each of these situations has its advantages, but if given the opportunity, you should incorporate all three simulation types into your training regimen. Be careful not to favor one type of training over another. There may be a time when you no longer have a team of individuals with whom to practice, and you will need to be well versed in training by yourself.

Before we delve into the specific drills, two factors must be addressed before beginning a robust combat simulation program.

Realism

A common phrase heard in combat training is "Train hard, fight easy." The more you are able to create the illusion of combat, the better prepared you will be during an actual zombie attack. When training with family or friends, it is easy to become lackadaisical and casual during your drills. **Do not let this happen.** The simulations discussed in group and partner training are only as effective as the individuals playing their parts. If you do not take your roles seriously, or do not authentically behave as an undead ghoul would in an actual combat scenario, then you all will suffer in the long run. Inauthentic behavior on any member's part may cause you to believe that fighting the undead is easier or harder than it actually is. Neither inaccuracy is worth your limited training time.

Safety

Just as realism is an important part of any combat drill, safety is even more so. Many of the drills described next require a great deal of speed, strength, and intensity in order to make the simulation as close to a real-world scenario as possible. It is important to remember that the people you are training with are teammates, not opponents. In an undead world, your true adversary is the one without a pulse. Ensuring safety during all combat exercises is paramount and especially critical during drills in which individuals are barreling full steam into teammates or fending off clutching hands. Always wear protective gear if available, including headgear and chest protection when appropriate. Use padded training tools instead of actual weapons. Always keep the intensity level high, but remember that a hurt or wounded teammate impacts his or her own fighting ability and the combat effectiveness of the entire group.

Group Training

If you are lucky enough to have a team of four or more individuals to train alongside, do not let this unique benefit go to waste. Your group sessions should focus on dealing with the more perilous undead combat situations—mob attacks. Undead mobs are often the most difficult to handle, and thus the most difficult to prepare against. Each individual in your group should alternate as the human defender as every other member simulates a zombie attacker, or *zuke* (pronounced "ZOO-key"). The following are combat simulations you can practice with your group.

Last Ghoul Standing

This basic exercise mimics the scenario of facing a group of zombies in an open area. Using a padded training tool approximate in size and shape to your preferred combat weapon, you should attempt to navigate around the pack and strike simulated blows to each zuke, just as you would in an actual battle scenario. If possible, use practice weapons that replicate each of your long-, melee-, and close-range arms. In advanced sessions, you can improvise the loss of a weapon midexercise to enhance your ability to switch armaments on the fly.

Because you are simulating blows to the heads of your teammates, be careful about the amount of force used in your attacks. Use a quarter to an eighth of your potential power level in your strikes, and if possible, have each zuke wear protective headgear. The purpose of this exercise is to train your agility when facing a pack of zombies, not to improve your delivery of destructive blows. In advanced training, conduct this exercise in a tighter, confined space, making the ability to dodge each zuke more difficult.

Red Rover

A variation on the classic children's game; the purpose of this exercise is to simulate the situation in which the only thing standing between you and safety is a group of walking dead. The safety point could be an exit, a weapon, or another human whom you are trying to rescue. This simulation should be conducted in a large room or outdoor setting, with the human defender standing on one side and the destination point forty to fifty feet in front of him or her. In between, your group of zukes should assemble in a random pattern. The object is to break through the group and reach the destination point, while the attackers attempt to grab and bite you. The exercise should be repeated several times to test the defender's ability as fatigue sets in, with the group assembling in a denser, more congested pattern each time. This exercise can also be used to practice the Bum's Rush maneuver.

The Maul Rat

The purpose of this drill is to become adept at fending off attackers while completely surrounded and to address attacks from unusual angles. In this difficult exercise, the training group should assemble in a circular pattern around the defender. With arms outstretched, the group attempts to grab and maul the defender as he or she tries to keep them at bay while being continually surrounded by the group.

The exercise should be conducted for a full five minutes, or until one of the attackers lands what would be a life-ending blow. The exercise is completed once every member has had the opportunity to play the role of defender. If your group is larger than ten individuals, break the team up into smaller groups to alleviate the monotony of having to portray a zombie for nine other teammates.

Partner Training

Training with a single partner can be quite useful in perfecting many of the combat and escape techniques described throughout this manual, and can help develop the unique feel for defending against a zombie in a one-on-one situation. All of the following drills can also be incorporated into group training, with the larger team splitting into pairs to conduct each exercise.

Ghoul Grappling

This drill trains you to counteract the common occurrence of a zombie grabbing your arms during an attack. With one individual again playing zuke and the other defending, the attacker should grab you on random locations on the arms—the wrists, forearms, or upper arms. With each grab, the defender should use one of the techniques outlined earlier and attempt to break the grip. Each time the defender is successful at dislodging the hold, the zuke should grab another region on either arm. The zuke should not attempt to bite, as the purpose of the exercise is to practice holds and releases. The zuke should, however, be as realistic as possible in clutching the defender as aggressively as possible until he or she is able to break free. Do not be concerned with gripping your partner "too hard." As strong a grip as you may believe you have, it is nothing compared to that of your standard undead corpse. This grip/release routine should continue unceasingly for at least four minutes, at which time the partners should switch roles.

Diablo's Mark

In traditional knife combat drills, partners rub their training blades with chalk, ink, or lipstick to determine the placement and gravity of wounds during dueling exercises. The Diablo's Mark drill is similar in concept. In this freeform exercise, the person playing zuke places marking balm on his or her lips and fingernails while the other defends against an attack. Any number of scenarios can then be created to simulate a unique zombie attack—unarmed encounter, handicapped defender, attacked while sleeping, and so forth. At the end of the drill, the defender determines how many times he or she was marked by the zuke's balm-coated lips and nails. Depending on the severity and location of the mark, each blemish can signify a failed zombie confrontation. After experiencing this drill, participants become acutely aware of the lethal nature of engaging the living dead.

Solo Training

At some point you may find yourself completely devoid of training companions, relying only on yourself to keep your skills in peak condition. It is a misconception that a training partner is always necessary to hone your combat abilities. You can perform a great many drills and exercises that require nothing but yourself and some minor training tools.

Solo training is also the most widespread type of conditioning carried out during large-scale zombie infestations; family is missing, friends are gone, and you must fend for yourself. In such an isolated state, the last thing you may feel motivated to do is conduct combat training. In actuality, it is precisely when you are alone that you must keep your fitness level and fighting skills at their sharpest. In these situations, you do not have the benefit of a partner saving you from the clutches of a ferocious ghoul attack. Here are several drills that can improve your solo combat skills.

The Splitting Headache

This long-range drill is ideal training if you find yourself often using a polearm weapon and attacking with a thrusting strike to the bridge of the nose, as depicted in the Skullcapper technique. Draw the outline of a zombie's head, including facial features, on a sheet of fabric. Mount the fabric to a solid surface and at an appropriate height for an adult zombie. Draw a pair of parallel lines on the face—one roughly one inch above and the other an inch below the eyes. This is your target zone. Using your actual combat weapon or a training staff, try to deliver as many consistent thrusts as possible between the drawn lines for three minutes. Keep count of how many strikes you execute during that three-minute period, and assess how precisely your strikes land.

The Maypole

This drill develops your coordination and footwork at melee range. Wrap a length of masking tape around an object that you can encircle, such as a tree, pillar, or mounted heavy bag. The height of the tape should mark the height of the average human skull. With your melee or training weapon in hand, begin moving around the target, circlestrafing just as you would if executing the StraCirs technique. As you circle, strike the tape with your weapon as you would strike the skull of an attacking ghoul. Complete five full rotations around the target, then reverse direction and complete another five rotations. You can also try switching the weapon to your nondominant hand during this drill in order to develop ambidexterity in your attacks.

The Nutcracker

If you still have never dispatched a zombie with a blow to the skull, most likely you have one question eating away at your conscience: Do you have the ability to do it? One obvious way to find out is to engage in combat with a ghoul, which is the worst time to find out that you are unable to do so. Another, more practical method is to train your muscles to deliver a devastating strike that can send skull fragments flying and drop the ghoul where it stands. The question is, how much force is required to deliver a ghoul-neutralizing blow? It is a difficult question to precisely answer, as there are many influencing factors, such as hair, cranium size, target area, and state of decomposition. However, you can better prepare yourself to deliver an adequately powerful blow through the Nutcracker drill.

Take a standard coconut (brown) and encase it in two

layers of duct tape. Place the fruit (a coconut is, in fact, not a nut but a fruit) in a double layer of plastic bags and suspend it from a structure so that it is roughly cranium height. Using the melee or long-range weapon you will wield in combat, strike the fruit just as you would a zombie skull. If you can shatter the hard coating of the coconut even when it is protected by the layers of tape and plastic, you have a good approximation of the strength and accuracy required to deliver a crushing blow.

Granted, a coconut is rather delicate and easily shattered. The taped covering in which you encase the fruit should somewhat compensate for its fragility, but if you find that you can splinter the target easily, a young, green coconut is much sturdier, and can present more of a challenge to the stronger combatant. An even greater challenge would be to use a durian, a fruit from Southeast Asia with a tough, spiked outer husk and available in many Asian markets. Be warned, the odor of the durian's interior pulp is so unpleasant that the fruit is banned from being eaten in certain public areas in Asia. The stench of the durian has been compared to that of rotting flesh, which, given what you are training for, is not a far cry from the odors you will encounter in zombie combat.

COMBAT REPORT: BRIAN DEVON

Green Beret, Free Republic of Dodge, Iowa

The burlap sack covering my head smells distinctly of fertilizer. Despite the feeling that hours have passed before we arrive at our destination, it has been only forty minutes since I was met and promptly hooded by members of the Dodge Security Force. When the hood is removed, I find myself in the finished basement of what appears to be a domestic residence. As previously agreed, I am stripped down to my underwear. My digital recorder, pen, and notebook are taken. My non-writing hand is shackled to my seat, and I am given several wax markers to transcribe my notes. "Remember Massoud[19]*," a member of the security detail says as he drops a sheaf of paper in front of me. The mask, strip search, and writing implements are all part of the precautionary measures taken by the DSF to ensure the safety of their leader, Brian Devon, Green Beret and now administrator of the Free Republic of Dodge. Devon places a plastic glass filled with water on the table between us and sits, flanked by his security personnel. Like many military professionals I've met, he exudes a fierce intensity tempered with an almost monklike aura of tranquillity. The following is the first and only interview given by Devon to a journalist.*

BD: This is not how I planned it. We were sent here on a very specific mission. Had the government held up its end of the deal, I would be sitting with a beer at home in the North Carolina secured zone. Instead, I'm talking to a half-naked reporter with a crayon in his hand.

ZCM: What was your mission?

19 Ahmed Shah Massoud, the famed anti-Taliban Northern Alliance guerrilla leader who was killed by assassins posing as journalists on September 9, 2001.

BD: DID—Domestic Internal Defense. With the amendments to the Insurrection and Posse Comitatus Acts, the military, specifically guys like us, was able to do the kind of work at home that we've been doing throughout our history in other parts of the world. In layman terms, we had to secure the city. Typically, at least a twelve-man ODA team would have been sent in for an operation like this, but given the defection of so many good operators to the private sector and the losses we suffered containing the initial overseas outbreaks, all they could afford to send was me and Charlie. Chuck was an X-Ray, part of the military program that recruited civilians straight into Special Forces. I know that those recruits were looked at sideways by many of the traditional guys for being "shake and baked" into SF, but Chuck was as talented as any other Green Beret I knew. He'd be the first to talk down about himself, loved to be self-deprecating. He would finish any suggestion he had with, "But what do I know, I'm an X-Ray." Anyone who worked with him even once knew better than to believe that.

We were under no illusions as to what we were facing in this operation. We knew exactly why the nature of our op was so ambiguous. Rumor had it that many of these missions were assumed to be one-way tickets. Chuck and I had no problem with that. But what actually happened, what the government did . . . but I'm getting ahead of myself.

We HAHO'd[20] in to minimize the announcement of our approach to unfriendlies, undead or otherwise. Opening our chutes high also allowed us to spend more time in the air for an immediate analysis of the region: a bird's-eye view to assess the vulnerability of the city and threats in the surrounding countryside. The satellite photos we were provided in our mission briefing were days old. For all we knew the town

20 HAHO: high-altitude, high-opening parachute insertion.

could have already been overrun in that time. But once we caught sight of the city and the terrain, I actually started to feel better about things. I looked over at Chuck as we floated down, and even though his face was obscured by the oxygen mask, I knew he was smiling. Dodge was primarily a manufacturing city—drywall and gypsum—and it looked like the townsfolk were smart enough to secure exposed perimeters with pallets of the stuff in preparation for any external aggression. The airfield looked serviceable, and the highways into and out of the city were clear of living dead. Things didn't look so bleak after all.

ZCM: How did the townspeople react to your arrival?

BD: They were ecstatic. Naturally, they felt that if the city was important enough to send us there, they were going to be all right. And we couldn't have arrived any sooner. All the ammunition in the town was gone, handed over during the National Voluntary Ordnance Sweeps[21] conducted months earlier. Other cities had only about a third of the population left, but most of the original townspeople, including the women and children, were still present in Dodge. The water supply was intact, the electrical grid was operational, and the city was DF—dead-free. But food supplies were running low, and outbreaks were being reported in the metropolitans farther east. The fear was that it would soon sweep through and decimate the town like a swarm of locusts.

The first task at hand was to finish the work that the residents had already started. We needed to fortify the city's perimeters and the entry and exits onto the highways. They did a good job before we got there, reinforcing the city limits with trucks and pallets of dry goods. The problem was that

---

21 During the National Voluntary Ordnance Sweeps, all U.S. citizens were asked to volunteer their personal stores of ammunition to the federal government. This act was later made mandatory and amended to include private firearms dealers, distributors, and manufacturers.

we saw plenty of homemade videos online showing collapsed reinforcements, resulting from a large crush of dead against a single structural weakness, as well as what Chuck called the "gory slope"—when enough zombies assemble against a barrier that they begin to climb on top of one another, cresting the fortification. Luckily, Chuck was 18C, an engineering specialist. He designed this staggered I-beam reinforcement perimeter using blocks of the city's drywall storage. He even built in patrol ramps in case any dead managed to reach the top of the reinforcements so we could scramble up quickly and chop them down. It was a thing of structural beauty.

The highways were another problem. Despite the image of zombies traversing the countryside, most made their way from city to city through manufactured pathways—roads, bridges, and highways. At that point, the government was still unwilling to render these pathways useless, not only because of the inability for commercial shipments to make it through, but also because of the potential cost of rebuilding the structures when order was restored. "When order was restored"—how goddamn ludicrous does that sound now? Regardless, we were under strict orders not to obliterate any public highway systems or roadways. Chuck came through with another stroke of tactical engineering brilliance. There was one major elevated highway running into and out of the city, making it easier for us to stanch the potential flow of undead. Chuck came up with the idea of jackknifing several sets of semitrailers, one row after another, which we could easily move in case a vehicle needed to enter the city. There was enough gas left in the pumps of the town's stations to fuel up the trucks and get them maneuvered into position.

With the city reinforced, we went about the task of training the townspeople. Men, women, children, no one was exempt. People have this ongoing misconception about Special Forces.

They like to think of us as cowboys, gunslingers—when in fact what we do most of the time is train people to take care of themselves. Chuck liked to describe us as the Peace Corps with M4s. Most of the time we're sent to the ass-ends of the world to teach people things they think they don't need to be taught; it was no different here. The women weren't an issue; they were the most willing to learn. Predictably, some of the men looked at us with a skeptical eye. A good number of them were former active military themselves. This is where Chuck really shone. I've seen him do it with tribal warlords in the Middle East, with Congolese contra-rebel troops, and here he was doing the same with ordinary U.S. citizens. Chuck had this innate ability, the kind you just can't learn, to be able to train people without being condescending. He didn't make the men feel like they were lesser men for having to learn from him.

ZCM: What type of training did you provide?

BD: Improvised combat. There were plenty of guns in the town, only no ammunition left to fill them. With no guarantees of a supply drop or additional troops, Chuck and I knew that the most practical training we could provide was to get everyone in town equipped to handle an improvised weapon. We separated them into appropriate ranks given their physical attributes and distributed tools taken from all the local hardware and agricultural supply stores. Everyone had to participate. Over the next couple of months, we ran drills for hours each day, cycling through each weapon range, until everyone in the town was capable of bringing down a ghoul at every distance possible. I must admit, these folks were quick studies. It usually takes more than two months to get a group this diverse trained up. These folks were good to go within six weeks. And it was none too soon. Shortly after the final training sessions were completed, Chuck smelled it in the air as he was checking on the highway reinforcements. Our first wave was approaching.

The strategy was pretty simple, but still a huge gamble. The tractor-trailer blockade created an elastic defensive zone that we hoped would disrupt most of the horde, but we weren't sure what would happen if a large enough swarm pressed against the rigs. Chuck and the townspeople who were most skilled with long-range weapons—shovels and pitchforks mostly—were the main line of defense after the trucks. Should any of the dead break through, it was Chuck and his team's responsibility to put them down or pitch them over the side of the highway embankment, where they would fall forty feet to the underpass. I was leading a group below the pass with short-range weapons that could finish off any dead that happened to survive the drop. If the blockades failed entirely, we would fall back while Chuck detonated the Semtex charges he'd mounted on the trucks.

The horde crested the top of the highway. As they drew closer and the moans began to reverberate in our ears, we realized that this was going to be a real test of Chuck's perimeter defenses. It was a huge mass, probably more than ten thousand zulus.[22] The first ones reached the trucks and began slamming their arms against the cabs. Others reached the first group and started pushing. And the ones after them started pushing. The trucks groaned against the pressing weight. As the bulk of the mass reached the blockade, things started to look ugly. We heard bones snapping. Skulls started to pop. We didn't think of it at the time, but I guess this was a good thing. The trucks were holding, but the mass of constant pressure was starting to force ghouls through the crevices and small openings between the truck cab and the trailer. As the group continued to ram themselves forward,

22 zulu: nonofficial military terminology for living dead combatants.

flesh was being forced through the cracks like sausage meat pressed through the holes of a colander. The smell was nearly unbearable. Once we got past the terrible sight of zombie flesh pouring out over the highway, we realized that the blockade was holding. Very few seemed to be making it past the first truck in one piece. There were some crawlers that got underneath wheels of the truck bed, but Chuck and his guys took care of those pretty quickly. He leaned over the side of the overpass and laughed, "I'll be a son of a bitch, looks like this is gonna work!" That's when we heard the fast movers overhead.

The air strike took out the entire blockade. There wasn't much gasoline left in the semis, but the contingency charges Chuck had rigged went up like the doors of hell were kicked open. Concrete and steel showered down on us in the underpass, but luckily most of my guys weren't injured. I wish I could say the same for Chuck and his team. They didn't stand a chance. When the smoke cleared, any zulus that were still intact continued to walk off the edge of what was left of the highway. The rest of us retreated back to the town. That's when we saw the rest of the damage.

ZCM: So it was a friendly-fire incident?
BD: Is that what you think?

ZCM: You don't believe the air strike was an accident?
BD: Why did they make four passes? Why did they target our gas stations and food storage facilities? Why did they destroy the airfield? Too many *whys*. Too many questions where we already know or no longer cared about the answers. They made their decision, and now we've made ours. As part of the Sovereign States Alliance, we no longer require the services of our federal support system.

These are good people. When our government asked the

public to stay in their residences when thousands were clogging the roadways, they stayed put. When they were asked to give up their ammunition reserves, they did so willingly while others waited until the sweeps were made mandatory. And when we didn't receive a single supply shipment even though there was a perfectly serviceable airstrip, they didn't complain. We thought the living dead were going to be the worst of our troubles. Turns out it wasn't even close.

ZCM: You've heard about the passing of the Repatriation Act?
BD: We have, and we have respectfully declined to participate.

ZCM: What happens if the government decides to retake Dodge by force?
BD: We'll be ready.

ACKNOWLEDGMENTS

To Matt Wagner, for believing that more needed to be said.

To my editor, Denise Silvestro, Meredith Giordan, Angela Januzzi, and the rest of the wonderful crew at Berkley who made it happen.

To G.A.R., for the foundation.

To Mr. William Fairbairn, Mr. Eric Sykes, and Col. Rex Applegate, the godfathers of CQC.

The Artists:

To John Fisk, for his design proficiency.

To Y. N. Heller, for the illustrations and his commitment.

The Medical and Conditioning Team:

To Kevin Ching, MD, pediatric emergency medicine, for the information on emergency crisis resource management.

To Dr. Phyllis Ho, for the dental and forensic information.

To Kathy Ma, MD, Orthopedics, for the anatomical research.

To Steven C. Schlozman, MD, child and adolescent psychiatry, for the insight into childhood development.

To David Osorio, for the fitness and conditioning data.

The Operators:

To Jimmy Buthorn, USPIS, for the information on CQB and room-clearing tactics.

To Frank Luongo, USN SEAL, for his knowledge of special operations.

To Michael Janich, for his extensive expertise on close-quarters combat.

To Brian Dillon, Suffolk County Police Department, for providing an authentic voice.

The Weapons Men:

To Justin "Sir Justyn" Webbe, for the historical and medieval context.

To Joel Bukiewicz, bladesmith, for demonstrating the process and for the tour of the workshop.

And to all the others who asked to remain anonymous and helped make this work a reality, your assistance was invaluable.